P9-DID-490

DISCARD

Mabel Manning Branch
6 S. Hoyne
Chicago, IL   60612

FUZZY NAVEL

OTHER WORKS BY J.A. KONRATH

Whiskey Sour
Bloody Mary
Rusty Nail
Dirty Martini

A Jacqueline "Jack" Daniels Mystery

FUZZY NAVEL

J. A. KONRATH

HYPERION NEW YORK

Copyright © 2008 Joe Konrath

All rights reserved. No part of this book may be used or reproduced
in any manner whatsoever without the written permission of the Publisher.
Printed in the United States of America.
For information address Hyperion, 77 West 66th Street,
New York, New York 10023-6298.

ISBN: 978-1-4013-0280-1

Hyperion books are available for special promotions, premiums,
or corporate training. For details contact Michael Rentas,
Proprietary Markets, Hyperion, 77 West 66th Street, 12th floor,
New York, New York 10023, or call 212-456-0133.

FIRST EDITION

10 9 8 7 6 5 4 3 2 1

R0414256528

Mabel Manning Branch
6 S. Hoyne
Chicago, IL 60612

This book is for George Dailey,
whose unwavering friendship and support
make him worth several times his weight in gold.
Or, in his case, barley.

Mabel Manning Branch
6 S. Hoyne
Chicago, IL 60612

FUZZY NAVEL

1½ oz. peach schnapps
3 oz. orange juice

Pour schnapps in a rocks or
old-fashioned glass filled with ice.
Add orange juice.

FUZZY NAVEL

4:38 P.M.

KORK

IT'S QUIET IN THE SUBURBS. The only sound is from the cab that has dropped me off, making a U-turn at the dead end, then heading back down the quiet, winding road. Its taillights quickly disappear, swallowed up by the multitude of trees.

I walk up the driveway and look at the house. It's a ranch, laid out in the shape of an L, occupying half an acre of green lawn speckled with fallen leaves. There's a double-car garage, the door closed. I see Mom through the front bay window. She's sitting in a rocking chair and reading a book—how much more stereotypical elderly can you get? I check the front door, and as expected it is locked.

I walk around the side of the house, running my hand along the brown brick, passing windows that should probably be washed. This is a big departure from the Chicago apartment. A lot more space. A lot more privacy. I've discovered that privacy is important. No neighbors for more than a quarter mile is a good thing. With all of the tree coverage, it's like being in the middle of the woods, rather than only five miles away from O'Hare Airport.

I stop at the back porch—a slab of concrete with the obligatory lawn chairs, a wrought iron sun table, and a veranda—and I close my eyes, breathing in the cool autumn air. Somewhere, someone is burning leaves. I haven't smelled that since my youth. I fill my lungs with the scent and smile. It smells like freedom.

The sliding glass patio door is open, and I decide to give Mom a lecture about that. Just because the suburbs are safer than the city doesn't mean that all of the doors shouldn't be locked.

I walk into the kitchen, catch the odor of home cooking. A pot is on the stove. I check the contents. Stew. I pick up the spoon, give it a stir, take a little bite of potato. Delicious.

Mom yells, "Jacqueline?"

I consider answering her, but decide a surprise is in order instead. I take out my gun and tiptoe into the hallway.

"Jacqueline? Is that you?"

I look left, then right, scanning for the psychotic cat that lives here. He isn't around.

"Jacqueline, you're frightening me."

That's the point, Mom.

I peek around the corner and see that Mom is standing up. She's in her seventies, short hair more gray than brown, her back bent with age. She's wearing a housedress, something plaid and shapeless. Mom's eyes dart this way and that way. They settle on me, and she gasps.

"Oh my God," she says.

"Did I scare you? You shouldn't leave the back door open, Mom. God only knows what kind of weirdos can get in."

Mom's chest flutters, and she says in a small voice, "I know who you are. My daughter told me all about you."

She reaches for the phone, but I'm on her in three steps, giving her a firm slap across her wrinkled face.

"I'm going to ask you this one time, and one time only. And then I'm going to start hurting you."

I smile, knowing how it makes the scar tissue covering most of my face turn bright pink, knowing how horrifying it looks.

"Where's Jack?"

MUNCHEL

THE TARGET IS two hundred and eighty-three yards away. James Michael Munchel knows all about mil dots, and how to calculate distance with the reticle, but he's using a laser measuring unit instead. This isn't cheating. A sniper can and should use every bit of technology available to him in the field, whether he's on a roof in Dhi Qar, Iraq, or crouching behind some shrubs in the Chicago neighborhood of Ravenswood.

Munchel is sitting on the lawn, legs crossed, the tip of his Unique Alpine TPG-1 rifle peeking out through the leafy green dogwood. He arrived here two hours ago, but had selected this spot three weeks earlier. The house is unoccupied, and Munchel has pulled the For Sale sign out of the lawn and set it facedown. Realtors probably won't stop by this late. If one does . . . well, too bad for her.

Munchel is wearing a camouflage jacket, leggings, and black steel-toed boots he bought at the army/navy surplus store on Lincoln Avenue. He can't be seen from the sidewalk fifteen feet away. Munchel knows this for a fact, because he's done several dry runs prior to today. He's practically invisible, even if someone is staring right at him.

To avoid arousing suspicion, Munchel didn't walk here in full camo. He came in street clothes—jeans and a blue shirt—and awkwardly changed while crouching behind the dogwood, putting his civvies in the black two-wheeled suitcase he towed along.

Munchel scratches his stubble, then peers through the Leupold scope, which has been zeroed out at two hundred yards. The crosshair is slightly above and to the right of the target's head, to adjust for the wind and the bullet drop. He'll never admit it, but he doesn't understand how to determine MOA—minute-of-angle. He can fake it online, while posting on the sniper message boards, but he doesn't really know how to calculate the actual degrees. In the forest preserve near his house, Munchel can hit a target from five hundred yards and keep the grouping within a four-inch radius. Who cares what the MOA is? It's good shooting no matter how you calculate it.

The target has his back to Munchel. He's in his living room, on the first floor of the two-flat, sitting at the computer. Just like he is every day at this time.

Predictability is a killer.

The blinds hanging in the large, three-section bay window are open, and Munchel can see straight down the hallway, all the way to the back of the house. He nudges the rifle slightly, to check what the target is surfing.

Pornography. Some weird shit with chicks wearing rubber aprons and wielding whips.

Freak, Munchel thinks. *Deserves everything he's about to get.*

Munchel glances at his watch, a Luminox 3007, the same kind that Navy SEALs use. Less than a minute left. Munchel's hands start to shake, and he realizes he's breathing heavy. Not from fear. From excitement. All the training, all the planning, it all comes down to this moment.

The butt plate is snug against his armpit, his face is tight against the cheek pad, the safety is off. The aluminum gun chassis is on the concrete planter behind the dogwood, a hard surface that ensures the gun will stay steady. Munchel takes a deep breath, lets it out through his teeth. His ears tell him there is no traffic coming, which is essential because he's shooting across the street—it would be bad if a car entered his line of fire at the moment of truth.

The target stands up, walks toward the window, seems to look right at him. Impossible, of course. He's much too far away, too well hidden. But it's still unnerving. Munchel chews his lower lip, begins the countdown.

The target turns. Munchel completely empties his lungs and waits . . . waits . . . waits . . . then squeezes the trigger with the ball of his finger, trying to time it between heartbeats like he's read about online.

There's a loud *CRACK*. The target's head explodes, and he pitches forward.

Munchel sucks in some air and lets it out as a laugh. *How ridiculously easy.* He checks to see if anyone around him noticed the gunfire. The sidewalks are clear. No one opens a door and sticks their head out. Everything is completely normal, just an average fall day in the city.

He reaches for his canteen—also an army/navy store purchase—and slurps down some purple Gatorade. His untraceable prepaid cell phone vibrates, and he stares at the number. It's Swanson. Anxious to see how it went, to meet at the rendezvous point and brag over beer and chicken wings.

Munchel ignores the call. He has other ideas of how to celebrate.

A streetlight comes on, its sensor activated by a timer. Munchel loads a round, aims, and takes it out. That's two shots now. Still, no one seems to notice. How disappointing.

He takes out his phone and dials 911.

"I was walking down Leavitt and heard someone shooting. I think my neighbor has been killed."

"What is your name, sir?"

"He's at forty-six fifty-two. I think someone shot him."

"Can you give me your name?"

Munchel hangs up, sips more Gatorade, and hunkers down to wait for the police to arrive.

JACK

MY PARTNER, Sergeant Herb Benedict, crams the last mini chocolate donut into his mouth, wipes a hand across his gray mustache, and then tries to heave his bulk out of the less-than-comfortable confines of my 1984 Chevy Nova. He has to rock, twice, before he gets enough momentum to break the tug of gravity between his ass and the seat.

"Thanks for not judging me," he says as we approach the yellow police tape.

"Because you ate two packages of donuts even though your doctor put you on a high-fiber diet?"

Herb nods. "Man cannot live on bran alone, Jack. Every day, as a snack, my wife mixes me a high-fiber sugar-free weight loss shake. Then she adds even more fiber."

"Sounds healthy."

"You want some? I got a zipper bag in my pocket full of the stuff. It's like drinking a stalk of wheat."

Dried leaves in shades of gold, red, and brown blanket the sidewalks. The cool air carries a crisp, woodsy scent. Spring and summer smell like garbage and sewage. Winter, like car exhaust. Fall is the only time of year Chicago smells nice.

The setting sun casts long shadows on the street, and ours walk ahead of us. I like September because the climate is moderate, and because I have brown hair and brown eyes, and 85 percent of my clothing matches this particular season.

"Does your wife know you're snacking between nutritious meals?" I ask.

Herb's basset hound jowls are turned down: his serious face. "She suspects. Last night she found some powdered sugar on my tie. I spent twenty minutes trying to convince her it was heroin."

A rookie guards the crime scene, keeping away reporters and gawkers. Young, curly hair, eyes intent. I don't recognize him, and he doesn't recognize us, asking for ID. This is perfectly acceptable. I'm wearing a pumpkin-colored Anne Klein jacket with a red chevron pattern, taupe Armani pants, and rust Gucci pumps. He probably thinks I'm a waif runway model looking for my photo shoot. Well, a retired one, maybe. There aren't too many fashionistas in their late forties.

I open my clutch—a Wal-Mart purchase, but hey, it matches the outfit—and remove my star, flashing it at the noob.

"Lieutenant Jack Daniels, Homicide. This is Sergeant Benedict."

The rookie—his name tag reads *Sakey*—doesn't seem impressed with either my rank or my outfit, but he lets us pass. We walk into the first floor of a two-flat vintage brownstone, the space already crawling with cops: uniforms, plainclothes, and techies taking pictures and video. I feel my stomach go sour, something that has been happening more and more whenever I visit a crime scene. Without letting Herb see, I remove a roll of antacids out of my jacket pocket and pop three. Not that I fear showing weakness in front of my partner. My concern centers around the fact that my antacids are mint flavored, and Herb likes mint. I haven't discovered a flavor that Herb doesn't like, even though I've looked. I only have a few tablets left, and I don't want to share.

"She's just trying to look out for you, Herb," I say.

"I know. But I have a feeling that the extra years this high-fiber diet may allow me to live will get cancelled out by the amount of time I spend on the john."

Herb and I each take some plastic booties out of the box by the door and slip them over our shoes. There are gloves as well, and I snap one on.

The house isn't very well lit, one thrift shop floor lamp and a living room chandelier with two bulbs not working. The CSU has brought in a portable halogen light, which illuminates the space to operating room brightness. There's a computer desk, empty pop cans, fast-food wrappers, and CDs randomly strewn over the top. The monitor is a flat screen, and there are speakers screwed into the walls. A red beanbag chair which doesn't match the red shade of the sofa which doesn't match the red shade of the drapes. The TV is an older model, sitting on a cheap pressboard cabinet. The walls are bare except for a poster of a topless Jenna Jameson.

The victim is a male Caucasian, average build, sprawled out face-down on the floor. He's wearing jeans and nothing else. His blond hair is matted with blood, and a halo of red has soaked the beige carpeting around his head. I've seen enough gunshot wounds in my day to recognize the cause of death.

I crouch down, squint at his right hand. In the webbing between his thumb and index finger there is a black tattoo of a tombstone. Written on its face is a number five with angel wings on it.

A bulge in the back of the vic's pocket appears wallet shaped, and I tug it out with a gloved hand. Driver's license shows me a picture of a man named Robert Siders who resides at this address. The hair seems the same. I pass the wallet to Herb, bend down, and gently turn the deceased's head to the side. No one looks like their driver's license picture, but in this case I can't even make a comparison—the victim's face has been blown off.

The wallet holds thirty-three dollars, a check stub from a local oil and lube place, and a wrinkled time card signed by the manager of same garage. No credit cards.

Without prompting, Herb yanks out his cell, calling Dispatch. I stand up, take a few steps away from the body, and let my eyes sweep the room while Herb speaks into the phone.

Sakey—the curly-haired rookie who carded me earlier—walks up next to me and peers down at the body.

"Roommate got angry," he ventures.

"One-bedroom apartment," I say. "No roommate."

"Girlfriend, then."

"No girlfriend. The house is messy, badly furnished, and there's a poster of a porn star on the wall. No woman would live here."

Sakey folds his arms and puts a hand on his chin. I watch the wheels spin. "Okay, drug deal gone bad. Dealer shot him in the face."

"No drugs. He's got ink on his hand. Prison tattoo. Did five years, got paroled. There's a signed time card in his wallet—he needs to turn it in to his PO, which means he's getting random drug tests. If he's holding down a job, he's keeping clean."

He nods. "Fine, we check for former associates. One of them must have came in and—"

"No one came in," I say.

Sakey raises an eyebrow. "Then who shot him in the face?"

"No one shot him in the face. They shot him in the back of the head."

"I've seen GSWs. He clearly was shot—"

"By a high-velocity rifle in the back of the head," Herb finishes for him, snapping his cell phone closed. "Higher velocity causes a shock wave in tissue, which makes big exit wounds."

"Record?" I ask Herb.

"In for ten and out in five. One count unlawful restraint. One count deviate sexual assault. One count aggravated criminal sexual abuse."

"Our vic is a rapist," I say, staring down at the body. "Herb, get the information on the woman he assaulted, and her family."

"You think they hired a hitter?" Sakey asks.

It's the first assumption he may have gotten right, but he says it to my back—I'm already at the window facing the street, letting my eyes roam back and forth, up and down. I find it at nose level.

The bullet punched through neatly, leaving a hole the size of a dime. No cracked pane or shattered glass—another indicator of a very fast round. I stand in front of it and face the apartment, looking from the window to the victim, and then down the hallway. I follow the path, scrutinizing the far wall, and locate the bullet's final resting place; another small hole, this one ringed with specks of blood.

I scan the CSU officers in the room and see one that I know, Dan Rogers. I call him over.

"Bullet wound up over here," I tell him. "But before you dig it out, I need to borrow your laser pointer."

I have no idea if he actually has a laser pointer in his box full of stuff, but he does, one of those thin models the size of a AA battery. I jam it into the depression in the wall, have Herb stand next to the window, and spend a minute lining up the holes.

"Who was first on the scene?" I ask Sakey.

"Beat cop named Rory. Out in back losing his lunch."

"Do you know when the call came?"

"A minute or two after five. Multiple 911s."

I nod, then throw him a bone. "Want to help find the hide?"

"Uh, yeah, sure."

I point to Jenna. "That poster still has the cardboard backing, so it should be stiff. Take it off the wall and meet us outside."

He immediately hops to it. I leave the house, put my plastic booties and latex glove into a different box by the entrance, then organize three teams of uniforms to do door-to-doors, checking for wits. When that's finished I take out a slim notepad from my clutch and jot down: *911 tapes, PO, priors, family,* and *freelance assassins/ViCAT.* Much as I loathe to get the FBI involved, their database will give me access to similar murders.

Herb and I meet Sakey where we'd originally found him, near the police tape. He doesn't seem pleased to be carrying a poster of a top-less woman. Especially since there's a crowd of onlookers, including a few members of the press.

"Why did I bring this?" he asks.

"Hold up the poster," I say.

Sakey does as he's told, and the TV cameras catch his frown. "They're filming us."

"No they're not," Herb says. "They're filming you. You're the one waving around the giant picture of the naked lady."

Sakey's unhappy face deepens, but he keeps the poster raised. "Now what?"

"Follow us," I tell him.

We push past the crowd, ignoring the questions being shouted at us, and stand on the opposite side of the street. I hold Sakey's shoulders, moving him left and right until the red dot from the laser pointer appears on Ms. Jameson's stomach. The TV crews creep closer, capturing our every move.

"Man," Sakey groans. "My mom watches the news."

Herb waves at the cameras and says, "Hi, Mrs. Sakey."

I tap Sakey on the back. "Just keep the dot on the poster and keep walking."

Sakey marches on, though he doesn't seem thrilled about it. Like many beat cops, he's probably fantasized about getting into Detective Division, working a major homicide. I guess I've deglamorized it for him.

We continue walking, following the sidewalk about a hundred yards down, then hop over a waist-high wrought iron fence surrounding a duplex. A slight breeze with a pinch of winter chill tussles my hair. Sakey's blows around as well, then springs right back to his original curls. I wonder what conditioner he uses.

"What's a hide?" Sakey asks. He holds the poster in front of his chest, the dot now on Jenna's hip.

"Where a sniper shoots from," Herb answers. "Now the problem is finding the catway."

"What's a catway?"

"About eight pounds."

Sakey doesn't laugh. Neither do I, having heard that joke several dozen times during the years Herb has been my partner. He also can't pass a cemetery without quipping, "People are dying to get in there." I never laugh at that one either.

We walk along the front of the building, up to a cluster of evergreen bushes. They're thick enough to hide a man. My gun comes out, a .38 Colt Detective Special snubby, my sights locking on the plant. A quick peek inside finds the bush to be devoid of snipers.

"Found brass," Herb says. He grunts, kneeling down on the lawn, teasing a spent cartridge into a clear plastic evidence bag with his fingernail. It's gold, shiny, almost three inches long.

"Three oh eight?" Herb guesses.

"I don't think so. Read the bottom."

Herb squints at it, peering down the front of his nose and making a farsighted face.

"The writing is scratched out."

Sakey nods his head and says, "Smart."

I've corrected him enough today, and he spared me the indignity of walking down the block with a nude porn star, so I don't give him a lecture. Instead I tell him to tape off the area and find out where the homeowners are so they can be informed their house is now part of a crime scene.

"You sure they aren't home?" Sakey asks.

I point. "Morning paper is still on the porch."

He looks at me with what might be admiration, then goes on his way.

"Don't forget your date," Herb calls after him.

Sakey picks up the poster and takes it with him, making sure Jenna faces him rather than the press. I turn my attention back to the bush, not expecting to find anything else, and being surprised when I see a white business card on the ground. I ask Herb for another bag and use the barrel of my Colt to nudge it inside. The front reads:

ONE MORE DEAD PERVERT
Courtesy of
T U H C

The ink on the card is slightly smeared, and the edges have a fine perforation to them. The killer probably printed it himself using his home computer and those blank business card sheets available at office supply stores.

I frown, not liking this at all. In my experience, killers who leave messages aren't likely to stop any time soon. I have a bad feeling that there's more to this than hiring a mercenary to avenge a rape.

I stare back at the apartment, viewing the line of site. Perhaps two hundred yards. With the proper rifle, not a difficult shot at all. My mom, a former Chicago cop herself, used to have a Winchester Model 70 she'd inherited from her father. During my teenage years we'd go on afternoon excursions down to southern Illinois farmland and regularly hit ears of corn from four hundred yards, and probably farther, with thirty-aught-six rounds. She'd sold the gun decades ago—not much use for long arms in an urban environment.

Herb gives the card the same treatment he gave the bullet, holding it at arm's length to read it. Glasses are in his future.

"*TUHC?*" His voice registers the same displeasure I feel. "I hate it when they leave us notes."

My cell buzzes. I free it from my inner jacket pocket and slap it to my face.

"Daniels."

"Lieutenant? This is Bobalik, Homicide from District 20, Ravenswood. Heard you got a sniper."

"News travels fast."

"Let me guess—one shot to the head, through the window from a few hundred yards away, vic was a sex offender?"

News must travel even faster than I thought.

"Yeah. How did you know?"

"I'm at a scene on Leavitt," she says. "Victim's name is Chris Wolak. Same MO."

"Got a time of death?" I ask.

"Call came at a few minutes after five."

Ravenswood is a Chicago neighborhood about five miles away from us, but Bobalik's victim died at the same time ours did. I frown at the obvious conclusion.

"It gets better," Bobalik says. "Guess what happened in Englewood at the same time?"

"One more dead pervert," I say, quoting the card.

I fill Bobalik in on the details, then hang up and relate everything to Herb.

"Three snipers," he says. "Jesus. Why don't we ever get the normal cases? A guy gets drunk, shoots his neighbor for playing his radio too loud?"

I look at the business card again and wonder the same thing.

O N THE CAR RIDE to Ravenswood my phone rings again. I inwardly cringe, hoping it isn't another sniper death. The fates smile; it's my fiancé.

"Did I catch you at a bad time?" Latham asks.

I picture him in his office, wearing a snazzy suit. Red hair. Green eyes. Boyish smile. Broad shoulders and trim waist. That leads to me picturing him without the suit. I almost say something dirty, but don't want Herb to hold it over my head for the rest of my life.

"Your timing is perfect," I say into the phone. "Are you calling to accept my mother's kind invitation?"

"I'll do my best to cram in as much of Mom's home cooking as I possibly can."

I live with my mother in the suburb of Bensenville. That's a big no-no for Chicago cops (living outside the city, not living with your mother). But the mortgage is in her name and so far I haven't been caught. I love Chicago, but Mom wanted a more laid-back lifestyle and I wanted to keep an eye on her because she's getting up there in years. So we bought a cute little ranch house in a woodsy area and I braved a daily one-hour car ride to and from the Job.

It's about as much fun as it sounds. To make up for the commute, I get to experience the joy of weeding, painting, home repairs, cutting the lawn, tarring the driveway, cleaning the gutters, and countless other homeowner tasks that I so enjoyed living without when I had an apartment in Wrigleyville.

But at least Mom is happy.

Since Latham proposed, Mom has been inviting him over more and more, foisting food, drink, and conversation on the poor guy. It isn't easy for Latham. Not just the travel back and forth from the city, but he had a bout with botulism earlier this year and hasn't fully recovered. He still retains some residual paralysis in his legs, and an aversion to food in general.

Thankfully, the paralysis doesn't extend to his other parts.

"It will be a few hours," I say. "I'll be tied up until at least seven or eight. Can we eat at nine?"

"That's fine. I'm on my way there now. I promised Mary we'd play some rummy."

"Mom guilted you into coming early?"

"Not at all. I enjoy spending time with your mother. Besides, we play for money. I've already won her pension, now I'm going for her Social Security."

I smile. "Mom told me she was up sixty bucks."

"She cheats, Jack. She looks all cute and harmless, but she's a wily one. I think she deals from the bottom of the deck."

Can a woman ask for anything more than her future husband hanging out with her mom? Plus he's caring, funny, attractive, and he puts up with me. Good sex sealed the deal.

"See you later," I say. "I love you."

"Love you too, Jack."

"Love you more."

"No, I love you more. See you tonight."

He makes a kissing sound and I grin and make a kissing sound back, then we hang up. I glance at Herb, who does a good job of ignoring me by occupying his mouth with a chocolate power bar. Herb insists he snacks on these for energy, even though he has more than enough energy already stored in the extra eighty pounds of fat he carries around.

"That probably doesn't have much fiber in it," I offer.

Herb licks some chocolate off his fingers. I once asked Herb what the difference was between power bars and regular candy bars, and he told me that power bars had more calories.

"For energy," he'd said.

When he had his heart attack a while back, he was the only one who seemed surprised.

"I thought we had an unspoken agreement, Jack." He's taken on a superior tone. "You don't question my eating habits, I pretend to ignore it when you make kissy-face on the phone."

"I don't make kissy-face on the phone."

"Yes you do. And for your information, this power bar does contain fiber. It's in the caramelized peanuts."

I snort. "The wrapper has more fiber."

"I'm eating that next."

This long-dead horse has been beaten many times, so I change the subject. "Are you thinking what I'm thinking about the last crime scene?"

Herb's turn to snort. "Yeah. Welcome to amateur night."

I drum my fingers on the steering wheel. "What kind of shooter grinds the engraving off the bottom of his bullets? Think about the misfires."

"He should be more worried about shooting himself in the face while he's filing it down. A pro would simply pick up his brass."

"A pro would also know we would find the slug. Hell, anyone who watched TV knows the word *ballistics*."

I left the cartridge with Rogers to take to the crime lab. He ID'ed it by sight, without needing to use acid etching to bring out the markings. A .338 Lapua Magnum. A caliber specifically designed for sniping, and hopefully unique enough to be able to track. I have a team doing just that.

"And did you see his hide?" Herb shakes his head. "Can you imagine the guy, squatting in a bush, facing the sidewalk?"

If you want someone dead, it's relatively easy to ring his doorbell and shoot him in the chest when he answers. Much easier than shooting him from two hundred yards down the street at a scheduled time.

"This isn't just about the death," I say. "This is a game. A bunch of knuckleheads playing soldier, getting their kicks shooting sex offenders long distance."

I leave the next part of my thought unspoken—that a knucklehead could kill you just as easily as a pro. In some cases, they're even more dangerous. Soldiers are taught patience and discipline. An amateur takes unnecessary chances and makes big mistakes, exposing more people to risk. This TUHC group might be easier to track down than an expert hired gun, but they might also hurt a lot of innocents before that happens.

My phone rings again. I find it on my seat without taking my eyes off the road.

"Daniels."

"Is this Jacqueline Daniels?"

A female voice, rote and professional.

"Yes. Who is this?"

"This is the Heathrow Facility, you're on the list of people to inform."

The Heathrow Facility is a maximum security center for the criminally insane. I've sent a few people there over the years. The arresting officer is always called if one of the inmates dies. They're also called when an inmate is released, or escapes.

"Who is this regarding?" I ask.

"Alexandra Kork."

A feeling overwhelms me, like the shower has gone from hot to cold. Kork is one of the most dangerous people alive. I'd met her under another name, and her entire family consisted of psychopathic killers. She almost murdered me, and several people I cared about, in horrible ways.

"What about Kork?" The words are hard to get out, sticking in my throat like chicken bones. A dozen thoughts run through my mind at once, the most pressing being *Please don't tell me she escaped.*

"Alexandra Kork died this morning."

I blow out air through my mouth, and my shoulders sag.

"It appears to be a suicide," the woman continues. "She set herself on fire with some aerosol spray."

That sounds like Kork. She'd kill herself in a horrible way like that.

"Are you sure it's her?" I ask. "One hundred percent sure?"

"The body was badly burned, but we confirmed it with dental records."

I picture Alex's face, pretty as a model's when I met her. Not pretty at all after we tangled. She'd gotten close, fooled me completely, made me doubt myself unlike I ever had before.

One of the things I've learned as a cop is that everyone considers themself the hero in the story of their life. Even bad guys who killed children and blew up hospitals believed they were good guys. Everyone can justify their actions. Everyone believes they're in the right.

Kork was different. She knew she was the bad guy, that her actions were evil. It didn't bother her at all. Or maybe it did. Maybe she finally realized what an awful person she was, and couldn't cope with it.

"Ms. Daniels? Are you still there?"

"Yeah."

"There's no next of kin listed. Would you like us to release her remains to you?"

"No. The state can bury her. Thank you for calling."

I hang up and pop a few more antacids.

"Are those mint flavored?" Herb asks.

"Alex Kork is dead," I tell him. "Suicide at Heathrow."

"World is a better place without her in it. Gimme one of those antacids."

I pass the roll to Herb, thinking about the last words Alex had said to me.

"You beat me this time. But it isn't over."

It's over now, Alex. You've haunted me in countless nightmares, but you won't haunt me anymore.

Not ever again.

"WHERE'S THAT PSYCHOTIC CAT you have?"

Mary Streng stares hard at Alex Kork. The woman who broke into their house is taller than Jacqueline, with broader shoulders. Her body is angular rather than curvy, and Mary can see the muscle striations in her bare forearms. Alex has straight black hair, shoulder length. This woman might have been pretty once, but the left side of her face, from her chin to her missing eyebrow, is a knot of pink scar tissue, puckered with patchwork skin graft zigzags and pockmarks from countless stitches.

"At the vet," Mary answers. "Bitten by a dog."

Alex winces. No—it only looks like a wince because the ruined half of her face stays immobile. It's actually a smile.

"That's a shame. Such a cute kitty, being mauled by a big, bad canine."

"He'll be fine," Mary says. "The dog isn't expected to recover."

Alex sits on the sofa next to Mary. She's tucked her gun—a small-caliber revolver—into the back of her jeans, which rankles Mary.

I'm an old lady, and she doesn't consider me a threat, Mary realizes.

It's true, and it hurts. Sharp as her mind still is, her body has grown old and weak. Osteoporosis is shrinking her. Rheumatoid arthritis has turned her hands into agonizing claws. Her figure, once a perfect hourglass, is now shaped more like the box the hourglass came in. What she would give to be young again, just for a minute, to show this young punk—

"Are you sizing me up?" Alex asks.

Mary lowers her eyes.

"Look at me when I'm talking to you, Mom. Or I'll start knocking you around."

Mary stares at her, projecting defiance instead of fear. Alex's face twitches into a half smile. Up close, the scars are white and look like rubber.

"I know you used to be a cop," Alex says. "I bet this really makes you feel helpless."

Mary doesn't answer. Jacqueline has told her all about Alex and her nightmarish family. Like most cops, her daughter kept her fears hidden away. But Mary knew that Jack feared Alex. And now she can see why. This scarred woman sitting next to her doesn't have a soul. Something, some vital part, is missing from Alex. The part that makes her a human being.

Mary had only seen it once before, more than forty years ago, on the Job. A homeless man had killed his friend over half a bottle of wine. Mary had hit the offender with her billy, over and over, but he wouldn't go down. He just continued to stare at her with those black, bottomless eyes. Eyes without a trace of humanity. Eyes that dared her to kill him.

The same eyes Alex has.

"I bet it hurt," Mary says, "when my daughter tore your face off."

Mary doesn't see the blow coming—it's too fast. But she feels it, the fist connecting with her mouth, the explosion of pain in her lips, her head snapping back. She had been punched before, in the line of duty, but never so hard or so viciously.

Then Alex is standing over her, running a hand through Mary's gray hair in a warped parody of kindness.

"Maybe later I'll show you how much it hurts," Alex says.

And Mary Streng realizes she's going to die.

It isn't as scary as she thought it might be. She's lived a long, full life. She's done everything she ever set out to do. She's made some mistakes, of course. Some big ones. A failed marriage. A child out of wedlock, put up for adoption when she was still a teenager. A feud with her mother that never got resolved before she died. But Mary managed to forgive herself, to learn from her errors, to keep on going. She knew she could meet death—even an unpleasant death—with grace and dignity and no regrets.

But this isn't just about her. Alex also wants to kill Jacqueline.

That scares Mary to the core. Mary would die for her daughter. She'd also want to die if her daughter were killed. Parents aren't supposed to outlive their children, and Jacqueline is too good a person to be murdered at the hands of this lunatic.

She has to warn Jacqueline. Has to make sure Alex can't get her.

"Do you bake?" Alex asks.

"What?"

"I know it's a stereotype, that all old women bake. But do you?"

"Yes," Mary says.

"What do you bake? Cookies? Bread?"

Mary doesn't like these questions. They seem too intimate. She forces herself to say, "I make pies."

"What kind of pies?"

"Peach. Cherry. Apple. I was going to make an apple pie today, for after dinner."

"You've got all of the ingredients?"

Mary nods.

"Okay, let's do it," Alex says. "Let's make a pie."

Alex takes Mary's hand, leads her into the kitchen. Mary doesn't understand where this is going, what Alex's ulterior motive is. But she has no choice other than to let it play out.

FUZZY NAVEL • 25

"What do we do first?"

"There's some dough, in the refrigerator."

Alex opens up the large stainless steel door and takes out a bowl with a wet towel covering the top. Mary stares at the gun in the back of Alex's jeans. She needs to get closer.

"This the dough?" Alex asks.

Mary nods. "Yes."

"It's done rising, or whatever?"

"Yes."

"What else do we need?"

"Apples. Brown sugar. Lemon juice. Flour."

"You want to lend a hand here, Mom? This pie isn't going to make itself."

It's silly. Mary has been slapped, punched, and threatened, and she stayed stoic. But a simple act of baking makes her eyes well up with tears.

Maybe it's the perversion of a normally enjoyable activity. Mary loves to bake. It's one of the simple joys of life. But being forced to by this murderer makes the whole experience seem tainted, dirty.

Alex acts normal the whole time. She rolls out the dough. She slices the apples. She's chatty and cheerful and asks many questions about the process. But she never lets down her guard and gives Mary a chance at the gun.

Jacqueline loathes baking, has no patience for it. Mary hasn't baked with her daughter since she was twelve years old. That fact makes this experience even worse. Mary should be bonding with her daughter, not with a psycho.

"Why do you bake if it makes you so sad?" Alex asks.

Mary wipes her face with the back of her hand, furious with herself for showing weakness.

"Or are you just upset because this is the last pie you'll ever make? There's a last time for everything, Mom. At least you can savor it, knowing it's the last time."

"The oven is done preheating," Mary says. "Put the pie on the bottom rack."

Alex obeys. Then she pats the excess flour off of her shirt and laughs at the cloud it makes.

"You never baked with your mother?" Mary asks.

"I might have. I don't remember. When I was small, Father tied her to a beam in the basement and whipped her until she died." Alex pops a stray apple slice into her mouth. "He made me help him, made me beat her."

"I'm sorry. That must have been horrible."

"Not really. He let me rest when I got tired."

Alex turns away, looks past the living room, out the large bay window facing the street. "Does Jack still drive that shitty Nova?"

Mary doesn't answer, sees a car coming up the driveway.

Not Jacqueline's.

Oh, no. It's Latham.

Mary takes a deep breath, ready to scream out a warning, but Alex is on her, tearing at her housedress, pulling off a sleeve and shoving it past her split lips, wadding it into her mouth. Then the gun is out again, pressed up against Mary's temple, and they both wait in silence for Latham to come in.

JACK

LEAVITT STREET BUZZES with activity. As in the previous crime scene, cops and onlookers surround the house, a walking, talking wall. The media already arrived, two news vans sending live feeds to their networks. I park in the center of the street, since nothing is getting through anyway. Herb extricates himself from my car with much grunting, but I refrain from making any jokes involving power bars or extra energy.

It's dark now. Dark and cold. The streetlight in front of the house isn't working, but there are enough emergency vehicles with their headlights on to provide adequate illumination.

We push through the crowd, duck under the cordon, and head for the house. This one is bigger than the two-flat we just left, a single-family home with a giant bay window in front. Through the open blinds I can see cops milling around inside. Herb and I don our booties and go in, seeking out Detective Bobalik to get an update.

She directs the crime scene from the front room, standing a few feet away from Chris Wolak's body on the floor. I pause, taking everything in. Ten, maybe twelve police officers in the room, most of them CSU. Decor is retro Norman Bates, stuffed ducks and pheasants and animal heads adorning the walls and shelves. A computer desk, the monitor showing porn. A large leather sofa. A framed picture of a smiling man holding the antlers of the buck he shot. An entertainment stand, TV, DVD, stereo. I examine the bay window, find the bullet hole, see the crowd outside looking back at me.

Bobalik is short, wearing glasses, and has really good hair, the kind that moves when she moves.

"I want ALS done before the ME arrives," she says to her team. "Bruen, organize the door-to-door. Let's move, people, I don't want to spend the rest of my life here."

I walk to her, my hand extended in greeting, and then her head explodes.

It looks a lot like someone kicking a pumpkin. The top of her scalp comes off, spins through the air, and bounces off the TV. A fine mist of blood rises up around her shoulders and hangs there even after she crumples to the floor.

"Down!" I yell.

A tug at my waist. Herb tackling me even as I dive for the carpet.

Another shot.

The bullet rips through Bruen's chest, blood erupting from the exit wound, splashing the wall several feet behind him.

Screaming. From in the house. From the street outside.

I look right. Herb on the floor, between me and the window.

The carpet below me is cold and damp.

Another shot.

A CSU member falls, the round slicing through the sofa he hides behind, taking a hunk out of his neck.

I look left. The victim, Chris Wolak, face-to-face with me, except there isn't much face left. A white male, in his thirties, a hole in the back of his head, just like Rob Siders.

I'm lying in his blood.

Another shot.

A detective. On the floor next to me, only a few feet away. The bullet enters his hip, exits up through his neck. A long way for a slug to travel through tissue.

We're not safe on the floor.

I scream, "Get away from the window!"

A uniform stands up, runs for the hallway.

Another shot.

A miss.

He makes it to the end of the hall.

Another shot.

He dives to the floor.

No—he doesn't dive. Blood volcanoes out of his back.

Herb gets to his feet, attempting to make the same run.

"Herb!" I yell.

He gets two steps down the hall.

Another shot.

The bullet smacks the wall, stripping off wood paneling.

Two more steps.

Another shot.

Over Herb's head, destroying a dome light.

Two more steps, and he's next to a door.

Another shot.

Herb falls through the doorway.

"Herb!"

Silence.

I roll, away from the vic, hands tucked to my chest.

Bump into Bobalik. Roll over her.

Another shot, tearing up the carpet where I was a second ago.

I continue rolling, angling toward the window.

Then I ram into the wall. The wall the window is on.

Out of the line of fire. Safe.

I reach up for the turning rod on the blinds, twist it, closing the slats on the window nearest to me, blocking the sniper's vision.

Another shot. Through the window.

Then another, higher up.

The blinds fall off the wall, clatter to the floor.

"Herb!" I yell with everything I have.

Herb doesn't answer.

Another shot.

Then another.

The gunfire isn't hitting the house. I open up my clutch, remove a lipstick, one that has a tiny mirror on the case. My back to the wall, I angle the mirror so I can see out the front window.

Most of the gawkers and media have fled. Cops are behind cars, weapons drawn. Handguns and shotguns, nothing long enough to hit a shooter two hundred yards away. Some are shrugging on bulletproof vests—Type IIIA—which won't offer any protection against high-velocity sniper rounds. A .338 will punch through them like they're tissue paper.

Another shot.

I watch a patrolman's head snap back—he's behind the trunk of the patrol car, and the bullet slices right through the metal.

I turn back to the room. Five cops down in here, plus the original victim. Five more cops tucked into corners and behind furniture. Plus me. And Herb, if he made it.

I know it will take a minimum of ten minutes for the Special Response Team to gear up and arrive. They'll have rifles, and heavier body armor.

But in the meantime, we're ducks in a pond.

I try again. *"Herb!"*

A second passes.

Two.

Three.

Four.

Then, "Jack!"

I blow out a pent-up breath, a million kinds of relieved.

"Are you okay?" I yell.

"Yeah! My wife called, hysterical. Saw us on TV. She said she'd hold you personally responsible if I'm killed."

I wonder if I should call Latham. Perhaps I won't have another chance.

I push back the maudlin thoughts, focusing on how to escape. I glance at the door, so far away. Then I lock eyes with a stag head, hanging on the wall.

Chris Wolak is a hunter. He'll have long guns.

"Herb! Check to see if there are any rifles in there."

"Hold on." The pause lasts forever. Then, "Found a gun locker. Need to break it open."

Another shot.

A crime scene techie, crouching behind the entertainment stand, wails like a siren, clutching the remainder of his foot. The pain must be unimaginable.

"Keep your head down!" I order the techie.

His keening cry goes on and on, and he rocks back and forth with his knee pressed to his chest, his head peeking out over the coffee table.

"Keep your—!"

Another shot.

The techie slumps to the ground, bleeding from the shoulder. A bad wound, gushing fast. He won't live until the SRT arrives. He needs medical help now.

I'm not the type who prays, but I beg the universe for Herb to find a rifle.

MUNCHEL

MUNCHEL PAUSES TO ADD another hash mark to the butt of
his rifle, using a black permanent marker. That makes nine so
far. The number pleases him, but he's angry at himself for missing that
fat cop, the one who came late to the party. Moves pretty fast for a
porker. He arrived with that good-looking split-tail who parked in the
middle of the street. That pisses Munchel off. Why should cops be
able to park wherever the hell they want to? It's bullshit.

Munchel checks his watch, figures he has a few more minutes before reinforcements arrive. Maybe he'll have another chance at Fatty,
and the double-parker.

His cell rings. Swanson again. Munchel picks up.

"What the fuck are you doing!" Swanson is yelling, his voice high
pitched and girlish. Not a soldier's tone at all.

"Hi, Greg. You at the rendezvous point, sucking down a cool one?"

"You asshole! You're live on CNN!"

"Cool."

Munchel pulls the bolt back, ejecting the empty cartridge, then
jams it forward to force another round into the chamber of his TPG-1.
He peers through the Leupold scope. All the cops in the street are
hiding or have run off. Of course they have. An entire platoon is no
match for a single skilled sniper. Munchel can shoot the petals off a

daisy at three hundred yards. Killing cops at less than two hundred is child's play.

"What if they catch you?" Swanson whines like a baby.

Munchel's voice is pure Stallone. "If they take me, it won't be alive."

Munchel puts his face against the cheek pad. Aims. Fires. Another head shot. He rubs his shoulder—it's getting sore, even with the built-in recoil damper—then he uses the marker to draw the tenth kill line on the stock.

"We're going after perverts, not cops!"

Munchel looks down, sees he's dropped the cell phone. Swanson is still bitching. He picks it up.

"You say something, Swanson?"

"You're going to ruin it for us!"

"Relax," Munchel purrs. "I'll make sure I kill all the witnesses."

"You dumb son of—"

Munchel hangs up. He doesn't need Swanson, or anyone else, telling him what to do. James Michael Munchel *knows* what to do. No matter what anyone else thinks. No matter who they are.

The memory comes, unbidden, and Munchel frowns.

"Military bastards," he says to himself.

He doesn't like to dwell on his rejection by the armed forces, but he dwells on it every day. All those stupid tests he had to fill out, being told by the recruiter that there were no wrong answers. A bald-faced lie. Obviously there were wrong answers, or else he'd be in a foxhole in Baghdad right now, killing insurgents.

Munchel chambers another round, imagines it's Osama in the crosshairs, not some stupid pig.

BANG!

That makes eleven, plus the original target. He doubts any marine sniper could do better. Another hash mark on the rifle. Pessolano will probably have a shit-fit when he sees how he marked up his precious gun. Maybe Munchel can buy the rifle from him. He respects Pessolano, because Pessolano actually toured, saw combat in Desert Storm. Pessolano always wears yellow shooting glasses, those high-contrast ones that block out blue light. Pessolano is hard-core, but he needs to lighten up. Him and Swanson both.

Munchel looks in the suitcase, finds the pair of yellow glasses he bought from that late-night infomercial. He slips them on, but they make everything too bright and give him an eyestrain headache. He takes them off again. Real snipers don't need fancy sunglasses.

Another glance through the scope, and Munchel grins.

Fat Boy is back. And it looks like the cop found a rifle. Some dinky little model, but a rifle nonetheless.

This might be interesting.

Munchel works the bolt, takes aims, and squeezes the trigger.

JACK

MY PARTNER'S LEG crumples beneath him when the bullet hits. He cries out, pitching forward, the rifle slipping from his grasp and taking flight.

Herb tumbles to the floor. The gun remains airborne, spinning like a Frisbee, the barrel aiming my way.

I bunch up my shoulders and cover my face—not much protection against a dropped weapon, but a reflex action.

The rifle bounces onto the floor without going off. But it's ten feet away from me, directly in the line of fire.

So is Herb.

I tug out my .38, aim where I'd seen the muzzle flash over a hundred yards away, and fire twice.

My bullets won't hit the mark. A snub-nose revolver isn't accurate beyond twenty feet. But Herb needs time to crawl back into hiding, assuming he can still move.

I press my back against the wall again, not wanting to leave my head exposed longer than necessary, and see Herb dashing across the carpet on all fours like a coked-up squirrel. Maybe those power bars have something to them after all. He makes it back through the doorway, leaving a spotty trail of blood.

"How bad?" I call to him.

"Calf! I'll be okay! Did you get the rifle?"

I stare at the weapon. Ten feet away might as well be a hundred.

"I'm working on it!"

I survey the room. Other than the injured techie, who is rapidly bleeding out, only four people are still alive: two uniforms, two plainclothes. I'm ranking officer, but I'm not about to order any of them to go after the rifle. Especially since I'm the closest one to it.

I imagine the sniper. Probably crouching in a bush, as the other had. Peering through a scope, his sites locked onto the fallen rifle, waiting for someone to try for it.

I've used scopes before. At distances longer than fifty yards, the slightest movement by the shooter throws them off target. If I distract him, then move quickly, I'll have two or three seconds before he finds me again.

Theoretically at least.

Or I can sit tight and wait for the cavalry to arrive. But I don't know if the injured cop can last that long. And I've had enough of people dying on my watch.

I look to my left, see a small end table. Metal, solid, manageable. I kick off my heels and holster my gun. Then I lift the table above my head, aim at the window where the last bullet went through, and heave it hard as I can.

Before it hits the glass I'm in motion . . . bending down for the rifle . . . hearing the window shatter . . . grabbing the barrel and hugging it to my chest . . . digging my bare heels into the carpet to change direction in case the sniper was tracking me . . . skidding . . .

Falling onto my ass.

The pain travels from my coccyx straight up to my neck like a lightning bolt, prompting instant tears and an immediate surge of panic.

I'm sitting directly in the sniper's sights. And he has an even clearer view of me now, because the window sports a large hole where the table broke though.

Though I don't remain still for longer than a second, it feels like a week, and my ears burn and my forehead gets hot where I imagine a bull's-eye to be, where the shot is going to hit.

The shot doesn't come.

I pull the gun closer to my body, drop my right shoulder, and quickly roll back to my original hiding spot alongside the window.

Herb says, "I had seven heart attacks watching you do that."

I look down the hallway, lock eyes with Herb in the mirror reflection of a music CD he's holding out the doorway. He's using it like I'd used the lipstick, to see around the corner.

Rather than respond, I do a quick inspection of the weapon. A Dakota rifle. Fixed sights. A twenty-four-inch barrel. Bolt action. I check the magazine. Three .458 rounds, plus one already chambered. I tuck the butt into my armpit and sight through the scope, aiming at the ceiling.

The lens is cracked, and bent to the left side.

"Scope's dead," I call to Herb. "Any more back there?"

A pause. Then, "No."

"Bullets?"

"I didn't see—"

The *crack* of the shot makes me flinch, and the CD disintegrates in Herb's hand. I look around the room at my men. They're hunkered down, terrified. I need to get them out of here. But I can't if they're too scared to move.

"Looks like our sniper isn't a music fan," I say. The joke sounds forced, mostly because it is.

"I can't blame him," Herb says. "I don't like John Denver either."

I unscrew the scope from its mount and toss it aside. Then I swing the barrel around, toward the street.

"Hold up another one."

"I could only find his greatest hits album."

I suck in air, blow it out hard, my cheeks billowing.

"How about Neil Diamond?" I yell.

I rest the tip of the barrel on the windowsill, an inch away from the glass. Not the best way to steady a rifle, but all I can manage given the situation.

"No Neil. Is Jim Croce okay?"

"That's fine."

"*Time in a Bottle*, or *You Don't Mess Around With Jim*?"

I'm about to tell Herb I don't care, but I reconsider. "*Time in a Bottle*," I yell.

I was never a fan of sappy love songs.

I stare down the street, waiting for it. The sniper's muzzle flashes before I hear the shot. The CD explodes.

"I couldn't save *Time in a Bottle*," Herb says.

I line up the sights, fixing them slightly above my target, knowing the bullet will travel in a parabolic arc.

"I'm going to fire four shots, four seconds apart," I tell the room. "So you have between twelve and sixteen seconds to get the injured, and yourselves, out of the house. There's an ambulance on the corner of Leavitt and Leland. You can get there using parked cars for cover. Understood?"

I count five *yeses*, including a weak moan from the injured techie. One voice is conspicuous in its absence.

"You too Herb."

"No way. I'm liking this CD collection too much. When was the last time you heard the Kingston Trio?"

"That's an order, Herb."

"I'm not leaving."

Goddammit. If Herb died his wife would kill me.

"Fine. Hold up the other Croce CD, then stay hidden. We go after I fire my first round. Everyone get ready."

I hold the rifle tight against my armpit and rest my chin on the stock, sighting down the barrel. I test the trigger pull, apply enough pressure to barely move it. Then I wait, breathing slow and easy so it doesn't throw off my aim.

It doesn't take long. The killer can't resist showing off his marksman skills, and he blows away the second Croce CD.

"Go!" I tell the room.

Then I squeeze the trigger.

MUNCHEL

MUNCHEL GRUNTS in satisfaction after the CD shatters, and then he moves the scope ever so slightly to watch the split-tail. He's ready for her to fire back. Hell, he *wants* her to fire back. That's why he didn't kill her when she went for the rifle, even though he had a bead on it. Confirmed kills are great, but real snipers must also contend with return fire. The cops in the street, they're all too far away, their guns not powerful enough to reach him. There's no threat or danger.

He wants a little danger. And the ultimate danger is when you go up against another sniper. An anti-sniper.

Munchel doesn't expect her to come close to him. Her rifle is a toy compared to his, and she doesn't even have a scope. But this will be a much better story to tell Swanson and Pessolano if the cops send a few rounds his way.

"Show me what you got, baby," Munchel says, baring his yellow teeth in a grin.

When her first bullet connects with the concrete planter he's resting his gun on, Munchel jerks like he's had acid thrown in his face. He drops the TPG-1 and ducks down.

How the hell did she make that shot?

"Lucky," he says aloud, his voice cracking.

As the word leaves his lips, another shot blasts into the planter, tossing up stone chips, burrowing a hole into it.

Munchel backs the hell away. He checks his clothing. Why isn't the camouflage working? Is she using night vision?

A bullet zips over his head, its wind practically parting his hair before burying itself into the building behind him. He hunkers down even lower, thinking he should be returning fire, *knowing* he should, but too scared to move.

One more shot, and the planter shatters, large chunks falling to the ground, a puff of dirt forming a cloud that settles in his eyes and on his lips.

Munchel holds his breath, waiting. His bladder feels like a water balloon being squeezed in a vise. Sweat pops out of his body in places he didn't even know he had pores. He doesn't dare move, convinced that she can see him.

A full minute passes.

He wonders if she's out of bullets, or simply toying with him. Maybe she has the shot, has him all lined up, and is enjoying watching him squirm.

Sirens, in the distance. Munchel knows that must be SWAT. He needs to break camp, get the hell out of here. His heart is thumping. His mouth is dry. His palms feel like he just soaked them in water. He's more scared than he's ever been in his life.

But he's also exhilarated.

This is what combat is like, he thinks.

The feeling is intoxicating.

Munchel knows the news cameras are rolling, knows that the split-tail can see him, knows that what he has in mind might be suicidal. But he decides to go for it anyway.

No one expects a pinned down man to charge. So Munchel charges.

The suitcase in one hand, the TPG-1 in the other, he sprints across the sidewalk, across the street, daring the woman cop to shoot him. He knows to zigzag, to make himself a harder target. He maybe even yells a little, an animalistic war cry, the sound of a hero facing certain death.

No bullets hit him. No one even shoots at him. Munchel pauses behind a car to catch his breath, marveling at his own bravery. It's dark, and the streetlight he shot out earlier helps him hide in the shadows. But if the cop has some sort of optical enhancer, it's possible she can still see him.

The sirens are getting closer. He needs some kind of distraction, something that will confuse the night-vision goggles the woman cop must be using.

He unzips the suitcase, removes one of two whiskey bottles. Inside is kerosene mixed with laundry detergent. Poor man's napalm. Munchel would have preferred real napalm, or a grenade, but he couldn't get those. He tried to order some, on the Internet, and the prick took his money and didn't send him shit. Hopefully the homemade stuff will be good enough.

Munchel unscrews the bottle cap and shoves in a braided wick from a camping lantern. He uses a Zippo to light the wick and then shouts, "Semper fi!" as he throws the flaming bottle at a parked SUV. It bounces off the hood and shatters on the sidewalk, soaking someone's lawn with liquid fire.

He doesn't stop to acknowledge his handiwork. He's on the move again, tugging the suitcase behind him in a crouch, changing direction several times, making it to the Chevy Nova parked in the center of the street.

The split-tail's car. He considers using his second Molotov cocktail to set it ablaze, to teach her a lesson, but changes his mind and reaches for something else instead. Something electronic, that Pessolano let him borrow.

This woman is a worthy opponent. It isn't enough just to destroy her car. Munchel wants to best her. To beat her. And he's already formulating a plan on how to do just that.

He turns on the device and attaches it to the underside of her rear bumper. Then he lights the second bottle of napalm, yells "Recon!" and chucks it at a patrol car.

Munchel runs back the way he came, slipping between houses, making it to his car a block away. It had taken him almost forty minutes of circling to find that parking space, and even though he was clearly the required twenty feet away from the fire hydrant, he still got a ticket. Assholes.

Rather than dwell on it, Munchel throws the suitcase and the rifle into the backseat, hops behind the wheel, and beelines for the rendezvous point, imagining Pessolano and Swanson watching his heroics on CNN and cheering him on.

KORK

ACK'S BOYFRIEND LATHAM is kind of cute. Red hair, a strong chin, broad chest. He doesn't cry out when I crack him in the nose with the butt of my revolver, and doesn't beg for his life when I stick the business end under his chin.

"On the sofa, next to the old lady."

He complies, but takes his time, fixing me with what he probably thinks is a cold stare. He's about as menacing as a teddy bear. If he wanted to learn cold stares, he should have grown up in my family.

"When's your girlfriend getting home?" I ask.

He reaches out, holds the woman's hand. Doesn't answer. Which pisses me off.

I've lost track of how many people I've killed, but I know I've killed men for annoying me less than Latham is doing right now. But I don't want to do anything permanent until Jack gets home and is able to watch. So I settle for smacking him with the gun again.

I hit him pretty good, opening up a cut on his cheek, and he refuses to meet my eyes. So much for the tough guy act.

"I don't like repeating myself," I say.

"She told me nine." His voice is soft, dull. "She's on a case."

FUZZY NAVEL • 45

I check my new watch. Heathrow didn't allow watches. Or jewelry. Or makeup. Or bras. Or shoes. We had our unisex cotton pants and top, and slippers with flimsy rubber soles. I could understand them keeping security tight. A few of the women in there were crazy. But my minders confused *insane* with *feeble-minded*. Big mistake.

My watch tells me I have about two hours left before Jack arrives. I'm hungry. Maybe I can get Mom to serve me some of that stew she's making. I also haven't gotten fucked in forever. The last time was with my so-called husband, and he was as ineffective in bed as he was at everything else. I eye Latham's broad shoulders, trim waist, then move my eyes lower, to his crotch. I wonder if he is up for the job. I know from experience that a man sometimes has problems getting it up when a gun is jammed in his mouth.

But when they can manage, the sex is mind-blowing.

Later, I decide. One more thing that Jack can watch.

"Who else is hungry?" I ask.

I smile, not the easiest thing to do when you've lost most of the nerves and muscles in half of your face. Mom grimaces. Latham stares at the floor.

"Both of you, stand up. Slow and easy. If you move too fast, or if I get the feeling you aren't going to behave, I'll shoot your knees."

They stand, and hero boyfriend puts his arm around Mom's shoulders. It's touching, the warmth. Really. When the time comes, I don't know which one I'll kill first.

No need to think about that now. We have all night. And what a night it will be. These aren't the only guests I'm inviting to this party. With some duct tape to keep everyone manageable, and some delivery pizza, we could keep this going for a few days.

First things first, Mom can serve some dinner. And I can warm loverboy up for our floor show later on. He looks to be the loyal type. Tough to break.

But I'll break him. When I was growing up, Father used the stove for more than just cooking. He used it for punishment. Showed me up close and personal all the ways a stove can make a person scream.

And I'm more than happy to share the knowledge.

JACK

WHILE I FIRE at the sniper the cops in the house clear out, carrying their injured team member. Herb comes up behind me, and we watch through the window as they make their way down the street. They join the others who were lucky enough to have gotten away, to the end of the block where the ambulances are.

We also watch our perp run around in jerky patterns, dragging a suitcase behind him and holding a huge sniper rifle, occasionally yelling something incoherent. He stops twice to throw homemade bombs at cars. Each one bounces off and causes a small fire on the sidewalk.

"This might very well be the world's stupidest criminal," Herb says.

I'm out of rifle ammo. Herb and I pull our service pistols, keeping the perp in our sights. Though he keeps zigzagging and ducking down, he would have been a cinch to shoot if he came within our range. We could even have nailed him without looking, because he kept whooping like a drunken sports fan, giving away his location. Unfortunately, he stays at least fifty yards away the entire time, and eventually disappears between two houses, running off into the night.

Herb and I meet the Special Response Team in front, and I send them in the direction the sniper had gone. By that time the small fires have almost extinguished themselves, and the cops who've been in hiding come out and attend to the dead.

The sniper might have been an idiot, or a lunatic, or both. But he still managed to kill ten of my men. I maintain a brave face for the TV cameras, but each time I see a body bag being loaded into an ambulance my throat closes up.

My boss, Captain Bains, arrives in a patrol car. He has his dress blues on, ready to make a statement for the press. Deputy Chief Crouch, the superintendent's right hand, is also present, setting up interviews with everyone involved. I'm first in line.

I'm bone tired, but I know I'll be debriefed over and over again for the next few hours, and there's no way to postpone it. I go back into the house and use the bathroom, doing a mediocre job washing off the blood. Then I call home, get the answering machine. Leave Mom a message that I won't make dinner tonight. I also call my long-suffering fiancé to let him know he's welcome to stay the night, and I'll make it up to him by cooking breakfast in the morning. I get his voice mail. Perhaps he and Mom are in a heated match of rummy.

Internal Affairs shows up—a bystander had been nicked by police crossfire. It wasn't by me, but they take my gun anyway; standard operating procedure so ballistics can rule out my bullets as the lethal ones. I'm too numb to argue. My phone rings, and I excuse myself for a minute.

"Jack, it's an emergency." Mom sounds frazzled. "You need to come home."

"Mom? Are you okay? What's going on?"

I'm talking to a dead line. I call back. Get the machine. Call again, get the same results. Try Latham once more, go directly to voice mail.

What the hell?

"I need to check on my partner," I tell the IA guys. Then I catch up with Herb as two paramedics assist him into the ambulance. The assistance involves a lot of lifting and grunting.

"I need a favor, Herb."

"No problem. I'll make a copy for you." He taps his jacket pocket, which held the Kingston Trio CD. "And yes, it's got 'Tom Dooley' on it."

I lean closer. "I need you to cover for me, for a few hours. The deputy chief wants answers. The Feds are coming, probably to compare this to every other sniper incident in the past seven hundred years. Plus I'm going to have to tell the same story again for IA."

"Are you going to tell them I stole folk rock?"

"No. I'm going to tell them to talk to you first. I just got a weird call from my mother, and something's not right. I have to run home. And as you're well aware . . ."

Herb finishes for me. "You live in the suburbs, even though you'd be fired if they found out, and even though there were many perfectly nice single-family homes in my neighborhood."

"I'll be two and a half hours, tops. Just make sure they don't go to my old apartment."

Because then they'll know I don't live in the city anymore.

"Take three hours," Herb says. "I use a lot of adjectives when I tell stories."

I pat his shoulder. "Thanks, Herb. Good luck with those stitches."

"If my wife asks, I didn't get shot. Tell her I was bitten by a monkey."

"Sure. She'll buy that."

"She's terrified of monkeys."

"Wouldn't a dog be more realistic?"

"She loves dogs. If it's a monkey, I'll get sympathy sex."

I speak to the deputy chief and inform him I have a family emergency, but he can debrief my partner at the hospital. I promise I'll be back within an hour. Which is an outright lie, because I live an hour away.

During the ride to the suburbs I obsess about my mother. If something happened to her, why hasn't Latham called? Or perhaps the emergency has to do with Latham, and Mom is too shocked to go into details.

I'm overwhelmed by mental snapshots of death: car accidents, strokes, heart attacks, earthquakes, floods. Are they en route to the ER? Is that why they couldn't pick up the phone? It can't be a fire, because the answering machine keeps going on—a fire would destroy the line.

Is it something to do with my father? Mom never forgave Dad for leaving us, and while I've been trying to rebuild a relationship with him, she refuses to acknowledge his existence. Maybe Dad had shown up at my house, which would cause Mom to go supernova.

Or is this something more insidious?

I look at my cell, find the call from the Heathrow Facility. The caller ID indeed reads *HEATHROW*, but maybe that can be faked. I dial 411, get the same number, and let them patch me through. I speak to three different people, all of whom confirm that Alexandra Kork is dead as dead can be.

Okay. I'm being paranoid. Even if Alex were alive—and she isn't—she still didn't know where I live.

Maybe Mom saw the sniper shootings on television and is simply worried about me. Not picking up the phone is a guarantee I'll rush home.

Or maybe Latham has some sort of surprise planned. I think of the mariachi band he hired when he proposed, and a smile breaks through my mask of worry. He truly is a sweetheart.

I get off the expressway on Route 20, heading for York Road. Whatever the emergency is, I'll find out soon enough.

My thoughts momentarily shift to the shooter. Finding sex offenders is a snap—thanks to Megan's Law, anyone can log onto the Internet and access the National Sex Offender Registry and get their names and addresses. But if this is some sort of warped vigilante group, why kill cops? Did the sniper simply get carried away? Or is he really out of his mind? And are his two partners just as unbalanced?

I turn left down my twisty road, heading home. I hear the dead leaves crackling under my tires, see glimpses of the moon through the canopy of trees, and wonder what Mom loves about this neighborhood so much. Can it even be called a neighborhood? We've never met our nearest neighbor, who lives a quarter of a mile away. Come Halloween, I wonder if parents drive their children house to house for trick-or-treating. If I had kids, I'd drive them—to the city.

Thinking of children makes me think of Latham, and I get sort of gooey inside. I pull into the driveway and park next to his car, convinced that this *emergency* probably has to do with Mom fudging points in their card game, or burning the apple pie. I do a quick mirror check, finger comb my hair, and hop out of my Nova.

The front door is locked, and the front room is dark. I notice a light in the kitchen through the bay window. I unlock the door and go in.

"Mom? Latham?"

I smell food. Stew, and some sort of baked goods. Maybe I'm right about the pie after all.

Mom is in the kitchen, sitting at the table. It takes me a second to realize she has duct tape over her mouth and around her arms, and then something appears in my peripheral vision, something blindingly fast.

I duck, but not quickly enough, and get knocked to the floor, my vision all lopsided and swirly.

"Welcome home, Jack."

I can't focus, but I recognize the voice.

Alex is alive.

And that means we're all going to die.

Jack's moment of realization is priceless. It's an expression of fear and helplessness, and it's so raw and honest that I feel like a peep-show voyeur watching it.

I want to hit her again, to turn her fear into pain. But there isn't any need to rush. Better to play it safe, make sure she's restrained first.

"Handcuffs," I say.

Jack doesn't answer. I don't think she's trying to defy me. I think she's so scared she can't even speak. I give her a kick in the ribs to help with her articulation.

"Handcuffs," I repeat. "You'll have plenty of time to be scared speechless later."

"Purse," she says.

I follow her eyes, see an ugly clutch on the floor. I keep the gun on her and walk over to it. There are handcuffs inside, but no gun.

"Where's that little toy Colt you carry around?"

"Internal Affairs. Had a shooting tonight."

I wonder if she's lying, then notice that she has blood on her skirt, her shirt. Looks like Jack has had a busy night.

It's about to get busier.

"Cuff your hands behind you," I say, tossing her the bracelets.

She complies, sneaks a look at Mom. I wait for Jack to say something like "Let her go, this is between us" or "If you touch her, I swear I'll kill you" or something equally meaningless. She surprises me by saying nothing. Perhaps she knows it won't do any good. Or perhaps she's saving her energy because she knows she'll need it later. For screaming.

I allow them their mommy/daughter moment, then wrap my hand in Jack's hair and jerk her to her feet. It doesn't take much effort. At Heathrow, I was able to catch up on two things—soap operas and exercise. The last time I'd encountered Jack, I'd been soft.

There isn't anything soft about me now.

I check to make sure Jack's hands are cuffed, then shove the revolver into the back of my pants. I'm still holding her hair, and I bring her face close to mine, letting her see the scars up close.

"See what you did to me? For a while, I wished you'd killed me. I bet you're wishing the same thing right now, aren't you?"

Jack stares back at me, but her eyes are glassy. She's fighting to keep it together.

"It took a long time for the pain to go away," I continue. "The state doesn't have the best plastic surgeons, as you can see. They had to graft on some skin from my leg. It actually grows stubble. Can you feel it?"

Jack tenses, strains to pull away. But my muscles are big and strong and it's like restraining a child. I rub my scarred flesh against her perfect cheek, letting her feel the pointy little hairs that used to be on my calf. She stops struggling. Her muscles relax. Jack knows she can't fight me, knows I can do anything I want to her.

I've been waiting a long time for this.

"Where's Latham?" Jack asks, meek, submissive.

"We'll get to him in a minute. First we need to call some old friends." I find her cell phone in her purse. "Is Harry on here?"

Jack nods.

"You need to convince him to come over."

"No."

I half smile, make a fist, and hit Jack in the gut so hard she spits up food she ate last year. While she's doubled over, I walk over to Mom.

"I understand the reason you're holding out," I say, standing behind Mom's chair. "You figure that you're going to die anyway, so why should you be helpful? That's not the correct mind-set. What you should be thinking about is all the things I'm going to do to you before you die."

Jack coughs, spits. "You'll do those things anyway."

"Of course I will. And eventually I'll get my way, and you'll call Harry. I know you're tough, Jack. Maybe if it was only me and you, maybe you wouldn't call. But we've got other people involved here."

I hold Mary's hand, her wrists bound to the chair with tape.

"I've heard arthritis is agonizing. I poked around in the medicine cabinet earlier. Mom is taking some major pills, isn't she?"

I swivel the chair around, give Mom a frown that only appears on half of my face.

"I hope you're not turning into a junkie. That's a road you don't want to go down. No matter how bad the pain gets."

I begin to squeeze her hand. Her eyes get wide, and I watch her shake with the effort not to make any sound.

"Look how brave your mother is, Jack. Trying to hold it in."

"I'll call," Jack says.

"I wonder if she'd scream if I broke a few fingers."

"I'll call!"

I release Mom's hand, give the old gal a pat on the head. Then I drill my eyes into Jack. She's pale, and appears close to collapsing.

"Convince him to come over here. Do I need to make any more threats?"

Jack shakes her head.

"Don't look so devastated," I say to Jack. "We're just getting started."

8:15 P.M.

JACK

MOM AND I ARE as good as dead. It's just a matter of how much we suffer before Alex kills us.

Seeing Alex again stunned me. Instead of acting, of fighting back, I'd been caught off guard. That opportunity has passed. But I might be able to create another one with Harry McGlade.

I need to somehow convince Harry there's a problem, without alerting Alex. Unfortunately, Harry's intelligence falls somewhere between a chimpanzee and a crescent wrench. This is going to take some finesse.

Alex dials the number, presses the speaker phone button, and holds it to my mouth.

"Harry's Den of Dyslexic Sex, where you can duck my sick. Harry speaking." His voice is nasally, Chicago through and through.

"Hi, Harry. It's Jack."

"Jackie! Good to hear from you. Looking for work? Since that Joliet thing I've been swamped. I could hire you part-time. You'd do some paperwork, answer some phones. I'm paying seven fifty an hour, clothing is optional."

Harry McGlade is a private investigator. A hundred years ago he used to be a cop, and my partner. I didn't like him much then, and don't like him much now, but he keeps popping up in my cases. Harry's tough to get rid of. Like an oil stain. Or a wart.

"Look, McGlade, if I asked you to come over to my house right now, as a personal favor, would you do it?"

"No can do tonight, Jackie. I've got a date with a very special lady. Very special. And if I cancel without giving her twenty-four hours notice, she charges my credit card anyway."

I glance at Alex. She rolls her eyes, then points her gun at Mom. Even though I don't have anything left in my stomach, I feel it rumble.

"Harry, I . . . I broke up with my boyfriend. I'm feeling kind of alone, kind of vulnerable."

"I get it. You're a chick, so you need to get laid to feel loved. I'm happy to step up to the plate."

That hurts to even think about.

"I just need a friend right now. Can you come over?"

"For sex, right? I don't want to be one of those guys, you cry on his shoulder, piss and moan for two hours, then I leave with snot on my tie and a trouser trout I have to smack around during the car ride home."

Someone owed me an Academy Award, because somehow I say, "Yes, Harry McGlade. I want to have sex with you."

Come on, you big dummy. You know there has to be something wrong.

"Pardon my skepticism, Jackie, but that didn't sound right to me."

Thatta boy, McGlade. Reason it out.

"Can you ask again?" Harry continues. "But using dirty words?"

Unbelievable.

"Just come over," I say.

"You mean make like Ward Cleaver and discipline the Beaver?"

"Yes, Harry."

"Say it."

Even if he saves my life, I'm still going to kill him.

"Come over, Harry, and discipline the Beaver."

"Are you drunk, Jackie? Is liquor impairing your judgment? Because I'm fine with that."

"I'm not drunk, Harry. I just need you here."

"I knew it. I knew those years of insults and dirty looks masked your true feelings. And I want you to know, the feeling is mutual. In fact, back when we rode together, and you got out of the car first, I'd sometimes lean over and sniff your seat."

Alex has to put a hand over her mouth to keep from laughing.

"Just make sure you bring protection," I say.

A gun, asshole. Bring a gun.

"Message received. Leave the front door unlocked. If I get there and you're already passed out, I'm hopping on anyway."

He disconnects. Does he know I'm in trouble? Is he playing along? Or does he really think he's going to get laid?

"Nice work, Jack. Now let's try another one. That intense guy with the killer abs. Phineas Troutt. I owe him too."

I stare at Alex. Her scarred face offers no reprieve. No pity. She's a monster.

But she's a monster who wants something from me, which gives me just a tiny bit of leeway. If I got in touch with Phin, all I'll have left to offer Alex is my pain and suffering. Best to stall that for as long as I can.

"Where's Latham?" I try to sound scared, which doesn't require any acting.

"Ahh, yes. Where is loverboy? I noticed he wore a ring. You too. When is the wedding, Jack?" She bats her eyes, but the scarred one simply twitches. "Can I be your maid of honor?"

"Where is he?"

Alex makes a show of looking at her watch.

"He's in the garage. How much air do you think is in one of those kitchen garbage bags? Think there's twenty minutes' worth?"

I bolt, running across the kitchen, heading for the door to the garage. My hands are behind my back, so I have to spin around to turn the knob. Alex doesn't run after me. She stays in the kitchen, hands on her hips, looking vaguely amused.

I manage to pull open the door, and find Latham in the middle of the garage, lying on the floor next to a giant stack of boxes. A white plastic garbage bag is over his head, duct tape wrapped around his neck.

He's completely still.

I run to him, drop to my knees, scooting around and grabbing the bag along with some of his hair. I dig my fingers in and pull. The plastic stretches, tears.

"Latham! Latham, please answer me!"

I feel him move.

"Jack?"

Thank God. I keep tugging, removing as much of the bag as I can, my fingers encircling his face. His cheeks are wet, with sweat or tears or both.

I shed a few tears too.

"I'm so sorry," I say, over and over.

"She put a hole in the bag. A little one. Didn't want me to die yet." He talks in a monotone, emotionless. Probably in shock.

"I gave him a choice." Alex stands in the doorway. "Fuck me, or die. He told me he'd do it if I put a bag over my head. Personally, I think it looks pretty good on him."

My fear vanishes, replaced by a hate so intense I can taste it. I get to my knees, then to my feet, and charge at her. Alex doesn't flinch. When I get close enough she sidesteps my attempted body tackle and trips me. Unable to break my fall, I land on my face, my lips kissing the dirty concrete floor, the wind rushing from my lungs.

"You want to play, Jack? We've got time to play." Alex puts her hands behind her back. "I'll even play fair. You're Little Miss Tae Kwon Do, right? Let's see if you can take me."

I'm so pumped up with anger and adrenaline that I get up before my breath comes back. I take a feeble gasp, shake away the stars, and run at her.

Alex kicks me in the stomach, so hard that it knocks my shoes off. I fall onto my ass, the handcuffs digging in and twisting my wrists, prompting a scream. I use the pain, continuing to stretch at the cuffs, pulling them up under my butt and over my feet.

My hands are now in front of me.

It won't help much fighting against Alex. She's stronger than the last time I'd sparred with her. But maybe if I could get to my bedroom, to my other gun—

I run for it, run like I have a freight train coming after me. Make it to the kitchen, to the front room, to the hallway. Then I stumble and eat carpeting.

"Is that how you got your black belt, Jack? By running away like a scared little bitch?"

I roll over, glare up at Alex. She grabs my handcuff chain and jerks me up to her level. Her strength is amazing.

"Pumped a little iron in lockup?" I say between breaths.

Half of her face smiles.

"A little."

Then she whips me forward, headfirst into the wall.

Everything goes from very bright to very dark.

SWANSON

JAMES MUNCHEL WALKS into the suburban sports bar with a big yellow grin on his face and a *hail conquering hero* swagger. He actually lifts up his hand for a high five when he reaches their table.

Greg Swanson can barely hold in his rage. His jaw is clenched, and his shoulders feel like a giant knot.

"Sit down, you idiot," Swanson orders.

Munchel darkens, lowering his upraised palm. But he complies. They're at a table in the back, and the place is crowded enough that no one is paying any attention to them. Like all sports bars, this one boasts an impressive number of TVs. The one nearest them is tuned to CNN, at Swanson's request, and it's still reporting live from Munchel's massacre scene.

"What the fuck were you doing?" Swanson asks.

"I was following the plan."

"The plan was to take out the target, not half the cops in Chicago."

"They were witnesses," Munchel says.

Swanson bunches up his napkin, squeezes it hard. He's bigger than Munchel, by five inches and sixty pounds. But the smaller man is flat-out crazy, and this scares Swanson.

Swanson looks at Pessolano, hoping for some assistance. Paul Pessolano is wearing those stupid as hell yellow shooting glasses, which make him look like a bee. His face is granite, impassive. He's had military experience, but he must have had his communication skills shot off during Desert Storm. Either that or he's seen *The Terminator* too many times.

As predicted, Pessolano offers nothing. Swanson turns back to Munchel, who is flagging down their server. He waits while Munchel orders a beer and one of those fried onion appetizers. When the waitress leaves, Swanson has to count to five in his head so he doesn't start yelling.

"I'm the leader of The Urban Hunting Club," he says, his voice as calm and patronizing as a grade school teacher's. "I'm the one who brought us together. I'm the one who picked the targets. I'm the one who came up with the plan."

Munchel rolls his eyes at Swanson, then nudges Pessolano.

"Hey, Paul, how many confirmed kills you got?"

"Eighteen." Pessolano's voice is rough, like he doesn't use it much.

"I'm almost caught up to you. I just got twelve."

"You got eleven," Pessolano says. "One of the cops lived."

Munchel shrugs. "Fine, eleven. Still pretty good my first time out."

Swanson realizes that he probably shouldn't have trusted guys who answered an ad in the back of *Soldier of Fortune*. But he didn't have a choice. Where else was he supposed to find mercenaries? Swanson works in a home improvement store, in the plumbing department. He isn't a killer.

Well, technically, he *is* a killer now. But he wasn't a few hours ago. And he wasn't a few months ago when he placed that ad.

When Swanson's wife got . . . *attacked* . . . five years ago, he'd been devastated. Jen was, is, his everything. Then the bastard who did it got out five years early—for good behavior, what a fucking joke. Swanson couldn't allow that. He had to kill the guy. For Jen. For himself. For society. It was more than just revenge. More than justice. The punk

needed to be killed, and Swanson felt the need to perform that particular public service.

But he knew that if he offed the guy, suspicion would immediately
fall on him. The authorities would look at his victims, following the revenge angle.

Unless it looked random.

Thus, The Urban Hunting Club was born. All Swanson needed
were a couple of like-minded guys who hated perverts, and then Rob
Siders's death would be blamed on vigilantes, not on an angry husband.

But Munchel has ruined the plan. TUHC has gone from being a
group that might have been respected, even admired, straight to Public Enemy Number One. Cops never forget when you murder their
own. They'll be hunted for the rest of their lives. All because Munchel
got himself a kill hard-on.

"We need to break up," Swanson says. "Go our separate ways,
never see each other again."

"Why would we do that?" Munchel asks. The waitress brings his
beer, and the idiot continues to talk in front of her. "We make a great
team. We got rid of some real scum today."

The server leaves, and Swanson leans over, jutting his chin at
Munchel.

"And now we're wanted for killing ten cops," he says through his
teeth.

Munchel smiles, takes a sip of beer. "Collateral damage. Couldn't
be helped."

Swanson looks at Pessolano, who is stoically picking his teeth with
his fork. He realizes he has to distance himself from these two loonies.
Hell, he should probably run straight home, grab Jen, and move to Cal-
ifornia. That might look like an admission of guilt, but Munchel is going to get caught, and when he gets caught he'll talk. Swanson doesn't

want to be implicated in any cop killing case, especially in a state that has the death penalty.

"I'm ditching the gun, and getting the fuck out of town."

Swanson stands. Pessolano clasps his hands together, puts them behind his head.

"You ain't ditching shit. Those are my rifles, and they're worth more than you make in a year."

"Fine. Let's go out to the parking lot, you can have your guns back right now."

Munchel finishes his beer, lets out a weak belch. He meets Swanson's stare.

"Before you go running home to Mama, crying like a little girl, we have to take care of one more problem."

Dread creeps up Swanson's shoulders and perches there, like a gargoyle. "What problem?"

"That chick cop. The one who fired back at me."

"What about her?"

Munchel wipes his mouth off with his sleeve. "She saw my face."

Swanson sits back down. This isn't happening. This can't be happening.

"Had some sort of scope," Munchel goes on. "Some infrared night-vision bullshit."

"Could she ID you?" Pessolano asks.

"Abso-fucking-lutely."

Swanson tries to think, tries to remember if his passport is up-to-date.

"We can go to Mexico," he says. "We can leave tonight."

Munchel snorts. "Hell no. I love America. I'm not leaving. Not because of some split-tail. Besides—there's another option."

Swanson's heart is beating faster than when he took the shot and killed the pervert. He should be feeling good right now. Satisfied. Complete. Maybe even a little excited. Killing Rob Siders had been easier than he thought, and every detail had been executed perfectly. But instead of celebrating, he feels terrified and ready to throw up.

"What option?" Pessolano asks.

"I put that GPS tracker you lent me on her car." Munchel grins wide, his teeth the color of corn. "I know where she lives."

JACK

"LET'S PLAY A GAME," Alex says.

I sit on the sofa. My hands rest in my lap, the handcuffs digging painfully into my wrists. My ankles are wrapped in silver duct tape. Latham has tape on his legs, wrists, and mouth. Alex dragged my mother, still bound to the kitchen chair, into the living room with us. Mom's eyelids are drooping. She doesn't look well.

Alex holds a nickel-plated revolver. It has a two-inch barrel and a rubber grip. A small gun. It probably only holds five bullets. My guess is confirmed when Alex swings the cylinder out and pushes the ejector rod, dumping five .32-caliber rounds into her palm. She thumbs one back into an empty chamber, spins the cylinder, and slaps it closed.

"I'm going to ask you some questions, Jack. If you get one wrong, I'm going to point the gun at either your mother or your fiancé, and pull the trigger. Like this."

Alex aims at my mother and fires before the cry can leave my throat.

The hammer falls on an empty chamber with a metallic *click*.

"A one out of five chance," Alex says. "Those are pretty good odds. Do you understand the game?"

I push the panic down, deep down, forcing myself to think rather than react to fear.

"What if I get the answer right?" I ask.

"Then I'll ask another one." Alex spins the cylinder. "Let's begin."

She walks over to me and stares down. Her eyes are empty. I wonder if she's enjoying this. She doesn't seem to be.

Alex doesn't have the classic male psychopathic response, because her particular mental disorder isn't linked to sex and testosterone. That means she stays calm, works within her peculiar kind of rationalization, without letting emotion take over. Her cruelty isn't hot and breathy. It's cold and calculating.

In my opinion, that makes it worse.

"How did I escape from Heathrow?" Alex asks me.

What is she looking for? Praise? Begging? Cowering? Or does she just want a wrong answer so she can shoot someone I love while I watch?

"You lured someone into your room, burned them, and took their ID. A guard, maybe."

"It wasn't a guard. Try again."

"Another inmate."

Alex snorts. "If I took another inmate's place, I'd be sitting in her cell right now. One more guess, then we play some Russian roulette."

I rack my brain, trying to remember what I know about Alex, about her past. She grew up with a family of psychos. She liked to kill animals. She was infatuated with her brother. She could act normal, function within society, until her peculiar tastes took over. She used to be a marine. She was an expert marksperson, and an expert martial artist. She murdered many people, torturing most of them first. She was of above-average intelligence. She had been analyzed by many specialists.

Many specialists.

"Your shrink," I decide.

Alex has killed several of her psychiatrists. She seems to get a particular thrill out of it, and I could easily picture her carrying on that legacy at Heathrow.

I know I'm right, because the unscarred half of her face smiles.

"Dr. Panko. Shorter than me, but the same hair color. She was a Freudian. Kept wanting me to talk about my parents. Saw me as a victim, a weak little girl who had been abused by the world. I had to fake a lot of tears in front of that bitch. It paid off."

"You got her to trust you," I say. As long as Alex is talking, she isn't shooting.

"So much that she allowed me to get a job in the laundry room. On our next session I snapped her neck and put her body in the laundry cart. Not easy to do in handcuffs and ankle restraints. When I did laundry rounds that night, I dropped her off in my room, switched clothes with her, and set her on fire after spraying her with three cans of Lysol. Then I walked out of prison while everyone stood around watching the blaze. How did I do that, Jack?"

"You took her keys. Her ID."

"Good. What else?"

I stare at Alex's cheek. "You also took her makeup."

"I needed a whole tube of concealer to cover up the scarring, and it wouldn't have stood up to close inspection. But no one even bothered to look at me. They were all too jacked up about the tragic suicide. I found Panko's car by pressing the alarm button on her key chain. She had this cute little gun in her glove compartment. A Freudian with a gun. I wonder if she ever thought about how ironic that was."

I steal a glance at Mom. She seems out of it. In contrast, Latham appears alert and determined. I try to tell him how much I love him using only my eyes.

"So how did I convince the authorities that Dr. Panko was me?" Alex asks.

I think about my earlier calls to Heathrow, how they insisted the dead body was Alex.

"You somehow switched dental records."

"Wrong." Alex holds up the revolver. "Who do you want me to shoot, your mother or your fiancé?"

My stomach falls to my ankles. "Give me another chance. You're smarter than I am."

"No. Choose."

I'm tempted to say *please*, but begging Alex won't help the situation. She feeds off of weakness. I promise myself I won't beg, no matter how bad it gets.

I look at Mom. She doesn't meet my eyes. I wonder if she's being strong, or if she's gone someplace in her head. Then I look at Latham. He nods at me. My sweetheart is giving me permission to shoot him.

"I refuse to decide," I say.

"Fine. Then I'll do both."

"Wait—!"

Alex points the gun at Latham and fires, then turns it on Mom and fires.

Two empty chambers, but something inside me breaks. The panic worms its way to the surface, and a soft whimper tears loose. I don't want to cry, don't want to let Alex see it, but some tears make it out anyway.

"Hmm," Alex says. "What were the odds there? A forty percent chance one of them would die? Looks like you got lucky, Jack. Now try again. How did I convince the authorities that Dr. Panko was me?"

I have no idea. My brain is mush, scrambled eggs. I'm being forced to watch the people I love get killed. Alex will keep going until they both are dead, then she'll start on me. How am I supposed to be able to think?

"The clock is ticking, Jack. You have five seconds."

I make myself focus, make myself reason it out. If Alex didn't switch records, there's only one other possible way to get a positive dental ID.

"You . . . you pulled some of your own teeth, put them in her mouth."

Alex claps her hands together.

"Bravo, Jack! But you make it sound so simple. It isn't easy, yanking out your own teeth. Especially without any anesthetic. Those suckers are in there tight! I used a toothbrush. Rubbed the handle against the cement walls until it got sharp. Then I jammed it into my jaw and pried the roots out. Does this look infected to you? Be honest."

Alex sticks her pinky into her mouth, pulls her cheek back. I see red, inflamed gums where teeth used to be, and her breath smells like meat gone bad. I turn away.

"Why did I do that, Jack? Why did I yank out my teeth? Why didn't I just get the hell out of there and not care if they realized I was gone?"

"For me," I say, my voice small. I stare at my lap.

"Exactly. I did it for you, Jack. Because if they knew I escaped, they would have warned you, and you would have gotten away."

Alex grabs me by my hair, twists my head until I look at her.

"How often did I think of you, when I was locked up? Take a guess, Jack. Guess how often."

I don't have to guess. I know the answer.

"Every day," I say.

"Every hour of every day I was in that hellhole I thought about you, Jack. About this moment right now. It made things bearable. Knowing one day I'd have you, and the people you care about, at my mercy—that was the only thing that kept me going. That was how I could look at my ugly, scarred face and not slit my own throat."

She releases my hair, and I force myself to hold her gaze.

"Tell me, Jack. Did you think of me?"

I don't know what she wants me to say. Rather than try to guess, I tell her the truth.

"Only in my nightmares."

"And what did you have nightmares about, Jack? Of me escaping?"

"Yes."

"Why didn't you kill me when you had the chance?"

"Because I'm not a killer."

"But I am. You should have taken that into consideration."

I don't want her to ask another question, so I blurt out one of my own.

"Do you think this is going to make everything right, Alex?"

She narrows her good eye. The other one just twitches. "What exactly do you mean, Lieutenant?"

"You can't get the time you did back. You can't get your family back. You can't get . . ." I force it out, ". . . your face back. Killing us isn't going to change anything."

Alex caresses my cheek, lets her fingers linger.

"I know that, Jack. I'm not doing this to make things right. The past is the past, and can't be undone." She winks her good eye. "I'm doing this because it's a lot of fun."

I don't want to provoke her, but I can't help whispering, "You're a monster."

Alex sighs. She looks at Mom, and Latham, and then at the ceiling, perhaps gathering her thoughts. When she speaks again, her voice is hard and even.

"Life is all about cruelty. You know that. You're a cop. You see it all the time. Nothing on this planet lives without something else dying. You call me a monster because I choose to accept my nature. I embrace it, rather than deny it. Here's a bonus question, since your moral compass is so true, since you're so sure you know right and wrong. Where has your morality gotten you, Jack?"

"Hurting others is wrong, Alex," I say.

Alex laughs, a harsh, cruel laugh. "Look at history. It's filled with atrocities. War. Murder. Torture. Rape. We call that kind of behavior *inhuman*. But maybe the terminology is backward. Maybe being *human* means hurting others. That seems to be what humans do best."

I shake my head. "Our species is successful because we nurture, not because we harm."

Alex spins the cylinder again, then twirls the gun around her finger like a cowboy.

"Let me clue you in on something, Lieutenant. Nothing is black and white. There are no universal standards that determine what's good and what's evil. It's subjective. You can't kill for money, or recreation, but you can kill during a war. Why is there a difference? Dead is dead. I set someone on fire, I'm bad. The state fries me in the electric chair, and people sell T-shirts and toast champagne. Right and wrong is a matter of perspective."

"Your perspective is warped. Killing is wrong."

"Yet you'd probably give up everything just to have a shot at killing me right now, wouldn't you? Let me enlighten you about something, Jack. Human beings are just animals, and all animals are selfish. Every single thing an animal does is selfish."

"People can be unselfish," I maintain.

"How so? Feeding the starving? Adopting unwanted babies? Sending aid when there's a natural disaster? Giving blood? Donating to charity? People do these things to feel good about themselves. They're all selfish acts, and pretty goddamn stupid as well. If you're going to be selfish, it should benefit your life, not take away from it. Now I'm asking you again—where has your morality gotten you?"

I know the answer, and hate the answer.

"Answer the question, Jack."

"Here," I whisper.

"Exactly. Your high regard for life, and justice, and the path of righteousness, has gotten you here. You're dead, and the people you love are dead, all because you're so sure that there's a right and a wrong. Be honest. Don't you wish that you had killed me after you tore off my face?"

I nod slowly and speak the truth. "Yes."

Alex half smiles. "Good. I'd hate for you to die without any regrets. And let me tell you something, Jack. For all I've done in my life,

I never put anyone that I cared about in jeopardy. Your loved ones are going to suffer, and it's your fault."

Alex sticks her face in mine, lets me smell her rotten breath.

"And you call me a monster," she says.

As if I'm not feeling horrible enough about the unfolding events, Alex helps add guilt to the fear, pain, panic, and regret I've been drowning in.

She seems to notice this, and I can sense it pleases her.

"Are we done with the philosophy?" she asks.

I don't answer.

"I'll take that as a yes. Moving on to the next question. And let me tell you, Jack, this one is a hard one. I've done some clever things in my life, but this one was truly brilliant. Are you ready for it? Are you ready to see if you're as smart as I am?"

I'm not ready. I'll never be ready. But I make myself nod. Alex smiles her half smile and comes in closer.

"How did I find out where you live, Jack?"

I don't have a clue. When I moved to the suburbs from my Chicago apartment, I didn't leave any forwarding address. All of my ID still lists Wrigleyville as my home. Except for Herb, Latham, and Harry, I didn't tell a single person that I'd moved. All the utilities here are in Mom's name. I pay my cell bill and credit cards over the Internet, using Mom's connection. No one knew that I live here.

But Alex knew. She came here directly after breaking out. How?

"You hired someone," I guess. "You had some money stashed, used a private eye to track me down."

"Wrong!" Her eyes twinkle. "Pick someone."

I can't speak.

"Hurry, Jack, or I'll shoot them both."

"Me," I croak. "Shoot me."

"Your turn will come later. And trust me—you'll be begging me to shoot you before we're through. But now you have to choose. Or we could do eenie-meenie-minie-moe."

I stare at Latham, my lower lip trembling, and somehow say, "Him."

The fact that Latham nods makes it even worse. Alex spins the cylinder and places the barrel up to his forehead. Latham closes his eyes. I want to close mine as well, but I owe it to him to watch.

Click.

I taste blood. I've bitten my tongue.

"Try again, Jack. How did I find you?"

I throw out a guess.

"You found out my mother's last name, called up the electric company or some other utility."

"Wrong."

Alex begins to pull the trigger, and I scream, "You have to spin it first!"

"No I don't. It's the same question, so no new spin."

I cringe, my whole world imploding.

Click.

"Looks like you get another guess," Alex says. "There's a one out of three chance that Latham will die if you get it wrong. Isn't this exciting?"

Latham's forehead has broken out in sweat, but he stays stoic, stays calm.

Think, Jack! Think!

"You tracked the home loan somehow, knew my mother moved here."

"Exactly," Alex says.

I slump back on the sofa.

"I just logged onto the Internet," Alex continues, "because they give full Internet access to the criminally insane. We were allowed two hours a day, right after our massage."

She begins to squeeze the trigger.

"Dr. Panko's office!" I yell. "You used her computer!"

"Sorry, Jack."

"No!"

Click.

Alex pats Latham on the head. "Down to a fifty-fifty chance, loverboy. Better hope your woman gets this."

How did she find me? How did she find me? How the fuck did she . . .

I stare at Latham, his eyes squeezed shut. Herb wouldn't ever give my address up, even accidentally. He's a cop, which means he's paranoid. So is Mom. Harry is an ex-cop, plus he has just as much to fear from Alex as I do. Dumb as he is, he's also naturally suspicious. Harry would know if someone was sniffing around for my address.

Latham isn't a cop. Latham is a nice guy. A trusting guy. He could have been manipulated.

"It was Latham," I say. "You got it out of Latham somehow."

Latham's eyes open, and there's so much hurt in them, so much betrayal, that I have to turn away. Alex begins to laugh.

"That's beautiful, Jack. Your fiancé has a gun pointed at his head, all because of you, and you're blaming *him*?"

I was wrong. Dear God, I was wrong.

Alex swings a leg over Latham and straddles his lap, caressing his lips with the barrel of the revolver.

"How does that make you feel, loverboy? Your fiancée must think you're really stupid."

"I'm sorry," I say to Latham. "I'm so sorry."

Latham says something, but the duct tape muffles it.

"I just have to hear this," Alex says.

She yanks the tape off. Latham stares right into my soul.

"After all we've been through, you still don't trust me?"

Alex couldn't have hurt me any worse.

"I figured you made a mistake," I say, my voice pleading. "You know I trust you."

"How could you think I'd do that?"

"She's smart. She could have tricked you."

Latham looks away.

"See," Alex says, patting his cheek. "You should have fucked me when you had the chance."

She presses the gun to his forehead, and then my mother begins to moan.

"Hold on," Alex says. "Mom wants to say something."

Alex gets off of Latham and walks to Mom. She rips off her gag, and my mother says, "Shoot me, not him."

Latham says, "Mary . . ."

I say, "Mom . . ."

Alex goes, "Shhhh! Let Mom make her case."

Mom doesn't look at Alex. She looks at Latham.

"Don't blame my daughter. She trusts you. She's just making wild guesses so you don't die. I'm an old woman. I've lived my life. I can accept this." Then she stares at me and smiles. Her eyes are warm, moist. "Jacqueline, my little girl. I'm so proud of you."

"No . . . Mom . . ." My words are mixed with sobs. Then I turn to Alex and do what I told myself I wouldn't do. I beg.

"Please . . . please don't do this. Do what you want to me, but let them go. Please."

Alex's face twitches into a half smile.

"The world-famous police officer Lieutenant Jack Daniels is asking me for mercy. But she didn't give me any mercy. She tore off half my face, and left me to rot behind bars. And now she's crying like a little girl, and I haven't even cut off her ears yet. I have to say, Jack, that I'm disappointed in you. I thought you'd be stronger." Alex cocks the hammer back. "Now pay attention while I kill your mom."

"NO!"

Click.

Alex laughs. "Wow! Can you believe the luck? If I were you, I'd go out and buy a lottery ticket."

I've got nothing left. All of my hope has been sucked out. My eyes wander around the room, and I try to fathom that this is it, my last few hours alive, and I'll have to watch Mom and Latham die before I meet my own horrible death.

"The next chamber has the bullet in it, Jack," Alex says. "No more odds. When I pull the trigger again, the gun will fire. It takes out some of the surprise, but it really does amp up the suspense. For the last time: How did I find you?"

I can't look anymore. I can't handle it. If I could have willed myself to die right then, I would have.

"I love you, Jacqueline," Mom says.

I want to say it back, but only sobs come out.

"Five seconds, Jack."

Alex hums the theme to *Jeopardy!* I decide to rush at her, try to get the gun away. My hands are cuffed and my feet are bound with tape but I have to try. I scan the room for a weapon, something that I could get to in time. A lamp on the end table, next to a stack of magazines. The TV remote control. A cat scratching post covered in carpeting.

Wait a second . . .

"Magazines!" I say, finding my voice. "I transferred my subscriptions here. You were at my apartment, you noticed I read fashion magazines. You called one of them, impersonated me, got my change of address."

Alex stops humming. She stares at me with her head tilted to the side.

"Nicely done, Jack. Very nicely done."

I know the relief will be short-lived, but every extra minute I have is like a gift.

"Now tell me which magazine it was," Alex says.

I subscribe to half a dozen magazines. I have no idea which one.

"Hurry, Jack. Answer quickly."

"I guessed right. I guessed it was a magazine."

"And now I'm asking which one."

It doesn't matter that I'd been correct. This isn't a game that Alex will let me win.

"Vogue," I say.

"Wrong."

She aims at Latham and fires.

KORK

THE LITTLE .32 BURPS in my hand and I hit what I'm aiming for. Latham's arm. He moans, and Jack throws herself on him, as if that will prevent me from shooting him again.

What actually does prevent me from shooting again is the simple fact that my gun is empty. If Jack were thinking straight, rather than having an emotional breakdown, she could have taken that opportunity to charge me. It wouldn't have done anything. I still would have overpowered her. But she could have at least tried.

I reload the gun, and the moment passes. I'm more than a little disappointed in Jack. She's the closest thing I've ever had to an actual adversary, but this has all been cake so far. I've spent many sleepless nights staring at the ceiling, wondering how she caught me. Now the answer is crystal clear.

She got lucky.

Anyone can get lucky. The fat kid scores the goal at the buzzer. The trailer trash wins the lottery. The dumb cop catches the brilliant killer.

This revelation makes me feel good. Damn good. I watch as Latham squirms on the sofa, Jack pressing an armchair cover to his wound, and I smile as big as my scarred face allows.

Dr. Panko, and the many headshrinkers who came before her, always tried to blame my unique outlook on a horrible upbringing.

That's just plain silly. Look at all of those people who were tortured and starved and sexually abused in the concentration camps during World War II. Did any of them become serial killers?

People don't become predators because of their environment. Some are born predators. My family had some . . . *social issues* . . . and not because of some ongoing cycle of abuse. It's in our genes. Dr. Panko might as well have been counseling a shark, trying to convince it that eating fish was wrong.

I know why I am the way I am. And I like it. Other human beings somehow connect and relate with each other on a level that I don't. They care.

It makes them weak.

I have no such compulsions. I'm unrestrained by sentiment. I've never known guilt, or regret.

I'm no robot. I can laugh. I can cry. I can reason. But I lack the capacity to empathize with others. Watching Jack fawn over Latham has no more effect on me than watching a man build a house, or a bird eat a snail.

But *shooting* Latham. That has an effect. That makes me feel powerful. Full of life. Complete. It produces a physical response within me, an endorphin rush.

Is this what love is? Is this how Jack feels when she looks at her fiancé?

I hope so. Because it will make taking that from her even sweeter.

I aim the gun.

"Move away from him, Jack."

Jack stares at me, face awash with tears, eyes confrontational. I wonder if she's going to make a move on me, decide in advance where I can shoot her without killing her. I'll go for the right knee.

But she backs off, returning to her spot on the sofa. Loverboy has lost a lot of color, and the makeshift armrest cover bandage is soaked through with red.

"I bet right now you kinda wish you dated someone in a different profession," I say to him.

It's funny, but no one laughs. Tough crowd.

The oven buzzes. It's the apple pie that I put in earlier. I'm anxious to try it. It's the first pie I ever baked, as hard to believe as that might be.

"Would you like to help me check on the pie, Mom?" I ask. I grab the back of her chair and tug her into the kitchen, warning Jack that she'd better behave, or I'll stick Mom's head into the oven, on the heating element. I know from experience how much that hurts.

I set Mom up near the oven door, and we both peek inside. It smells great.

"Is it done?" I ask.

She nods. Earlier, while we were baking, she'd tried to connect with me by making small talk. Perhaps, after shooting her potential son-in-law, we've lost some of that earlier closeness.

I find some pot holders hanging up next to the sink—they say *Home Sweet Home* on the front—and take out the pie. It's brown and bubbling and looks delicious. And hot. I bet this thing would cause some serious burns if it got thrown in someone's face.

"If this tastes as good as it looks, maybe I'll let you live long enough to bake another."

Mom doesn't seem happy with the thought. I leave the pie on the counter to cool, then drag her back into the living room. Jack and Latham are where I left them. I half hoped Jack would have hopped over to the front door and tried to get out. It would have been fun chasing her down again. But she just sits there, a whipped dog.

"I'll pay you," Jack says.

This surprises me. I didn't expect the bargaining to begin so soon. At least, not before I did some breaking and cutting and burning.

"With what?" I ask. If I let her think I'm entertaining the notion, it will hurt Jack even more when I crush her hopes.

"We have some savings bonds. A few thousand dollars' worth. And jewelry. An antique diamond necklace that my mother inherited from her mother."

"And where is this cache of treasure?"

"In my bedroom. I can show you."

Jack pushes herself up to a standing position, balancing on her taped feet. Now I understand. She has extra weapons in the bedroom. She's hoping to grab one.

"Sit down," I say. "That can wait. First let's call up our friend Phin. Maybe he won't be a limp dick like Casanova here."

Jack sits, lets out a long breath. "I don't know how to contact him."

"Then we break one of Mom's poor arthritic fingers for each minute you take."

"I really don't know. He doesn't have a phone."

I move behind Mom, put my hand over hers.

"I guess we're not going to make any more pies," I tell her.

"I don't know how to find him!" Jack screams at me.

I decide to start small. The pinky. Then I hear a car come up the driveway. I glance out of Jack's big bay window, facing the front yard, and see a Corvette pull up. I point the gun at Mom's head.

"Stay quiet, or she dies," I say.

I pull Mom toward the front door, then wait. There's a knock.

"Jackie! You naked?"

Harry McGlade.

Jack begins to yell, but I've already got the door open, got the gun in Harry's face.

"Aw, hell," Harry says. "It's Frankenbitch."

I touch the barrel to Harry's nose.

"Come on in. Join the party."

Harry walks in. He's as I remember him. Average height, a beer belly, three days' growth of beard. He's wearing black leather pants—yuck—and a yellow silk shirt with the top few buttons open, showing off a blanket of gray chest hair. He's also wearing enough aftershave to be smelled from another zip code.

I stare down at his right hand, and am surprised to see it still attached. But closer scrutiny reveals it isn't a real hand. It's fake, prosthetic.

I pat Harry down, taking his keys, a cell phone, three condoms, and half a bottle of baby oil. Then I feel his artificial hand. The flesh is made of rubber, but there's something solid underneath. I tug the covering off and look at the mechanism inside. A three-fingered metal claw, grafted to his wrist.

"You're not even wearing a gun," I say. "If I'm Frankenbitch, you must be Robodope."

Again, no one laughs. Maybe this show needs a two-drink minimum.

"You have to give me the name of your plastic surgeon," Harry says, "so I can buy him another drink."

That warrants a kick in the balls. He doubles over. I pull him by his hair into the kitchen. I ran out of duct tape on Jack's legs, but I have an idea that should work until I find some rope.

"Open up the robot hand," I tell him, "and grab the refrigerator."

Jack has one of those expensive double-door stainless steel fridges, and it's big and solid. Harry does what I say, and locks his claw onto the freezer handle.

"Now take out your batteries."

"They're up my ass," Harry says. "Stick your head up there and take a look."

I introduce the butt of my gun to Harry's jaw, and he falls to his knees. I spend a minute pressing and probing his prosthesis until I find the ejector for the battery pack. I pull it out and shove it into my pocket. Then I grab Harry's collar and pull his face close to mine.

"Aren't you happy to see me, Harry? Didn't you miss me?"

"You should run away while there's still time," Harry says. "Before the villagers come with torches."

I smile, give him a peck on the cheek. Then I whisper in his ear.

"Remember what I did to your hand? That's nothing compared to what I have planned."

Harry doesn't have a smart-ass reply for that. I go back into the living room, feeling smug and powerful.

"I warned you, Jack. No yelling. I'm going to have to punish you for that. But first we need to invite Phin to this reunion." I press the speaker button, then toss Jack her cell phone. "Call him."

"He doesn't have a phone," Jack says.

"Then you'd better think of some other way to get in touch."

I go over to Mom, squeeze her hand. Mom gasps.

"I'll try the pool hall I've seen him at," Jack blurts out. "I need to call information."

"If you dial 911, you watch your mother die."

Jack wisely chooses 411, asks the computer voice for Joe's Pool Hall in Chicago, and gets connected.

"Pool hall," the phone says.

"I need to speak to a guy there. Name is Phin Troutt. Blond, crew cut, probably wearing a white T-shirt and jeans. Tell him it's Jack, and it's an emergency."

"Hold on."

We wait, listening to the background noise.

"Hey, Jackie!" Harry, from the kitchen. "Does this mean we're not gonna have sex?"

I think back to the last time I killed several people at once. A family. Mom, Dad, teenage girl. I couldn't remember the reason. But did I ever need a reason?

"Hello?"

"Phin!" The relief in Jack's voice is obvious. "I need you to come to my house. Right away."

"You don't need another wedding date, do you? The last time didn't work out well for me."

"I . . . need your help."

Jack gives Phin the address. Phin doesn't answer.

"Hello? Hello? The call got dropped." She presses a few buttons. "It isn't working."

"Let's try Harry's phone," I say.

"How about instead, you try eating that gun, you freak-of-nature gargoyle!"

I make a mental note to cut out Harry's tongue when I go back into the kitchen. Then I toss Jack the cell.

She presses some buttons then says, "No service."

I pick up the cordless phone on a table. No dial tone. Latham's phone doesn't work either. How strange. It's almost as if someone is blocking the—

A bullet comes through the front window and the revolver jerks from my hand, flying across the room. I see the blood on my fingers, feel a sting, and realize that someone has shot me. My previous military experience makes me drop to the floor and elbow-crawl away from the window.

Jack yells, "Get down!" and she drags Latham to the floor. Then she inchworms over to Mom and pushes her chair over. Another shot hits the TV, causing the screen to explode.

"What the hell is going on!" Harry cries from the kitchen.

I see terror on Jack's face. She says, "I think my work followed me home."

"HOLD YOUR FIRE!" Swanson barks into the radio. Some moron, probably Munchel, started shooting before he gave the signal. Swanson isn't in place yet. Munchel's rounds could cut through the whole house and come out on his end. Getting shot isn't on Swanson's list of things to do before he dies. Especially getting shot by friendly fire.

They'd tracked the GPS Munchel put on the cop's bumper to this secluded house in Bensenville. The setup is good. Lots of trees, no neighbors, nice and dark. The plan is to form a triangle around the house, keep an eye on doors and windows, and wait until the cop shows her face. But everyone needs to get into position first.

Munchel's voice comes through the radio. *Just zeroing out my scope.*

"Can't you do that without shooting?"

"Yeah, but it isn't as much fun."

The radios, like the rifles, the scopes, the suppressors, the GPS, the portable cell phone jammer, and various other bits of military and spy gear belong to Pessolano. Pessolano also crept up to the house earlier and cut the phone line and cable connection, so the cop can't call for help using the Internet.

So far, so good, but Swanson is still nervous as hell. The targets they'd eliminated a few hours ago had been easy, Munchel's rampage aside. But that had been the result of weeks of training, planning, and surveillance. Even with Pessolano's equipment and experience, this all seems slapped together at the last minute.

If given the choice, Swanson would have fled. But he fears that running might project a certain lack of trust, and then his handpicked teammates would feel the need to eliminate him as well.

So here he is, crouching behind a tree two hundred yards away from a woman cop's house, ready to kill for the second time this night. Just to save his own ass.

The lights in the house are on, and he has a view into the living room from a forty-five-degree angle. Besides the large bay window in front, there are ten other windows around the house, and none have drapes or shades or blinds. There's also a front door, a side door by the garage, and glass patio doors around back, which lead into the kitchen.

Swanson focuses the Leupold scope and squints through it, searching the living room.

It appears empty. Then he notices a foot protruding from behind a couch. That dumb-ass Munchel—his shot made the cop take cover. Swanson fumbles for the radio.

"Is everyone in position?" he asks. There's no answer. He realizes he's pressing the wrong button, finds the correct one, and asks the question again.

"Affirmative," says Pessolano.

"Yeah," says Munchel. *"I see where two of them are hiding."*

Two of them?

"The cop is with someone?" Swanson asks.

"She's with four other people."

Five people? This keeps getting worse and worse. While the authorities did a piss-poor job keeping his wife's attacker behind bars, they still caught him in the first place. They're the good guys. Swanson wants to be one of the good guys too. He doesn't see how killing cops and their families can be considered good.

Swanson hits the talk button and says, "Who is with her?"

"One of them is a chick with a gun. Another is a grandmother. And two men. One is sitting next to the refrigerator, the other is tied up."

"Why is he tied up?"

"Don't you ever tie up your old lady, Swanson?"

Swanson does a slow burn. He's told Munchel what happened to Jen. Munchel is either so ignorant that he forgot, or he is throwing it in Swanson's face.

Swanson lets it go. The sooner they get out of here, the better. He presses the talk button.

"We're just going for the woman cop. The others are innocents."

"Bullshit they are," Munchel says. *"I'm shooting anything that moves. I'm not leaving witnesses alive to come after me."*

"This is my team!" Swanson shouts into the radio. "I say we leave the civilians out of this!"

"You may have put this team together, but this here is a democracy. I say we vote on it. What do you think, Pessolano?"

There's a pause. Then Pessolano says, *"We kill them all."*

Swanson wonders how far he'll get if he climbs into the car and just takes off. Will he make it to Mexico? Will these jokers track him down? Over the previous weeks, meeting and planning and training, Munchel and Pessolano had become his friends. But now they seemed like entirely different people. Crazy people.

"Fine," Swanson says. He doesn't have a choice. "We go on my mark. Get ready."

Swanson squints through the scope, guesses where the head is in relation to the shoe he sees. The suppressor screwed into the barrel makes the rifle almost a foot longer, and more than a little unbalanced. Pessolano lectured them during the car ride over, saying that the suppressor won't silence all of the noise. Silencers are fictional, because nothing can completely muffle a gunshot. The suppressors will also throw off the aim and reduce the bullet's speed.

Earlier tonight, they wanted the gunshots to be heard. They wanted the media attention. Now, working as quietly as possible is the way to go, because they have no idea how long this is going to take.

"One . . ." Swanson says, "two . . ."

Someone fires before he reaches three. That asshole Munchel. Then Pessolano is firing too. Swanson takes aim and squeezes the trigger.

The shot is off. Way off. And it's still pretty loud, even with the suppressor. He loads another round, searches for a target, and can't find any. He seeks out the radio.

"We get them?"

"Negative," says Pessolano.

But Munchel hoots, so loud he can be heard without the radio.

"I think I nailed me a grandmother!"

JACK

"*WHEN ARE WE GOING to go shopping for drapes?*"

Mom has been asking me that since we moved in. But whenever free time came along we used it to see a movie, go out to dinner, or catch up on the TV shows we recorded. I always assumed that Mom didn't push the issue because she liked seeing woods on all sides of her.

Now I wish she had pushed the issue.

After the first two shots rip through the house, I tip Mom's chair over, intent on dragging her into the hallway. While our house has a lot of windows, the hall bathroom boasts the smallest one, and the glass is frosted for privacy.

"Save Latham first," Mom says.

I look at my fiancé, see he's taken cover behind the sofa. The large bay window offers a wide view of the entire living room. I can't get to him without making myself an easy target.

"He's in the line of fire," I tell her. Then I grab her chair leg and pull.

The chair doesn't come easy. It keeps catching on the carpeting, and my movements are restricted by my bindings. But I find a rhythm and inch by inch I drag Mom out of the living room.

Halfway to the hall, all hell breaks loose. Bullets tear through the couch Latham is hiding behind. Windows shatter. Walls shake, the plasterboard throwing off powder like smoke. I cover Mom's body with my own, realize that makes us a bigger target, and get on my knees and pull for all I'm worth.

I feel the impact vibration in my hands, know that Mom has been hit, and a moan/growl leaves my throat. Shots whistle past my head, and I tug Mom all the way into that bathroom, afraid to look at her, afraid not to look at her.

"Mom! Are you hit?"

Her eyes are closed. I can't tell if she's breathing.

I find scissors in the medicine cabinet, hack away at the duct tape, see the smoking bullet hole in the chair's wooden seat.

"I think I've got splinters in my keister," Mom says.

I cry in relief, give Mom a hug. The shooting stops.

"Latham!" At the top of my lungs.

"I'm okay!"

Thank God.

"I'm okay too!" Harry yells. "If anyone cares!"

I use a Dixie cup to get my mom some water from the sink. Then I holler at Harry, "Where's Alex?"

"Don't you care that I'm okay?"

I use the scissors on my legs, cutting away the tape.

"Dammit, Harry, do you see her?"

"I don't see her. But her gun is in pieces."

I stare down at my wrists. My handcuff keys are in my purse, in the kitchen. But I have extra handcuff keys, and an extra gun, in my bedroom. Unfortunately, it's a handgun, and won't help against the psychos outside. But it will help against the psycho in the house.

"Stay here!" I order my mother.

Then I rush out into the hallway, and bump right into Alex.

She stands there, hand bleeding, eyes wild, apparently uncon-cerned that she might get shot at any moment.

I still have the scissors. I thrust them at her, and she grabs my wrist with one hand and swings at me with the other, a roundhouse punch. I bunch up and take it on the shoulder, then jerk my head for-ward, aiming for her nose.

I connect solidly, and Alex releases me, staggering back, hitting the hallway wall directly behind her. We face each other. A bullet whips through the small space between us.

"Lock the door!" I scream at my mother.

"Jack . . ."

"Dammit, Mom! Listen to me!"

I hear the door close, feel it press against my back. A bullet digs into the ceiling, raining bits of plaster on Alex and me. Her face twists in a half smile.

"What are you going to do with those scissors?" she asks. "Give me a haircut?"

I have other ideas. Gripping the scissors with both hands, I hold them before me like a sword, and feint a poke. She moves to dodge the fake attack, and I launch my real attack—a spin kick aimed at her ribs. Alex spins away and I miss, my foot making a dent in the wall.

"Jack!" Harry yells. "I think Alex is in the hall!"

I turn around, feel a breeze, and blink as a bullet passes in front of my face. Alex kicks my wrists and the scissors go flying. I throw myself at her, driving my shoulder into her side, using all of my 135 pounds.

Alex stumbles, falls. I sprint for my bedroom at the end of the hall. I open the door and see my cat, Mr. Friskers, sitting on the re-mains of a down pillow, surrounded by feathers. We keep him locked up in the bedroom because he has the tendency to destroy things and attack people. The shooting must have agitated him, because all the hair on his back is sticking straight up, as is his tail.

I keep one eye on the kitty—he isn't an animal you turn your back on—and head for the closet.

Alex tackles me from behind, driving me to the floor. She lands on top, and she forces her arm under my chin, around my neck, and begins to squeeze.

It's like having my head in a noose. I can't take a breath and everything gets blurry. I look to my right, see Mr. Friskers staring. Apparently my looming death doesn't interest him, because he trots out of the room. I look left, see a bunch of stuff under my bed, all of it covered with dust, none of it useful.

Alex lets up a bit on the choke hold—I guess she doesn't want to kill me yet. I still can't pull free, but I'm able to lower my chin just enough to clamp my jaws on her forearm.

She yelps. I bite. She pulls away. I twist onto my side, make my fingers stiff, and shove them into her kidney.

Alex grunts, rolling off of me. We both get to our feet, Alex cradling her bleeding arm. I've bitten pretty deep. Her eyes narrow to slits, and her scar tissue flushes bright pink.

"Is that what you got your black belt in?" Alex says. "Biting?"

"No."

I pivot my hips, whip my leg around, and reverse-kick her upside the head. She staggers, but doesn't fall. I follow it up with a flying kick, knocking her backward over my bed.

"Hey, Jackie!" Harry calls. "Is your cat friendly?"

My extra handcuff keys are in the jewelry box, on the dresser behind her. My gun is in the closet, zippered up in my shooting bag. If I go for the gun, there's a chance Alex might wrestle it away from me before I get it out. But if I leave the room, she might go searching for it.

Alex stands up. I tug open the closet door, grab the bag, and head for the door.

"JESUS CHRIST! THE CAT HAS MY JOHNSON!"

A shot comes through my bedroom window, making a hole in my sleeve but missing my arm. Alex and I both drop to the floor. I take the opportunity to unzip my bag, and Alex gets onto all fours, poised to come at me. I toss the bag onto the bed, into the line of fire. The sniper proves my hypothesis by shooting the bag. Alex doesn't reach for it. Neither do I. Instead, I scramble for the door.

"HE'S BITING ME! HE'S BITING ME!"

I feel her hand brush my ankle. I twist free and run in a crouch. Through the doorway. Down the hall. Into the kitchen.

Mr. Friskers has latched on to Harry's crotch. Harry is unsuccessfully trying to yank him off.

"Don't pull," I say, running past. "It just makes him dig in."

"HE'S GOT THE TWINS!"

Harry tugs on the cat's tail, which Mr. Friskers *really* hates. He becomes a blur of fur and claws, hissing and scratching as Harry screams.

I search the floor for my purse, find it, dump the contents.

My handcuff key. I snatch it up just as Alex appears in the kitchen.

Two more shots ping through the windows, both of them hitting the fridge. Rather than duck down, it looks like Harry is trying to stick his groin in front of the bullets.

Then Alex pounces, coming at me low, arms outstretched and eyes crazed.

I go at her even lower, aiming for her ankles. I hook my elbow around her foot, tripping her, then roll to the side, bumping up against the dishwasher. I still have the handcuff key. I fumble with it, trying to find the keyhole.

Another shot, very close to Harry. Mr. Friskers screeches, jumping high enough to hit the ceiling. He lands on the floor and streaks out of the kitchen, apparently having had enough. Harry, bleeding and pissed off, points a finger at me.

"Why would you have a cat like that? Why?"

I get the key in, turn it.

My hand pops free. I yank open the dishwasher, intent on grabbing a knife.

Alex kicks the dishwasher door closed, and I barely escape with my arm. I thrust the knife, stabbing at her leg, and realize I have a spoon instead. She hits me with a right cross that brings the stars out, but I've been hit harder and I gather up a handful of her shirt and deliver an uppercut that sends the bitch staggering.

Then I'm on my feet. On my feet, hands free, angry as hell. I swing lefty, not making a fist, catching her just above the eyes with the handcuffs hanging from my wrist. I open up a gash on her forehead, and the blood trickles into her eyes, making it hard for Alex to see.

I scan the countertop, see the apple pie. I pick it up, still steaming hot, and chuck it at Alex's head.

She ducks. The pie hits Harry, in the groin.

"JESUS CHRIST, IT BURNS!"

He slaps at the apples, which must only add to his discomfort. I fly back to the counter, grab the coffeemaker, and bounce it off Alex's chest. Then I tug the toaster from the wall and swing the appliance around my head like a lasso. I'm not aiming to knock her out. I'm aiming to knock off her fucking head.

I release the cord. Alex puts up her hand to protect her head, and both her hand and the toaster smash into her face. Somehow she stays on her feet. I charge at her, snarling, ready to tear her throat out with my bare hands.

But before I can get to her the kitchen becomes a firing range, bullets zinging into cabinets and countertops. Glasses and plates shatter, pots and pans ding-dong with ricochets. Alex and I kneel on the ground and cover our heads, and McGlade pulls food and drawers and shelves out of the refrigerator as fast as he can, trying to fit himself inside, which is like trying to stuff a pot roast into a tube sock.

"Jack!" Mom cries from the bathroom. It's a cry of concern, not pain.

"Stay there, Mom!"

The shooting eases up again. I look around for something to hit Alex with, and then I glance up and she's standing over me, holding up the tabletop microwave oven, ready to cave my skull in.

"Hey, pork chop face!" Harry says.

Alex turns.

"Got milk?" Harry asks. Then he smacks her in the head with a full jug of moo juice, hitting her so hard that she spins 360 degrees before sprawling out onto her back.

Her eyes are closed. She's out cold.

Harry points to the milk all over the floor.

"Now promise me you won't be crying over this, Jack."

I can't help myself. I have to grin at that.

"I promise, Harry."

"Good. Now bring me that goddamn cat. I want my foreskin back."

HERB

"WHERE IN THE HELL is your partner?"

Herb stares at Blake Crouch, Chicago's deputy chief, and says, "I don't know."

Crouch resembles a mole, with a long, sharp nose and tiny black eyes. Came from out of state, so he didn't rise up through the ranks like much of the brass. Because of this, Herb suspects, Crouch thought he had to be a hard-ass to gain respect. Hence his nickname, *Deputy Grouch*. Someone needed to lecture this man about flies and honey and vinegar. Someone other than Herb, who spent an hour getting stitches in his leg and then even longer tap dancing with the Grouch in the ER, waiting for Jack to return.

Herb had called Jack on her cell and at home, several times each. No answer. Which worries him. Jack is the poster girl for being responsible. Being incommunicado isn't like her at all.

"I'm going to send a team to the lieutenant's apartment," the Grouch says. "If I find out she's deliberately hiding something . . ."

Herb shakes his head, his jowls wiggling.

"She's not hiding anything, sir. It went down like I said."

"I still need her statement. There's blood in the water, and the sharks are circling the wagons."

Herb has no idea what that means, and he guesses the Grouch doesn't either. But he can't let the deputy chief find out that Jack lives outside the city.

"She's not at her apartment," Herb says. "She's with her mother. Her elderly, sickly mother."

"Her mother is sick?" the Grouch asks.

"Very sick."

"Which hospital is she in? I can meet—"

"She's sick in the head," Herb says.

"Is it pyromania?" the Grouch asks.

"Huh?"

"I had an aunt with pyromania. She'd knit sweaters, then set them on fire."

Herb tries to judge if the Grouch is being funny, but he sees a tear in the corner of the man's eye.

"I think she's just failing mentally," Herb says. "Jack ran out to the suburbs to check on her."

"Do you know where?"

Herb shakes his head. The Grouch gets in close, so close his pointy nose almost touches Herb's. Herb rears back slightly, afraid he'll lose an eye.

"I will bring your partner before a disciplinary committee if I don't hear from her within the hour. So if you have any clue where she might be, Sergeant, I suggest you find her."

"Jack saved lives today," Herb says, his voice steady.

"I don't care if she saved the mayor's daughter from being eaten by sharks . . ."

What is with this guy and sharks?

". . . I want her debriefed right now. Do I make myself clear?"

"Yes, sir," Herb says.

The Grouch backs off a few feet.

"Good. Now I've got to talk to the media. They're having a field day with their cockamamie theories."

"Are they jumping the shark?" Herb asks innocently.

The Grouch doesn't respond, already walking away from Herb's hospital bed. Herb looks for nurses, then discreetly picks up his cell phone, which isn't allowed in the ER. He can't reach Jack at either number.

Herb knows his partner well. If Jack's phones are off, that means something really serious is happening, something so serious it is making Jack neglect her responsibility here. Though Herb made up the story about Jack's mother failing mentally, he knows she has some health problems. Could that be what's taking Jack so long?

Herb tries the two hospitals nearest to Jack's suburban home. Neither has admitted Mary Streng, or any elderly Jane Doe. He calls Dispatch, has them check suburban 911 calls. While he's on hold, he digs into his pocket stock and eats a power bar. For energy. He considers drinking the bag full of bran-fortified breakfast shake, but dismisses the idea. Dispatch comes back, informs Herb there haven't been any calls from Jack's house.

The Novocain numbness makes it difficult to put his pants back on because he can't feel if his leg is in the hole, and he can't really see it either, thanks to a belly forged by decades of poor dietary choices. But he manages, and then he straps on his empty holster—IA took his gun to rule out friendly fire from the crime scene—and puts his jacket on.

Then Sergeant Herb Benedict heads to the suburbs to find his partner.

MUNCHEL

JAMES MICHAEL MUNCHEL takes another sip of Gatorade from his canteen, wipes the sweat off his eye, and peers through the scope again. So far, he's been the lucky one. He has the kitchen covered, and that's where most of the action has taken place.

From what he's figured out, the tall bitch with the messed-up face is causing all sorts of problems for the female cop, the guy next to the refrigerator is stuck there because he has some kind of James Bond mechanical hand that won't let go, and there's a cat in the house in serious need of a distemper shot.

Munchel could have ended it for all of them, at any time. But he didn't. He made sure his shots came close without hitting any of the targets. Scaring them, but not wounding them. He's having too much fun for this to end.

That tight-ass Swanson is looking to kill everyone, then hightail it out of here, quick and dirty. But this should be savored. There's a real-life drama going on inside the cop's house. It's far more interesting than Munchel's everyday life, punching a clock at the English muffin factory. Munchel is the gluer there. His job, for eight mind-numbing hours from ten p.m. until six a.m., five days a week, is to add glue chips to the melter, which is then picked up by the roller, which paints glue on the flat cardboard blanks prior to them being folded into muffin packages. His work is literally about as much fun as watching glue dry.

He's going to miss his shift tonight. Maybe he'll even be fired. But he doesn't care. Right now he feels like he's watching a movie. No, like he's starring in a movie. Starring in it *and* directing it. He decides who dies first, who dies last. He has the power.

"Did you hit anyone yet?" Swanson, through the radio.

"Negative," Pessolano answers.

Munchel hits the talk button. "I came close. They're hiding. Don't have a shot."

He squints through the scope. The chick cop is right in his crosshairs. All he needs to do is pull the trigger, and it's game over.

But where's the challenge in that?

That gives Munchel an idea. A way to make this even more interesting, and to get the same adrenaline rush he got in Ravenswood. But he needs to get back to Pessolano's pickup truck, which is parked in the woods half a mile away.

"I gotta take a leak," he tells the guys. "I'll be back in a minute."

Then Munchel stands up, stretches, and heads off to get another rifle.

AFTER A SEMI-FRANTIC SEARCH I find the handcuff key on the kitchen counter. I unlock the remaining bracelet, drag Alex across the floor by her hair, and secure her wrists around the U pipe under the sink.

"See if she's got my battery pack in her pocket," Harry says.

I don't like touching Alex—even restrained and unconscious she frightens me. But when I reach for her pocket she doesn't leap up, break free, and then plunge a knife into my chest. She just lies there, unmoving. I locate the bulge in the front of her pants and tug out Harry's battery. Well, a few pieces of it.

"Shit hell damn," Harry says. "Kick her in the head, from me."

"Can't you pry open your hand?

"Yeah, why didn't I think of that? Then I could have actually tried to hide, rather than just squat here like an idiot."

I frown. "Maybe we could pull off the handle."

"I already tried. Who the hell made this fridge? Brinks?"

Harry reaches inside, helps himself to one of my Goose Island India Pale Ales.

"Latham!" I call to the living room. "We got Alex subdued. You holding up okay?"

My honey answers affirmatively, but his voice is weak.

"How about you, Mom?"

"I'm good. Did you punch her lights out?"

"Harry did."

"Nice job, Harry!"

"Thanks! But your daughter hit me in the dumplings with a hot pie."

"Jacqueline!" Mom scolds. "Why did you do that?"

"It was an accident, Mom."

"Did you apologize?"

I mutter, "Sorry, Harry."

"She didn't sound sincere!" Harry tells my mom.

I roll my eyes, then fish out a bag of peas from the freezer. I hold it to my sore chin and consider the situation.

Alex, for the moment, is secure. We have no cell phone service, which means the snipers are jamming the signal. My landline is also out. Since my home phone goes through my cable connection, I assume my cable Internet is gone too.

I ponder the likelihood of someone hearing the gunshots and calling 911, and realize the chances aren't good. The shooters are using suppressors, and the trees do a decent job of stopping the echoes.

Latham is still bound, still bleeding. I need to get to him, but between us is a vast open space, all of it viewable by the snipers. I counted at least two shooters, but I'm guessing that all three are here. I have no clue why. Are they pissed off I didn't die in Ravenswood?

Harry picks an apple slice off of his shirt and pops it into his mouth. "I never got to thank you for inviting me over. We should do this more often."

"Alex forced me, Harry. I tried to warn you."

"No biggie. Who needs balls anyway? They make your pants fit funny."

"It's bad?" I ask.

Harry pulls out his waistband and peeks inside.

"I don't think they're supposed to swell up this big."

"You need to see a doctor."

"I need to see Mr. Ripley."

"Mr. Ripley?"

"The *Believe It or Not* guy. I should make a plaster mold for his museum."

I toss him the frozen peas. He stuffs them down his pants.

"COLD!" Harry yells. "SO COLD!"

I stare at him, hopping from foot to foot, and then I look at the freezer door of the stainless steel refrigerator. It's pockmarked with bullet holes, each in the center of a huge dent. Strange. Full-metal jacketed slugs should have punched right through without denting it. I crawl up to Harry to get a closer look.

"So what shitstorm did I wander into?" McGlade asks. He drains the beer, tosses the bottle at Alex's head, misses, then reaches for another.

"Three snipers. They kill sex offenders. Call themselves TUHC."

Harry belches and says, "The Urban Hunting Club."

I appraise him. "You've heard of them?"

"No. But there's a producer of DVD adult entertainment called TUBC. *The Urban Booty Club.* Lots of college girls taking off their tops and eating Popsicles, stuff like that. The first DVD is only nine ninety-nine, but that's how they sucker you in, because they send you two new DVDs every month for twenty-nine ninety-nine each. And they're only forty-five minutes long, which is a real rip-off." Harry scratches his nose. "So I've heard."

The Urban Hunting Club sounds right. That's something a group of disgruntled blue-collar Grabowskis would call themselves.

"They killed three rapists tonight, then gunned down ten cops," I say. "Looks like they followed me home."

"You think?"

I open the fridge, can't find where the bullets have gone through on the inside. The door seems to have stopped them. I shake it, and hear some slugs rattling inside. I use a spoon to pry back the plastic molding, and a gray bullet drops out. It resembles a mushroom. The snipers have switched from jacketed rounds to soft points. A soft point has more stopping power, expanding on impact, but not the penetrating power of a full-metal jacket slug, which didn't deform as much.

"You know, Jackie . . ." Harry stares down at me, "the top of your head is really sexy."

"This is the only time you'll ever see it, McGlade."

He takes out his cell phone and snaps a picture.

"Hot," Harry says. "I especially dig the gray roots coming in. I like a woman with decades of experience."

I ignore him, something I'm particularly good at. "We need to turn off the lights. We've got two in the kitchen, three in the living room, the hallway, the bedroom, and the garage. Then, when it's dark, I can grab the gun bag in the bedroom, pop outside, and sneak up on these bastards."

"You can kill all the lights at once," Harry says. "Got a circuit breaker?"

"End of the hallway, in the laundry room."

"I'll wait here." Harry shakes his prosthetic for effect.

"Actually, Harry, I'm thinking we use this refrigerator for cover."

"You want to push this heavy thing all the way across a carpeted hallway? Good luck."

"*We're* going to push it."

"And give the psycho kitty another chance to use Acorn Andy as a scratch post? No thanks."

I reach into the refrigerator, take out the squirt gun we keep in there for when Mr. Friskers disagrees with guests.

"Just spray him if he gets close."

"Like this?"

Harry squirts me in the face. Big surprise there. Then he sprays me in the chest a few times, squinting to see through the material. I take the gun away from him.

"Grow up, Harry." I yell over my shoulder, "Mom! Latham! We're going to shut off the electricity!" I face Harry again. "Let's do this."

Harry grins, then adjusts his peas. "All right, but I'm warning you—if it's really heavy, I'm going to make you check me later on for a hernia."

"I can't wait," I deadpan. Then I unplug the fridge and we begin to push.

PESSOLANO

PAUL PESSOLANO PEERS THROUGH the yellow lenses of his aviator sunglasses, trying to find his backpack in the darkness. He can't see shit. Pessolano feels around in the grass where he's sitting, and locates one of the straps. He pulls the bag closer, lifts up his glasses so he can see inside, and removes a magazine filled with five Lapua .338 Mags. He pops the old magazine out of the TPG-1 and clicks the new one in place. Then he gives it a slap, like he's seen in a thousand war movies.

Even though he told the others differently, Pessolano was never in the armed forces. The closest he ever got to the sands of Kuwait was Miami Beach. Six months ago he worked in a chain video store in Tampa. Then his elderly mother died. He quit his job, sold her house, and used the money to buy some top-of-the-line sniper rifles and surveillance equipment. His plan was to become a mercenary. Or a hit man. Or a wandering gun for hire, like George Peppard on *The A-Team*.

Work wasn't easy to find. He tried reading the police blotter and calling up the parents of juveniles involved in illegal activities, asking if they wanted to hire him to make their lives easier. He never got any takers, and after cops showed up at his apartment (he hid inside and didn't let them in) he fled the state.

Swanson's ad in *Soldier of Fortune*, asking for *"civic-minded mercs who wanted to make things right,"* is the first freelance job Pessolano has actually been on. It doesn't pay anything, but that's okay. This is all about getting some experience. Once he turns this corner, he's sure he'll find other jobs. Because Pessolano is now, officially, a killer.

It was easy, killing the pervert. Pessolano had been worried about it, afraid he wouldn't have the guts to pull the trigger when the clock struck five. But he pulled that trigger. And he shot that pervert in the back of the head. Baptized by fire, a culmination of the greatest few weeks of his life.

All the preparation, all the practice up to this point, didn't seem real. Pessolano felt like he was living someone else's life. He liked the feeling, but didn't fully believe it. But he believes it now. He's not a pretender. He's the real deal. And he's got the dead body to prove it, and good friends to share it with. Though Swanson seems a little soft, and Munchel a little crazy, they are his friends. That's why he doesn't mind them using his guns and equipment.

And now the thing Pessolano wants to do most is impress his friends. He knows they look up to him. If he can kill all five of the targets by himself, they'll revere him even more. That's why he's using the better bullets. The Lapuas, which can shoot through a brick wall. These are the last of the full-metal jacket rounds. He gave Swanson and Munchel cheaper bullets—soft points. They work fine, but they aren't as deadly as the Lapuas.

He pulls back the bolt. The brass flies out. He chambers a round and spends a minute tracking down the ejected cartridge and pocketing it. Then he presses his cheek against the pad and sights his target: the hallway. He can see all the way down to the laundry room. If he switches position, he can see into the bedroom where the two women were fighting over the black bag.

Perfect. Now all he has to do is wait.

The wait isn't very long. After hunkering down for only a minute or two, something appears in his scope. Something large and silver.

A refrigerator. The woman cop and the guy with the fake hand are pushing it into the hallway, trying to use the doors for shields.

Pessolano smiles. One of his bullets could shoot through five of those fridges stacked side by side. He lines up the mil dots in the scope, aiming at the door she's hiding behind, right where her heart should be.

JACK

"DAMMIT, HARRY! PUSH!"

"Hold on. I need to hydrate."

Harry reaches in the refrigerator for another beer. I've been in life-and-death situations with him before, and being flip is Harry's normal MO. He lacks the ability to recognize the severity of his position. Either that, or he recognizes it and chooses to ignore it. I suppose the attitude has served him well so far, because despite the efforts of many people, Harry McGlade isn't dead yet. But I don't want to get my head blown off because he thinks everything is one big joke. Harry might have delusions of immortality. I don't.

So I take the beer from his hand and shove it back in the fridge.

"Stop acting like an idiot and let's push this thing. On three. One . . . two . . . three!"

I half expect him to reach for the beer again, or shoot me with the squirt gun, but Harry knuckles down and pushes. The fridge is a high-end model, the rollers heavy-duty. It moves easily on the kitchen linoleum. But when we get onto the carpet, every inch becomes a battle. The hallway isn't long—no more than twenty-five feet—but it might as well be a mile. We strain and shove and grunt, putting our weight into it, digging our heels in. In less than a minute we're both winded, and the fridge hasn't moved down the hallway more than three feet.

"Do you need help?" Mom, from the bathroom.

"Hell yeah!" Harry says.

"Mom, stay where you are."

"She wants to help, let her help."

"She's not—"

The bullet punches cleanly through the refrigerator door, and I feel it tug against my jacket's shoulder pad. I drop onto the ground, hugging the floor, thinking, *Oh my God, that wasn't a soft point.*

"Uh-oh," Harry says.

He kneels next to me, but his mechanical hand prevents him from lying down. Another bullet hits the fridge, a few inches above his head. I consider crawling down the hall, back into the kitchen, but that would leave Harry stranded in the hallway, an open target.

"Run, Jack!"

I can't believe it. Harry isn't the heroic, self-sacrificing type.

"Run in front of the bullets!" he yells. "Shield me!"

I stand up, put my palms on the refrigerator door, and scream at him, "Push!"

We push. And we're surprisingly effective. Funny how someone shooting at you can give you extra motivation. We move the fridge two feet, then four, a bullet barreling through the door only two inches from my hand, then we get some momentum going and we're really making headway. Then another shot rings out and Harry falls to his knees and cries, "I'm hit!"

We're less than a foot away from the bathroom. If we make it there, we can duck inside and dodge the gunfire. But Harry is useless, clutching his shoulder.

I suck in a big breath, find some deep, hidden reserve, and put everything I have into pushing that refrigerator another two feet, Harry on his knees and barely able to keep up. I reach the door, then help Mom drag Harry into the bathroom, to safety.

Harry sits on the floor, his metal hand still holding on to the refrigerator door. Mom takes another pair of scissors from the medicine cabinet and begins cutting off his shirt, looking for the bullet hole. True to his name, Harry has the hairiest chest I've ever seen. It looks like he's wearing a brown and gray sweater. Mom cuts all the way up to the shoulder, but Harry refuses to take his hand away from the wound.

"I don't want to look," he says, hyperventilating.

My mom pats his head. "It's okay."

"If I die, I want you to make the funeral arrangements, Jack."

"I will."

"I want strippers there."

"Okay, Harry."

He removes his hand, reaches out for me. I hold it. Mom pulls away his shirt and reveals—

"It's a scratch," I say.

"Don't sugarcoat it," Harry moans. "I can handle the truth."

I release his hand and peer at the thin red line. I've given Latham worse injuries with my fingernails.

"It's not even worth a Band-Aid, McGlade."

"You got a mirror?"

I hand him the tweezing mirror from the vanity. He holds it on an angle and looks.

"We cut my shirt off for this? I paid sixty bucks for that shirt."

I sigh, stand up. Mom, however, stares down at Harry with a strange look on her face.

"Mom, you all right?"

"Harry . . . *McGlade* is your last name, right?"

"Yeah. Harrison Harold McGlade. I see you're loving my chest hair. The ladies think it's cute. I go into bars, ask them if they want a fuzzy navel. Then I lift up my shirt and jiggle. If it gets a laugh, I ask them if they'd like something stiffer."

Mom seems transfixed.

"Is that a birthmark on your chest?"

"Port-wine stain. Looks like a fish, doesn't it?"

Harry uses his fingers to part the gray, giving us a better view. His birthmark is several inches long, and indeed shaped like a fish, with an ovalish body and a triangle-like tail.

"Yes, it does," Mom says. "It's very distinctive. How old are you? Forty-nine?"

"Yeah. But the doctor says I have the body of a thirty-year-old, if the thirty-year-old was really unhealthy and close to death."

I don't like where this is going. My mother seems way too interested in Harry. "Mom?"

She ignores me. "Were you born in March?"

Harry's eyes narrow. "On the twenty-ninth. How did you know that?"

Mom's knees begin to shake, and I put my arm around her for support.

"Mom? What's wrong?"

"One last thing," Mom says to Harry. "Were you adopted?"

Oh my God, no. A thousand times no.

Mom had told me that before she met my father, she had a baby out of wedlock. A baby boy. With a sailor she had a one-night stand with when she was a teenager. When I became a cop, I'd tried to track my half brother down, tickled that I had a sibling out there. But I never thought that my brother could be someone like . . .

"No," Harry says.

Thank Christ.

"I was raised by the state," he continues. "In an orphanage."

Mom's jaw hangs limp. So does mine. Harry puts two and two together and says, "Are you saying that I might be your son?"

Mom nods.

Harry grins, his smile as wide as a canoe.

"Mom! Sis! It's so good to be home!"

JACK

I F KARMA IS REAL, I must have done something unspeakable in a previous life.

"This has to be some kind of mistake," I say to my mother. I may have actually been pleading a little. "He doesn't look anything like you."

"He looks like his father."

Harry makes puppy dog eyes and says, "Mom? Tell me about Dad."

I don't have time for this. Latham is bleeding and we're surrounded by snipers. I need to kill the lights and grab the gun.

I poke my head into the hallway, on the opposite side of the fridge. While FMJs can shoot through it, the snipers can't *see* through it. That means I can run to the laundry room and hit the circuit breaker without being spotted.

"He was a sailor," Mom says. "I never knew his last name."

"I'm going for the fuse box," I say.

"What was his first name, Mom?"

Mom pats Harry on the head. "His name was Ralph." She used the same soothing voice on me when I was younger and sick with the flu. "You have his eyes."

"I'm going now," I announce. "I hope I make it."

"Did you love him?" Harry ask.

Mom says, "For about three hours."

"Wow," Harry says. "Three hours."

"Latham!" I call out to my fiancé. "I'm going for the circuit breaker!"

I hoped for a *be careful*. Instead I got: "Is that creepy private eye really your brother?"

I rub my eyes.

"Ralph had a lot of body hair too," Mom says. "All over."

That's my cue. I duck low, suck in a breath, then hustle out the door and down the rest of the hallway, skidding into the laundry room. No one shoots me. The circuit breaker is on the wall, next to the dryer. I hook a finger through the metal ring on the door and tug. It's stubborn, and doesn't want to open. The panel isn't broken, it has a strong spring inside that makes sure it's always closed. I pull really hard, my finger aching, and then it finally gives. I squint at the rows of breakers, and press the large black button that reads *MAIN*.

The house goes dark, and the panel door slams back into place. I don't hesitate, scrambling back into the hall, using memory and feel to find my bedroom. I take four steps inside before bumping into the bed. Then I spread my hands out over the top, seeking the ammo bag. My fingers brush the carrying strap, and I jerk the bag to me. I work the zipper, stick my hand inside, and yank out my competition pistol, a Kimber Eclipse II .45 ACP. I flip the safety and jack a round into the chamber. I feel around for extra clips, find three. They're all empty. Bullets have been on my shopping list for a while.

There's also a nylon holster in the bag. I shrug that onto my shoulder, the straps getting twisted in the dark but still doing the job.

Then I head for the window to sneak outside and round up the bad guys.

PESSOLANO

WHEN THE LIGHTS GO OUT in the house, Pessolano takes the Leupold optics off the quick-release mount, puts it back into his bag, and attaches a Gen 3 starlight scope to the rifle.

Night vision works by using an image intensifier with a photoelectric effect to amplify ambient light. At least, that's what the instruction manual says. Pessolano doesn't understand it, but he knows that it turns images from pitch-black into a phosphorescent green.

He peers through the scope, and there, silhouetted at the bedroom window, is the female cop. He has one remaining Lapua FMJ round left, so he aims carefully, trying to adjust for the wind that has picked up.

BANG!

He sees the bullet strike the cop in the head, sees her jerk back, and smiles as she collapses.

"Bull's-eye," Pessolano says to himself.

This is so much more rewarding than working at a video store.

9:34 P.M.
MARY

MARY STRENG IS STILL TRYING to wrap her mind around the possibility that this strange man in her bathroom might actually be her son.

Almost fifty years have passed since she gave up her infant boy. She doesn't remember his exact birthday, only that it was before Easter, and bitterly cold. Labor had been lonely, frightening, miserable, the pain of childbirth exacerbated by the knowledge that she wasn't going to keep her baby. She'd gotten pregnant at eighteen years old, still in high school. Dropped out when she began to show. Left home soon after that, never telling her parents the reason why, preferring their protestations to their judgments. Got a job at a deli in another part of town. Lived in a fugue for a few months, then moved back home and finished school when it was all over.

She used to fantasize that someone adopted her son. Someone rich and caring, who spoiled him with extravagant gifts. A year later she met her future husband and got on with her life. Mary still thought of her son sometimes, on cold days in March, but she managed to forgive herself.

Hearing that Harry had been raised by the state, and not by Mary's imaginary perfect family, reopened a long-sealed box of regret.

She wants to ask him about his life. If he's happy. If his childhood was okay. If he hates her.

Then she hears the shot, hears the *thump* of her daughter hitting the floor, and all thoughts of her past flit away.

"Jacqueline!"

No answer.

A feeling of dread unlike any she's ever experienced drops over her like a shroud. Without giving it a second thought she grabs a flashlight from the bathroom closet and rushes into the hallway.

"Be careful," Harry says after her. "Keep low."

Mary doesn't bother doing either. She moves as fast as she can, hurrying into the bedroom. Jacqueline is on floor, beside the bed. Her eyes are closed. Her hair is soaked with blood.

Oh no. Oh no no no no.

Mary kneels next to her daughter and directs the light onto the wound, her hands trembling. She can't see the injury—there's too much blood. Mary grabs a pillow, pulls off the case, uses that to mop at the spot that's bleeding.

It's a deep gash, three inches long, an inch wide. Mary presses the fabric to Jacqueline's scalp, pulls it away, and can see her daughter's skull bone, a startling white, before the blood begins to flow again. The bullet must have grazed her head, digging a trench in her skin. Thank God the bullet didn't strike an inch lower.

Mary's relief is short-lived, because the blood keeps coming. She estimates Jacqueline has already lost close to a pint, and she's still pumping it out. Mary wraps the already-soaked pillowcase around her daughter's head, tying it under her chin like a babushka. In the bathroom, there's a first-aid kit. She could go and get it, then come back, but she's unsure if the kit will be enough to stop the bleeding. Better to bring Jacqueline into the bathroom. Then Harry could help.

Keeping low, Mary pulls the comforter off the bed, and then the sheet beneath it. She lays the sheet on the floor, and with a deep grunt she rolls Jacqueline on top of it, placing the flashlight on her daughter's chest. The effort leaves Mary gasping for air, but she doesn't pause, instead crawling to the foot of the sheet and grasping it as hard as she can in her arthritic hands. Then she scoots back on her butt and pulls.

Pain, like sparks, shoots from Mary's knuckles, up her arms, where it meets with other pain from her shoulders and back. Mary grits her teeth, squeezes her eyes shut, and fights against the pain. Arthritis produces a deep ache, like a migraine in the bones. Mary takes drugs to control the worst of it, even though they make her dizzy. She's missed her last pill. The agony is worse than childbirth. Worse than a toothache.

Jacqueline slides across the carpeting, about a foot.

Mary doesn't rest. She scoots back again, takes a deep breath, and pulls.

Another foot.

And another.

And another.

She reaches the bedroom doorway, her whole body shaking. The pain in her knuckles has become so bad that she's moaning. She can't make a fist anymore, so she wraps the sheet around her hands, around her wrists, which presses her inflamed knuckles together.

Pull.

Pull.

Pull.

"You're almost there, Mom!" Harry shouts. "Just a little more!"

To take her mind off the agony, Mary thinks about Jacqueline's birth, of holding her for the first time and saying, "Hello, my angel. I'm your mother. I'm going to be taking care of you, for the rest of my life."

How those words meant so much to Mary, because she'd given up her previous child. How she swore to keep that promise, even if she lived to a hundred.

Pull.

Hurry.

Pull.

Save your daughter.

Pull.

The most important job anyone can ever have is being a mother. Remember your promise. Now dig deep and move it, old lady!

"Gotcha!"

Harry stretches out, touches Mary's shoulder, then grabs a fistful of sheets. He tugs Jacqueline up to the bathroom, and they both muscle her through the door.

Mary tries to stand but she's too weak. Her hands are screaming. She shoves the flashlight into her armpit, crawls to the closet, finds the first-aid kit, fights with the damnable zipper on the nylon case, and opens it up.

Inside are Band-Aids, antibacterial ointment, smelling salts, packets of Tylenol, gauze pads, cotton balls, an Ace bandage, and various other items. Mary selects a roll of white medical tape.

"Harry, get this roll started."

Harry picks at the end, trying to get his fingernails under it. He manages, and Mary tears off a strip with her teeth, the only part of her body that still works. She crawls back to her daughter.

Jacqueline is still unconscious, but she's panting. Mary feels her heart, and it's like she has a hummingbird trapped in her rib cage.

"She's hyperventilating."

"Tachycardia," Harry says. "She's going into hypovolemic shock."

Mary stares at him. "What does that mean?"

"She's lost so much blood that her body isn't getting oxygen, so her heart is pumping faster to compensate for it."

"What do we do?"

"Stop the bleeding, and get her a transfusion. Then feed her some liquids."

Mary stares at him, impressed.

Harry shrugs, says, "I've got the first three seasons of *ER* on DVD. Great show."

Mary hands Harry the flashlight, then turns her attention back to her daughter. She soaks up some blood with a hand towel and then pinches the wound closed and tries to use the tape to keep the edges together. It doesn't work; the blood comes too fast, getting on the adhesive so it won't stick.

"I need another piece," she says.

Harry follows her example and rips off a strip of tape with his teeth. Mary tangles the tape in Jacqueline's hair, unable to stop the bleeding.

"Do you have a sewing kit?" Harry asks.

Mary holds up her gnarled hands. "I haven't sewn in twenty years."

"How about safety pins?"

Mary checks the first-aid kit, doesn't find any safety pins. She has to go into her bedroom.

"Hold the towel," she tells Harry. "Keep the pressure on. I'll be right back."

Mary takes the flashlight and hurries into the hallway, heading for her room. She finds the box of safety pins in her desk drawer. She also sees an inkjet refill kit for her computer printer and takes that as well.

When she gets back into the hallway, the shooting resumes.

Mary drops down to all fours, her old bones creaking with pain. Round after round hit the refrigerator, but none penetrate it. Mary guesses they're using hollow points, or something similar. They must have night-vision scopes as well. And suppressors; the gunshots aren't nearly as loud as they should be. Mary wishes she still had her father's Winchester rifle—she'd be happy to show these men how to shoot.

The onslaught ends. Mary hopes that one of their neighbors heard the shots, called 911, but quickly dismisses the notion. Their neighbors all know that Jacqueline is a police officer. They won't call the cops on a cop making too much noise.

Mary crawls back to the bathroom.

"Help me open these safety pins."

Harry is almost as useless with his left hand as Mary is with both of her hands combined, and they drop pin after pin without getting one open. It's an exercise in frustration, made unbearable because neither one of them is keeping pressure on Jacqueline's wound, and the blood is just pouring out of her.

"Got one," Harry says.

Mary grasps the open safety pin, holding it up like a rare jewel.

"Hold the light."

Harry aims the beam while Mary goes to work on Jacqueline's head. It's slippery, hard to see, and neither the pin nor her hands want to cooperate. But Mary stays focused, fights the pain, and she gets the pin through both sides of her daughter's gash.

Closing the safety pin is even harder than opening it. She pinches it, again and again, but it resists her every effort.

Jacqueline's breath becomes shallow, weak. Mary wants to cry.

"Staples," Harry says. "TV doctors use those all the time."

That might work. Mary tries to stand, but she's too weak. Harry helps her up.

"You can do it, Mom," he says.

Mary nods, takes the flashlight, and heads into the hallway again, back to her bedroom. She has a senior moment, unable to remember where her stapler is, but sees it on the desk. She opens the top, checking to make sure it's loaded.

A shot comes through the window, knocking the computer monitor off the desk. Mary considers dropping down to the floor, worries that she might not be able to get back up, and hurries for the door instead.

In the hallway, the fridge is once again being used for target practice, round after round dinging into it. Mary stays low, makes it back to the bathroom, and sits next to Jacqueline. The safety pin is still in her daughter's head, pinching the ends of the wound together even though it isn't closed.

Mary swings out the stapler base, presses the magazine to Jacqueline's head, and pushes down.

It works. The staple holds.

She repeats the process eight more times, the bleeding slowing to a trickle.

"There's witch hazel in the vanity," she says to Harry.

"Witch hazel. Stat."

He hands it down, and she pours it on Jacqueline's head, hoping that's enough to sterilize it. Then she towels off the excess and uses the medical tape to seal the wound completely.

"Once again, the day is saved by television," Harry says. "Eat your heart out, George Clooney. I kind of look like him, don't I?"

Mary lets out a long breath. "You're practically twins."

Now for the transfusion Harry mentioned.

"I don't have any IV needles," Mary says. "But this came with my ink refill kit."

She reaches into the box and takes out a twenty-cc syringe, still in its package.

"Is that even sharp enough?" Harry asks.

"I'm going to find out."

Mary bites the wrapper off. The needle is long, pointy. She stares down at her own arm, looking for a vein.

"What blood type are you?"

"Does it matter? I'm her mother. I should be compatible."

Harry shakes his head. "That's not how it works. What are you?"

"Type A."

"What's Jack?"

"Type O."

"Type O is the universal donor. Jack could give you blood. But if you give her blood, you'll kill her."

Mary stares down at Jacqueline, watching her gasp for oxygen that her body isn't absorbing. Mary almost starts crying again. Seeing her daughter suffer, and not being able to help, is the worst torture a parent can endure.

"I'm Type O," Harry says. "She can have some of my blood."

Mary touches his face and says, "Thank you, son."

Harry smiles. The smile quickly falls away when she jabs him in the arm with the needle.

"Jesus!" He shirks away. "I think you hit bone!"

Mary pulls the plunger, filling the syringe with blood.

"You don't have any diseases, do you?" Mary asks.

"Nothing that can't be cured with antibiotics," Harry says through his teeth.

Jacqueline has thin wrists, and her veins are easy to find. Mary's hands are curled into painful claws, and the syringe is hard to hold, but she manages to give Jack twenty ccs of Harry's blood.

"How many pints do you think Jacqueline has lost?" she asks Harry.

"Two, maybe more."

"How many syringes is that?"

Harry turns very white.

"How many, Dr. Clooney?" Mary asks again.

Harry mumbles a number.

"Pardon me?"

"Forty or fifty," Harry says, rubbing his eyes.

Mary takes his hand. "Jack and I won't forget this."

Harry yelps when she sticks him again.

THIS IS TAKING FAR TOO LONG. The more time Swanson squats here, waiting for a shot, the more time he has to dwell on why this is the granddaddy of all bad ideas.

So far, he's only killed one man—the one who attacked Jen. That scumbag deserved to die. It isn't Swanson's fault that Munchel went butternuts and wasted all of those cops. Swanson had nothing to do with that. But this—staking out a police officer's house and trying to murder everyone inside—Swanson is a full participant in this colossal mistake. Prior to this, a savvy lawyer could ensure that he wasn't charged with Munchel's murder spree, and a sympathetic jury might even let him off for wasting the pervert. But he'll get the death penalty for what he's doing right now.

The temperature has dropped, the wind picking up. Swanson wipes the sweat off the back of his neck, finds it cold as a mountain stream. He's on his stomach, legs behind him, and his right pants cuff has ridden up, exposing his calf to the cool night air. He wastes a moment reaching back, covering his skin, and his shirt untucks and bares his belly to the breeze.

Noise, to his right. Swanson tries to swing the cumbersome TPG-1 around, gets the barrel hung up on the ground. He moans in his throat, getting onto his knees, ready to run for it.

"Easy, Swanson. It's me."

Pessolano.

"Dammit! You scared the crap out of me! I could have shot you!"

"Hard to shoot while running away."

Swanson thinks about correcting him, about insisting he was ad-justing his position for a better shot. For some reason, even with everything going to hell, Swanson wants the respect of his men. He's still team leader, still the one calling the shots.

But instead of making excuses he takes control, asking, "Why didn't you contact me over the radio?"

"Didn't come here to talk."

Pessolano hands something to him. A scope.

"Night vision," Pessolano says, "to see inside the house."

Swanson takes it. Of course Pessolano has night-vision scopes. If everyone in the house turned into vampires, Swanson would bet that Pessolano also came equipped with stakes and garlic. "Did you give one of these to Munchel?"

"I went to his spot. He wasn't there."

Swanson frowns. "Munchel is gone?"

"Said he wasn't there, didn't I?"

"I heard shots coming from his direction a minute ago."

"That was me. I put a few into that refrigerator. That's a seriously heavy-duty appliance. I may pick one up for myself."

Swanson feels like a kite in a high wind, his string unraveled to the end and ready to break.

"Maybe we should go too," Swanson says.

Pessolano hawks up a big one, spits it in the grass where Swanson had been lying.

"I got the cop," Pessolano says. "Head shot."

Another cop dead. Swanson feels like cringing, but doesn't. Pes-solano is wearing those stupid yellow sunglasses, and Swanson doesn't know if he can see his expression in the dark. So he forces himself to say, "Good work. Then we can get out of here. I bet Munchel got bored and went back to the bar."

"We're staying," Pessolano says.

"Why? The cop is dead."

"There are witnesses."

"How can there be witnesses? They can't see us. We're two hundred yards away."

"Munchel said the cop had an infrared scope."

"Munchel's gone!" Swanson yells. "How do we know he was telling the truth?"

"Vehicle approaching," Pessolano says.

They both drop to their bellies. A dark sedan rolls into the cop's driveway and parks behind the other three cars.

Pessolano begins unfolding his bipod, setting his rifle up.

"What are you doing?" Swanson hisses.

Pessolano pulls back the bolt and loads a round. "What does it look like I'm doing?"

"We don't even know who it is!"

"Who cares?"

Swanson stares, overcome with impotence, as Pessolano shoots out a tire on the sedan. The car shifts into reverse, but Pessolano puts two quick shots into the engine, forcing a stall. The driver parks the car, kills the headlights. Swanson uses the night-vision scope, sees a portly man get out on the passenger side, opposite the rifle fire. The man has a badge hanging around his neck.

Another police officer.

"It's a cop," Swanson hisses. "He might have called for backup."

Pessolano slaps another magazine into his Alpine.

"He didn't. I've been watching."

"But he still can. I'm sure he has a radio in the car."

Pessolano squeezes off another shot, and the sedan's window shatters.

"Not anymore," Pessolano says.

Swanson looks behind him, in the direction of their truck. He can still run for it. He's only killed the one pervert. He's still one of the good guys.

"I don't have a shot on the fatty," Pessolano says. "I'm changing position. Cover me."

Swanson continues to stare off into the darkness, away from the mayhem going on around him.

Pessolano's voice is soft, menacing. "During Desert Storm, we executed deserters."

Swanson turns back, locks eyes with Pessolano. Though Swanson knows diddly-squat about the military, he's pretty sure that they don't kill the people who run away. They get court-martialed, or arrested, or something less serious. He wonders, not for the first time, if Pessolano has been lying about his war record. Or if the man has even served at all.

"Are you threatening me?" Swanson asks.

"We started this war," Pessolano says. "We have to end it."

Jen leaps into Swanson's mind. His sweet, innocent, damaged wife. She isn't aware of Swanson's plan, has no clue he just killed the man who attacked her. It's supposed to be a surprise for her birthday. He's pictured the scene in his mind a thousand times: He shows her the newspaper, she sees that it's finally over, that she can finally go back to the way she used to be, then he admits that he's the one who pulled the trigger, and she embraces him, calls him her hero, and everything goes back to the way it used to be.

Will Jen still think he's a hero if he kills a bunch of cops? Will she understand that the only way to see this thing through is if some innocent people die?

No. Jen will never understand that. She will never forgive him.

"Are you going to cover me or not?" Pessolano asks.

Swanson makes his decision. A decision Jen can never know.

"I'll cover you," he tells Pessolano. "Just show me how to change scopes."

10:00 P.M.
HERB

SQUATTING IS NOT A POSITION that Sergeant Herb Benedict enjoys, and he enjoys being shot at even less. He doesn't even have a gun to return fire, thanks to Internal Affairs. Not that it would do much good. The sniper is at least two hundred yards away, well out of range for a handgun. Herb can't even pinpoint his location. The darkness, and the woods, make him invisible.

Though he realizes how dire this situation is, years of experience prevent Herb from panicking. Though his heart rate is up—more from surprise than fear—he keeps a clear head and is able to focus on survival.

He's hiding behind the front wheel, on the passenger side, opposite of the shooter. Hubcaps and axles offer more protection than aluminum and upholstery, but he doesn't know how much more. He needs to find better cover.

Herb tugs out his cell, can't get a signal. He plays the *hold up the phone and wave it around* game without success, then tucks it back into his jacket pocket and fingers the plastic zipper bag full of high-fiber sugar-free weight loss shake—his allotted mid-afternoon snack and what he should have consumed earlier instead of all those power bars. He briefly considers cracking it open—he's suddenly very thirsty—but he holds off. Being a career cop, Herb has contemplated his own death many times. He's watched his own funeral in his mind's eye, and doesn't want the mourners' chatter to revolve around: "Did you hear he died with a diet drink in his hand?"

Plus, the sugar-free weight loss shake tastes a lot like mud, with grit in it. His wife mixes one for him every morning, adding extra fiber per the doctor's orders.

If she added something better, like grated cheese, then he'd drink the damn things.

Herb squints. There's no light anywhere around. Jack's house is roughly forty feet away, completely dark. Though hefty, and getting up there in years, Herb can move fast when he has to. But if the door happens to be locked, he'll be stuck out in the open. And he knows he isn't a terribly difficult target to hit.

He shifts his attention to Jack's large bay window. If he got up enough speed, perhaps he could crash through it, though the possibility of being cut to hamburger doesn't please Herb, even though he really likes hamburger. Besides, it's likely Jack is just as pinned down inside as he is outside.

Herb is operating under the assumption that his partner is still alive, still okay. Why else would a sniper still be in the area?

He considers his options. The car is trashed, as is the radio. Jack's car is ahead of his in the driveway, along with two others—a Corvette and a sedan—but he doesn't have keys for them. There are no neighbors in sight, though Herb passed a house maybe a quarter mile up the road. Plus, there's always the *run away screaming* possibility.

Herb guesses the sniper has night vision, and also guesses, from the previous angle of fire, that he will change positions to get a better shot. There's also a good possibility that more than one sniper is on the premises. They could have followed Jack home from the Ravenswood crime scene. They may be lining up their shots right now, as he squats here, knees aching, wondering what to do next.

Running away screaming is holding more and more appeal. Unfortunately, there's no place to run. It's thirty yards to the nearest tree,

and it's a sapling that won't provide any cover. He'll be picked off before he gets halfway there.

A shot impacts the driver's door. Then another. *Only three pay-
ments left*, he thinks, ducking down even lower. He touches his pants.
His stitches have ripped, and blood has soaked through. When the
Novocain wears off, that's probably going to hurt.

The tire he's squatting beside explodes. He jerks in surprise, rocking backward onto his ass. Another shot plows into the side of his
Chrysler, where he was only a second ago.

He's in a crossfire. No place to run. Nowhere to hide.

Herb's a practical guy, and he understands his chances of survival
aren't good. But he's not ready to die quite yet. He and his wife were
planning on visiting Italy for the holidays. He's never been, and has
heard the food is spectacular.

Thinking fast, he stands up, filling his lungs, and makes a mad
dash up the driveway.

After four steps the shot comes. His whole body jerks to the left,
bouncing hard into the rear fender of Jack's car. Herb staggers, takes
two zombie-like steps forward, a short step backward, and then drops
to his knees.

He moans, just once, a moan of pain and surprise, and his hands
seek out the sudden dampness soaking his right side.

Sergeant Herb Benedict thinks of his wife, pictures her kind
smile. Then he stops breathing and falls onto his face, his eyes wide
open and staring blankly into the dark night.

10:06 P.M.

PESSOLANO

PESSOLANO WATCHES the fat cop die.

It's bloody.

Counting the woman cop by the window, this brings Pessolano's death toll to three. Not the eighteen confirmed kills he lied to Munchel about back at the bar, but not bad for his first day as a real-life mercenary. Not bad at all.

He points the Gen 3 starlight scope at the large bay window, looking for number four.

THE SMELL OF AMMONIA spikes up my nostrils, and I wake up to the worst headache I've ever had. I open my eyes, squinting against the flashlight in my face, realizing I'm on my bathroom floor.

Mom stares down at me, her face a picture of worry.

"You okay?" I ask her. My throat is really dry, and my tongue sticks to the roof of my mouth.

"I'm fine, dear. How are you feeling?"

"Sleepy. Wake me up in a few hours."

I close my eyes again, get another whiff of ammonia.

"Mom! Quit it!" I reach up to push the smelling salts away.

"Harry says you shouldn't sleep after a head injury."

Harry?

"You need to wake up, sis," he says. "We're still in a lot of trouble."

It comes back to me in a big, ugly rush. Alex. The snipers. Finding out Harry McGlade might be my brother. I raise my hand to my head and gently probe the spot that hurts the most. I touch matted hair and tape, and what might be a staple.

"Did I get hit in the head?" I ask.

"You were shot," Mom says. "You've been out for over half an hour."

"That long? I remember turning off the circuit breaker. But nothing after that."

"You're lucky," Harry says. "I'm going to remember this last half hour for the rest of my life."

I cough. "I'm thirsty."

Harry sticks his hand out the bathroom door, and comes back with a bottled water from the refrigerator. Mom shines the flashlight on him, and I can see that he's been crying. I take the water, oddly touched by his concern. He must really be worried about me.

Mom puts her hand on my face, strokes my cheek.

"One more," she says.

Harry vigorously shakes his head. "No. Please. Thirty-eight is enough."

"Just one."

"I can't take it," he says. "I'm one big hematoma."

"Don't be a baby. You have plenty of blood left. Let's try your leg."

Mom holds up a syringe. Harry tries to back away, but he doesn't have anywhere to go.

"Not that leg!" Harry cries. "The veins are all collapsed!"

My mother doesn't heed him, jabbing him in that leg.

"Holy hell, it hurts so bad!"

Fresh tears flow down his cheeks. So much for him worrying about me.

"Harry's such a brave boy," Mom says. "Aren't you, Harry?"

He moans. "I need aspirin. A shitload of aspirin."

That seems like a good idea. I sit up, intent on visiting the medicine cabinet. Vertigo kicks in, making everything lopsided, and the pain gets so bad I see spots. I sip some water, try to get my vision to track correctly.

"Is Jack okay?" Latham, from the living room.

"She's a bloodthirsty demon!" Harry moans. "Draining me dry!"

"I'm okay," I call to him. "How are you doing?"

"Getting drowsy."

"Maybe he needs a transfusion," I say to Harry.

"Don't worry." Mom yanks out the needle and pats his thigh. "Harry's a universal donor."

"Harry needs some pain reliever," he says, "because he feels like he just doggy-styled a cactus."

Harry reaches into the vanity over the sink and finds the Tylenol bottle. He pries off the cap with his teeth, pours a bunch in his mouth, then washes them down with a beer he liberated from my fridge.

"This might hurt," Mom says to me.

She sticks the needle into my arm, next to dozens of other marks. I look like a junkie after a bender from hell. There isn't much pain, though. My throbbing head is too much competition.

I drink more water, Harry tosses me the Tylenol, and I swallow three. Mom finishes shooting me up, and then takes a few pills herself. We help each other up. I'm still a little dizzy, but I can function. I give Harry a pat on the shoulder and he shouts.

"Sore! Very sore!"

I consider myself a kind person, but showing kindness to Harry McGlade takes Herculean effort.

"Thanks for the blood, Harry."

His eyes soften. "Hey, that's what family is for. We already share the same blood, right?" Then he adds, "And if you develop any kind of itchy rash in the feminine area, I've got some cream left over from my last doctor visit."

I don't want to think about that.

"What next?" Mom asks.

I finish the water, toss the empty bottle in the trash can. Sort of a silly gesture, worrying about being tidy when there's a shot-up refrigerator sticking out of the door.

"I'm going back to the bedroom, to get my gun. Then I'm going to find a way outside."

"They can see in the dark," Mom says. "They have those scopes."

That makes sense. The lights were out and they still managed to hit me.

"I'll move fast. They can't shoot what they can't hit."

Mom hugs me. I hug her back. She's trembling.

"I thought . . ." Her voice cracks. "I thought I lost you."

I want to say something meaningful, something poignant, but I'm getting pretty choked up too. So I settle for kissing her on the forehead and telling her I love her. Then I disengage, heading for the door.

Harry blocks my way.

"Gotta go," I say.

He holds open his arm.

Oh God. He wants a hug.

I brace for it, stiffening as he encircles my waist. But rather than the sleazy feeling I normally get when Harry touches me, this time it isn't too bad.

"Be careful, sis."

I give him a perfunctory pat on the back, and he whimpers in pain.

"Your back too?"

"She stuck me everywhere I had skin."

I pull away, saying, "Keep an eye on Mom."

He doesn't say anything glib or smart-ass. He simply nods.

I slip past him, switch off the flashlight, and duck into the hall.

KORK

I OPEN MY EYES and wonder where I am. I try to lift my hands, and see I'm chained under a sink. My body hurts all over.

I must have been a bad girl. Father punishes us when we're bad. He calls it Penance. I'm afraid of Father, afraid of his punishments. I feel like crying.

Then my mind clears. I'm not ten years old anymore. I'm all grown up. And this isn't our house. It's Jack's.

I'm in the kitchen, all alone.

Anger replaces fear.

My eyes sting. I rub my face on my shoulder, wipe away some blood. My forehead is cut. My head aches. My right hand still stings from when the gun was shot from my grip. None of the damage is serious.

I test the pipe I'm chained to. It's cold, metal, two inches thick. A drain trap, under the sink. I give it a hard yank. Then another. It's solid.

I scoot up closer, rest my head on the bottom of the cabinet. It smells like dish soap and moldy sponges. I can't see very well—so I work by feel, palpating the U pipe, seeking the joint. I think *righty-tighty, lefty-loosey,* and lock both fists around the octagonal coupling. It isn't a pipe wrench, but it's all I have.

I twist. My hands are strong, from thousands of fingertip push-ups while in Heathrow. My arms are bigger than most guys'. But the pipe doesn't want to cooperate. It refuses to turn, preferring instead to dig a nice trench of skin out of my palm.

I twist and twist until it feels like my veins are going to burst out of my temples. The joint won't budge.

I stop, then spend a few minutes trying to use my handcuff chain as a tool, levering and turning and pulling.

My efforts leave me with sore wrists, but no closer to escape.

I close my eyes, let the solution come to me. I broke out of a maximum security prison for the criminally insane. I should be able to get out from under a stupid sink.

Voices, elsewhere in the house. I make out a few words, but they don't interest me. I'm not the only one trying to kill Jack and her family. But I don't believe those jokers outside pose much of a threat to my plans. If they had any skills, everyone would already be dead. They're jackals. I'm a lion. Lions don't fear jackals.

I feel the pipe, higher up, where it meets the sink. The joint here is plastic, bigger, the size of a peanut butter jar. And it has nubs on it, to grip when attaching the drain to the pipe. I form my fingers around them and twist.

Red and yellow spots form in my vision, and my head begins to shake. I strain and strain until my entire world is reduced to five square inches of force and pain.

I release it and forcibly exhale. My hands are trembling.

But it moved a fraction of an inch.

I crack my knuckles, then go at it again, a smile enveloping half my face.

1 0 : 1 5   P . M .

JACK

I'M GRATEFUL I CAN'T REMEMBER being shot, because that might
have made me reconsider my actions. Though I've never used a
night-vision scope, never even saw one in real life, I'm familiar with how
they work, thanks to Tom Clancy movies. The hallway is pitch-black to
me, but to the snipers I am an easy target, glowing bright green.

Thanks to Mr. Clancy, I also have an idea how to mess with their
aim.

I stick out my left hand, reaching for the wall. When my fingers
graze it I run forward four steps. I lift the flashlight up to chest level,
switching it on and pointing it through my bedroom door, out the
window. Then I immediately dodge right.

The light will temporarily blind anyone peering through a night-
enhanced scope, causing a bright flash. If someone has a bead on me,
they might reflexively shoot when the light goes on. Hence the change
of direction.

The shot doesn't come.

I toss the flashlight into the bedroom, toward the far corner, and
jog toward the window in a crouch. I duck down, beneath the pane,
safe. Then I feel around the floor. I find my dropped Kimber.

Hurt isn't strong enough a word for the feeling in my head,
and my stomach isn't happy with the bottle of water I chugged. I rest

for a minute, slowing down my breathing, picturing what I need to do next.

Unlike my Colt, the Kimber is bigger, badder, and more accurate. This is the gun I use in marksman competitions. I need to get outside, locate the bastards, and get within a hundred feet of them. Once they're within range, my handgun is more effective than their long guns. They're using bolt action, single fire, and it takes a few seconds to load each bullet. My .45 holds seven rounds, and it shoots as fast as I can pull the trigger.

If I can get close enough.

Originally, I intended to sneak out the bedroom window. Getting shot in the head made me think about other possible exit points. My house is built in an L shape, but that still means four right angles. There are only three snipers, so they can't completely cover all four sides.

The trick is to find an exit they aren't covering.

The front door won't work. The large bay window in the living room offers too good a view inside. Mom's room has a window, but it's on the same wall as mine, and a shooter can easily watch both. The kitchen patio doors lead into the backyard. Again, they're big and offer a full view, but I can get through them quicker than climbing out a normal window. The garage has a window, but it's behind an endless stack of boxes that we never unpacked after moving in. The bathroom window is frosted, and no one has shot through it yet, but it's decorative and doesn't open. If I break it, that will leave Mom and Harry exposed.

Life would be so much easier if I'd just bought a house with a basement. I could have crawled up a window well, gotten out at ground level, and come at them low, under their noses. I'm sure these guys are amateurs. They'll sweep left and right, but won't know to sweep up and down.

My concentration shatters when the window above me does, glass shards sprinkling my hair and shoulders. Something thumps to the floor in front of me, and I recover from the startle and extend my arm, pointing the .45, pulling the trigger halfway before stopping myself.

It isn't a person in the room with me. The flashlight in the corner is pointing in this direction, and it silhouettes a familiar shape, nestled in the broken glass on my carpeting.

A rifle.

I stand up and stick my gun through the hole in the window, looking left, then right, for the person who threw a rifle into my bedroom. I catch a dark shape turning the corner into the backyard, but it's gone before I can squeeze off a shot.

I don't pause to think. I use the butt of my gun to brush away the jagged glass still jutting out of the pane, lift my knee up, and climb through the window frame. I hear my mother calling my name, but don't want to answer, don't want to give my position away.

I'm dizzy, winded. I touch the brick wall, use it steady myself. Then I half run, half stumble toward the backyard, to the corner the man disappeared around. I pause, my back against the house, both hands on my Kimber. The evening has cooled off, and there's a strong enough breeze that I feel it through the bandage on my head. The lawn is cold and tickles my bare toes. I hold my breath and listen.

Night sounds. Leaves rustling. Crickets. The faint whistle of the wind. Just your average autumn night in the suburbs.

I count to three, then spin around the corner, gun pointing in front of me. I can't see much in the dark. I make out some low shadows on my patio, chairs and a table. My lawn goes back about twenty yards, and beyond it is the tree line. Enough cover for me to disappear into. If I can't find the snipers, I'll go into the woods and come out the other side, to a major highway, and bring back help.

Before I take a step forward the ground spits up dirt and grass a few feet to my right.

"Go back inside!"

A man's voice, coming from deep within the same woods I want to enter.

I backpedal, firing blindly into the trees, wasting two bullets. I press my back against the wall, not too far from my bedroom window.

The next shot eats into the brick less than a foot in front of me, digging out a chunk big enough to stick my hand into.

"I told you to get back in the house!" the man yells. "Go get your rifle, or I'll shoot you where you stand! I ain't asking again!"

I think about running in the opposite direction, toward the front of the house. Less cover there, but maybe I can make it to my neighbor, up the road.

Probably not smart. My shooting has assuredly caught the attention of the other two snipers. They'll be waiting for me.

Not seeing any other choice, I go back to my bedroom and climb through the window, careful not to step on any glass.

"Jacqueline!" Mom.

"I'm okay!" I call back.

My eyes trail down, to the rifle. Why did the sniper give it to me? Some kind of trick or trap?

I reach over slowly, like it's a rattlesnake ready to strike, and wrap my fingers around the barrel. I pull it close, see a piece of paper rolled up in the trigger guard. I unroll the note and read the semi-legible words scrawled on it:

> *There are three of us.*
> *You have three bullets.*
> *Let's play.*

These assholes actually think this is a game.

I holster the Kimber and check the rifle. It's a Browning, bolt action, walnut stock, a twenty-inch barrel, weighing about seven pounds. No scope, no sights. I open the ammo tube and find three .22 LR hollow point rounds. Much smaller than the ammo the snipers are using, but still potent enough to drop a deer. I roll them between my fingers, shake them next to my ear, give them each a sniff. They seem like the real thing. I feed them back into the tube, yank the bolt, and chamber a round.

If they want to play, I'm happy to oblige.

MUNCHEL

MUNCHEL WATCHES the split-tail climb back through the window, and he feels every hair on his arms stand at attention. He isn't tired. He isn't scared.

He's electrified.

This has been the greatest day of his life. And when that cop returns fire, it will take everything up to the next level. He imagines this is the desert, hot wind blowing in his eyes, sand in his teeth, his platoon pinned down by enemy fire, and Private Munchel—no, *Sergeant Munchel*—is called to take them out with extreme prejudice. But the insurgents have a sniper of their own, a famous Taliban bitch who's a dead shot at a thousand yards, and only Sergeant Munchel has the skill to—

"Where in the hell are you?"

The radio startles Munchel, jolting him out of his reverie. He swears, unclips the radio, then presses the talk button.

"What's the problem now, Swanson?"

"The problem is that you disappeared for an hour, and when you come back there's gunfire. Loud gunfire, not our silenced rifles."

"They're suppressors, not silencers." Pessolano, cutting in.

Swanson sighs like a drama queen. *"I don't give a shit what they're called. Tell me what's going on."*

"The woman cop," Munchel says. "She had a gun in the house, shot at me through the window."

"I already killed her," Pessolano says.

"You must have missed, because she was shooting at me just a minute ago."

"You sure it was her?"

"'Course it was her. Looked just like her."

"Could of been her twin."

"Her what?"

"Her twin sister. Like that Van Damme movie."

"It wasn't her goddamn twin, Pessolano. You just goddamn missed."

"Enough!" Swanson cuts in. *"Her gun is too loud. Someone is going to hear it and call the cops."*

Munchel grins. "Well, it's about to get even louder, boyo, because I gave her a rifle."

He pictures Swanson's face turning bright red with anger. It amuses him greatly. Ever since they first got together, Swanson has been playing leader. But he sucks as a leader. He's too scared of everything, and has zero creativity.

And what is this shit Pessolano is talking about twins? That guy has been bragging and boasting about his war record nonstop, but he can't even confirm a kill.

Munchel knows that he's the alpha male of the group. He proved it earlier, in Ravenswood. And he's about to prove it again.

"What. Did. You. Say?" Swanson probably thinks pausing between each word makes him sound tough.

"I gave her Pessolano's Browning, and three bullets. Make this a little more interesting."

"I better get that gun back," Pessolano says. *"Or you owe me seven hundred bucks."*

"You'll get it back." Munchel laughs. "Might have to wash the blood off it first."

Another sigh from Swanson. *"We need to finish this shit up, and get out of here before more cops come."*

"How?" Pessolano asks. *"Everyone is hiding. We can't get any shots."*

"Then we get closer."

Munchel nods. That's the first thing Swanson has said all night that he agrees with.

He clips the radio to his belt, picks up the rifle, and creeps closer to the house.

THE FIRST THING I need to do is minimize my disadvantages. And there are many.

They're three people. I'm just one.

They have cover. I have people to protect.

They have unlimited bullets. I have three.

They have scopes, both normal and night vision. I have a head injury.

But I do have one advantage. Never underestimate a woman fighting for her life.

I stick my head into the hall and shout.

"Latham! We're going to get you in the bathroom with Mom and Harry. It's the safest place in the house."

"Don't risk it, Jack. Too many windows."

"I've got an idea about that. Be ready to move when I get there."

I crawl over to the flashlight in the corner of my room, then get into a crouch. The Tylenol has kicked in, taking my headache from excruciating down to merely agonizing.

Don't think. Just act.

I point the flashlight out the window and run out the door, through the hall, into the laundry room. I tug open the fuse box door, hit the main breaker, and the house lights come back on. I assume the snipers still have their night-vision scopes on. Now they'll be all lit up.

I hurry back into the hall, flipping off lights as I go.

"Hold this," I tell Harry, passing up the bathroom. He takes the rifle.

"Santa come early this year?"

"Scissors," I say.

Mom hands me the scissors.

I squeeze past the fridge, run into the living room, catch a quick glimpse at Latham still by the sofa, but head straight for the front door instead. I turn on the outside lights—front porch, garage light, driveway lights—and kill the lights inside the room. I also kill the flashlight. That leaves only one light on in the house. The kitchen.

I creep over to it, reach for the switch while keeping my eyes on Alex. She's still on the floor, handcuffed to the pipe under the sink. She regards me.

"I'm a better shot than you," she says. "Let me go and I'll take care of those snipers."

I flip the kitchen light off. Then I jog over to Latham, kneeling next to him, seeking out his face in the dark.

"How you doing?" I ask.

"Some guys say the excitement goes out of a relationship after the first year. I'm not one of those guys."

I give him a quick peck, missing his mouth and hitting his cheek.

"This is going to hurt when the circulation comes back."

I go to work on his duct tape, cutting, peeling, ripping, until his hands come free.

He groans, and my heart breaks. I do his legs next.

"Think you can move?"

"I'll do my best."

I help Latham up, try to get his wounded arm over my shoulder. He cries out, so I switch sides.

"Lean on me," I tell him.

We make it three steps, then he collapses.

"Legs," he says. "Having some problems."

I check the front window, look out onto the lawn, and have a clear view. The combination of darkness inside and lights outside will make it hard for the snipers to see us using either regular or night-vision scopes.

"Keep going," I grunt, trying to pull him to his feet.

Latham manages one step before falling.

"I'm sorry," he says.

He's breathing as heavy as I am.

"Legs not working?" I'm referring to the residual paralysis from his bout with botulism.

"Not working."

This time I find his mouth, press my lips against it.

"It's okay," I say. "I have legs for the two of us."

I prod Latham to his feet once more, then have him stand behind me and put his arms over my shoulders.

"Piggyback?" he says into my ear.

"Just hold on tight."

His good arm locks around my chest. I lean forward, taking his weight, and manage four staggering steps.

"I kind of like this position," Latham says.

I stop, lowering him down, catching my breath.

"Don't like it too much," I say between puffs. "I can only concentrate on one thing at a time."

The *BOOM* of a gunshot, and the room gets a hair darker. I glance out the window.

The snipers are shooting the outside lights.

I focus ahead, down the hallway. Maybe fifteen feet to the bathroom. I pick Latham up and go five more steps before losing my footing. We fall, Latham on top of me. My head feels like it has exploded, and I can't take a breath.

Another shot. Another outside light winks out.

There are only four lights left. Then Latham and I will be completely exposed.

PESSOLANO

THE COP IS SMART, doing that with the lights. Pessolano's night-vision scope is too bright. Useless. He switches back to the Leupold scope, and the outside lights still make it impossible to see inside the house.

No big deal. He just needs to shoot out the lights, then switch back to night vision.

The first two are easy. Especially since he moved eighty yards closer. Even a child could have made those shots.

Pessolano doesn't have any tree cover this time. He's flat on his belly, legs out behind him, the TPG-1's bipod legs resting on the wild grass across the street from the house. His pose is identical to the sniper that came in those packages of plastic green army men he used to play with as a child. Pessolano wishes he had a bazooka—he can picture the toy figure on his knee, a rocket launcher perched on his shoulder, ready to rain hell upon the enemy. That guy was his favorite.

He nudges left, seeking the lights on the garage, and frowns.

The dead cop—the fat one he shot on the driveway.

He's gone.

What the hell is going on? First he shot the woman cop in the head, and she got back up. Now this.

Pessolano shakes his head, trying to clear it. He peers through the scope again.

Definitely gone. Just a small puddle of blood where he's fallen.

No. It's not blood. The liquid on the driveway isn't red.

It's brown.

Chocolate milk, Pessolano thinks.

The fat cop tricked him.

Pessolano begins to sweep the grounds, looking for where he ran.

HERB

THE KEY TO THE RUSE was night vision.

Herb knew that night-vision scopes produced an all-green image. That meant blood would be green too. Surviving depended on two things: the sniper missing, and Herb's acting ability.

Since he had no place to run or hide, he simply got up and jogged toward the house, hoping when the shot came, it would miss. Then it was simply a question of falling over, breaking open the bag of chocolate high-fiber shake in his pocket, bugging out his eyes, and holding his breath until they left him alone.

And it works. It works perfectly.

Until the outside lights come on.

When that happens, Herb knows they'll switch from night vision back to their regular scopes. They'll be able to tell the difference between brown and red, and they'll shoot him where he lies.

Herb doesn't wait around for that to happen. He gets up on all fours and beelines for Jack's car, hoping to get inside and use the radio to call for backup.

The doors are locked. Herb bends down, peers under the car. He could fit his head under there, but nothing else. That might work for an ostrich, but not for him. Herb needs a different hiding place.

He scans the house, eyeing the shrubs. Too small. There are a few trees on Jack's lawn, but they're too thin; it would be like an orange hiding behind a pencil.

A shot. Herb bunches up his shoulders, lowers his head, trying to make himself small. But they aren't shooting at him. A light above the front porch blows out. Followed by another.

Good. If they shoot out all the lights, then they might not notice . . .

The third shot drills through the windshield of the Nova, missing Herb by less than a foot. Herb flinches, recovers, then rears back and smacks his palm into the window, trying to break it. The safety glass fractures into several thousand cracks, but it's still held in place by its protective coating. Herb hits it again. And again. The sheet finally gives way with a loud *pop*, tiny squares of glass falling onto the driver's seat.

Herb reaches a hand inside, fumbles for the lock.

Another shot punches through the back window, blowing apart Jack's radio. Bits of plastic shrapnel embed themselves in Herb's cheek. He ignores the pain, opening the door, reaching across the seats, tugging open the glove box, finding the remote control for the garage door.

Another shot. Latham's car window shatters. The different angle means it's a different sniper. He's caught in another crossfire.

Herb raises the remote above dashboard level and presses the button.

Nothing happens.

He presses again.

Nothing.

Two shots in quick succession, taking out two more of the Nova's windows. Herb is out of ideas. He puts his hands over his head and waits for the inevitable.

JACK

MY TEMPLE THROBS in time with my heartbeat, but I manage to get both feet under me one more time, supporting Latham on my back.

More shots are fired, but the outside lights stay on. I stagger the remaining few steps to the bathroom, and Mom meets me in the hallway, helping to drag Latham inside. We lean him against the sink. I flip on the overhead light and gently peel back his shirt, getting my first look at his injury. An ugly black hole, just above his armpit. No exit wound. The bleeding is minimal.

"I think you're going to make it," I tell him, my mouth near his.

"Good. I was worried you carried me all the way here for nothing."

I put my hands on his face, stare into his eyes. "I love you, Latham."

"I love you, Jack."

"I love you more."

"No, I love you more."

We briefly touch lips.

"So he doesn't need any of my blood, right?"

I pull away from Latham, frowning. "You're safe for the moment, Harry."

"Actually, I'm not." Harry motions for me to come closer.

"What?"

"It's important, Jackie. Come here."

I get within whisper range.

"I have to go," he says.

"It was great seeing you. Come back soon."

Harry makes a face. "The beer I had, Jackie. It wants to be set free."

I blink. "You have to go to the bathroom?"

"Yeah. So can you, like, distract Mom while I piss in the sink?"

"You are *not* urinating in my sink."

"Fine. Just open up the toilet and I'll aim for it."

I glance over my shoulder. The toilet is five feet away.

"Absolutely not."

"I can hit it. I'll arc the stream."

"I don't have time for this, Harry."

"I'm going to wet my pants."

"Not my problem."

"Fine. I want my blood back."

I consider my sink, realize I'd never use it again if Harry violates it, but don't see any other alternative. I cross my arms.

"Okay, Harry. Make it quick."

"Stand between me and Mom. I don't want to sully her high opinion of me."

I hit the lights and play blocker. More shots, outside. But no familiar tinkling of window glass, or slugs impacting the fridge.

"I need help with my fly," Harry says.

"No way in hell."

"Please."

"No."

"Come on. I haven't had a single obscene thought about you since I found out we're related."

I turn, pat his cheek. "Bad news, bro. You're going to have to wet your pants."

Mom is taping and gauzing Latham's wound, her hands so gnarled that he has to help. More shooting. No sounds from inside the house. What are they firing at? Each other?

"I have to check something out," I say. I pick up the rifle and sneak into the hallway.

The remaining outside lights still glow brightly. I move slowly, hunching over, peering out the living room window, trying to find the snipers' locations. Another shot. They've moved closer, to within a hundred yards. I check to see what they're aiming at, see the wreck that is my car. And in the car . . .

Herb!

I run to the front door, second-guess myself, and backtrack to the garage. I swing it open, hitting the garage door opener button on the wall, planting both of my feet, and snugging the rifle up against my shoulder.

"Herb!" I scream.

I fire my first round across the street, aiming where I'd seen the muzzle flash. I immediately load the second round and shoot again.

Herb doesn't waste time. He slides face-first into my garage before the door even gets halfway up. I hit the button again, and Herb rolls to the left, bumping up against the wall of cardboard boxes. Two bullets ping off the garage floor, chewing hunks out of the concrete. I rush over to Herb, hooking my elbow around his, straining to get him back to his feet.

He bellows. Herb's hands flutter around his knee, as if indecisive about whether or not to touch it. My partner had hit the ground hard—especially hard considering his age and weight. His pants are bloody, but I don't know if his earlier gunshot wound has opened up or if this is a new injury.

"Did you get shot again?"

He shakes his head, his jowls flapping. "Knee!"

"Broken?"

He replies through his teeth—a keening cry that makes my stomach vibrate.

A round punches through my garage door, making a hole the size of my fist.

Then another. And another.

I have to get Herb out of here.

"We need to get you in the house."

"Leave me here."

Bullets continue to ventilate my garage door, and the light coming in from the holes dims. They're shooting the outside lights again. Once those are gone, they'll switch back to night vision.

Then we're screwed.

"On three," I say. I set down the rifle and take hold of his collar. "One . . . two . . . three!"

Herb moans deep in his throat, and I pull while he uses his three functional limbs to drag his broken one. We reach the doorway into my house, then I collapse next to him, both of us breathing like asthmatics at a hay festival.

"There's a saw." Herb points to the workbench at the back of the garage. "Cut my leg off. That will hurt less."

My chest heaves. "At least you still have your sense of humor."

"No joke. I'll pay you twenty thousand bucks to saw off my leg."

I blink away the motes, wipe some sweat from my forehead. "Let's go again."

"Please, no."

"On three."

"Why do you hate me so much?"

"One . . . two . . . three!"

Another strangled cry from Herb, but we make it into the house, across the living room, and to the front of the hallway before fatigue drops me to my knees.

"Here is good," Herb wheezes. He's directly in front of the bay windows. The only possible way he could be an easier target is if he had antlers.

"We . . . we have to get you to . . . to the bathroom."

"I . . . I like it here."

Another shot. The last of my outside lights blows out.

"On three."

"Jack . . . if I . . . if I don't make it . . ."

"No time for this now, Herb. One . . ."

"I just want to say . . ."

"Two . . ."

"That I'm cutting you out of my will . . ."

"Three!"

Herb cries out again, but he gives it his all, and so do I, and even though my knees are rug burned and even though he can barely move and even though bullets tear up the carpeting around us, we make it all the way to the refrigerator, and to the bathroom.

Safe. For the moment.

"Did you?" I gasp at Harry, pointing at the sink.

He shakes his head.

"Where?" I ask.

Harry reaches into the fridge and removes a pickle jar.

"Remember to throw this away later," he says.

I stick my face under the faucet and take gulps of water so big they hurt going down. Mom fusses over Herb, winding an Ace bandage around his knee. I eventually catch my breath, and give Herb half a dozen Dixie cups' worth of water.

"Now what?" Mom says.

The five of us are crammed into the bathroom pretty tight. We couldn't have fit someone else in here if we buttered them. I stand near the sink, next to Harry. Latham sits on the toilet. Mom leans over Herb, who occupies most of the floor. The temperature in here is ten degrees warmer than the rest of the house.

"Anyone up for charades?" Harry asks. He points at Herb. "Lemme guess . . . Moby-Dick!"

Herb and Harry don't get along, from way back.

"How's the pain?" I ask my partner.

"Hurts," Herb says.

"One to ten?"

"Ten. Blew the knee out. And the medication has worn off from my gunshot wound." His face is pouring sweat. "I'm hoping I pass out."

Mom uses scissors to gently cut up a side of Herb's pants leg. His stitches have ripped open, and his knee is swelled up to the size of a honeydew.

"Does anyone know you're here?" I ask.

He shakes his head, wincing from the movement. "No. The Grouch, he wanted to talk to you. Threatened to go to your old apartment. I came here to find you."

"So you didn't call for backup?" Harry asks. "Smooth move, Ironside."

"Nice fridge," Herb says. "Maybe you'd like me to cram your head in the crisper."

"Quiet," I tell them.

I rub my eyes, trying to force a brilliant thought.

Amazingly, one comes.

"I've got one rifle round left. In the garage, there's a pull-down ladder to the attic. I can get up there, get on the roof, and take out one of the snipers from a vantage point."

"You can't get from the attic to the roof," Herb says. "That's not how houses are built."

"You sure?" Harry asks.

"You want to drag your refrigerator up there and double-check?"

"Why don't you go check, Jumbo? I've got a buddy with a crane."

"Enough," I say. "How else can I get up to the roof?"

"Do you have a ladder?" Latham asks.

"No good," Herb says. "They'll see the ladder, know she's up there."

"One of us could take the ladder away," Latham says.

"Who?"

Herb has a point. No one in the room is in any shape to help out.

"Why don't we just set the house on fire?" McGlade asks. "Cops will come, and bring reinforcements."

"Good idea," Herb says. "We'll start with that shag rug on your chest."

"Sis, the mean fat man is picking on me."

Herb raises an eyebrow. "Did he just call you *sis*?"

"Long story. And we're not setting the house on fire."

Harry appears crestfallen.

"Can't we wait them out?" Latham suggests. "Maybe they'll leave when the sun comes up."

I shake my head. "They'll rush the house before then. Or set fire to it themselves, and pick us off when we run outside."

"How about a decoy?" Harry says. "We'll kick Alex outside, and while they're shooting her you can run for help."

"Alex?" Herb asks. "I thought she was dead."

"Another long story," I tell him. "And we're not kicking anyone outside. The snipers are surrounding the house. There's nowhere to run."

Herb tries his cell phone. Harry found half a bottle of Grey Goose vodka in my freezer and he takes a swig. Latham has his arm around Mom. I wonder if I can get on the roof by climbing onto the veranda in back. Maybe I can stand on the patio table and pull myself up. But even if I manage, I'll probably be seen doing it.

"I was saving this, because I wanted to keep a clear head," Mom says. "But I think we could all use a couple."

She holds up a bottle of OxyContin—her prescription arthritis pain medication. It has an extra-large cap, and she spins it off like a pro.

"Who needs a hit?" she asks.

Herb takes four. Latham takes two. Mom takes two. I decline—opiates aren't wise with a head injury. Harry takes two, and washes them down with a swig of Grey Goose.

"You shouldn't mix codeine and alcohol," Mom chides. "It intensifies the effect."

"I sure as hell hope so."

Harry passes Mom the bottle. She takes a nip, as do Latham and Herb. I get it last, and since I'm not mixing it with drugs, I take the biggest swallow. It burns going down, and sits in my empty stomach like a lump of charcoal.

We're all quiet for a moment. It isn't hard to read everyone's thoughts, because we each have the same one: *We're all going to die.*

"Okay," I say. "I bet I can pick one of them off from the living room."

"That will still leave two," Herb says.

"But it will be tougher for two to watch the whole house. If I get one, then I'll have a better chance at getting away, getting help."

No one argues. I pull out my Kimber, offer it to Harry.

"If they get in," I say.

"You know I suck lefty."

"Latham's never shot a gun, Mom can't fit her fingers in the trigger guard, and Herb just took enough codeine to kill Keith Richards."

Harry takes the gun.

"You've got five rounds left. Use them wisely."

Harry nods, then says, "When we get out of this. I want to go to one of those department store portrait studios. Get a family photo. I've never been in a family photo."

I consider making some sort of comment about waiting for the DNA test first, but instead I pat his shoulder.

"Hematoma!" he yelps.

"I'll be back in a minute," I say. "Everyone stay put."

Then I slip out into the hallway.

KORK

I GIVE THE DRAIN JOINT one last turn and it comes loose. My fingers are torn and bloody, and my hands feel like lead weights. I raise them up, pull the handcuff chain between the sink and the pipe, and then I'm free.

I don't waste time celebrating the victory. Jack had turned off the lights in the kitchen, so it's tough to see, but I locate the utensil drawer from memory. I feel forks and spoons and assorted cooking supplies until I find what I'm after—a lever action corkscrew. The curly end fits nicely into the keyhole of my cuffs, and I have them off within a few seconds.

Even if the house wasn't surrounded by snipers, running wouldn't be an option. Before I leave here, Jack Daniels, and everyone in this house, must die.

I bump against the counter and spread my hands over the top, seeking out the knife rack.

SWANSON

SWANSON IS TEMPTED to move farther away. Those two shots the woman cop fired from the garage came very near him, kicking up dirt just a few feet in front of his face. But he's the one who gave the order to get in closer, so he's determined to stick it out.

He and Pessolano shoot the last of the outside lights, then change back to night scopes. The constant juggling of scopes bugs Swanson. A lot of things about this situation bug Swanson. But this will all be over soon. When the cop fires her last rifle round, he's going to order his men to break into the house and finish the job point-blank. Enough of this long-distance bullshit.

In concept, The Urban Hunting Club was brilliant. Dazzle the police and the media with three sex offenders who all die at the same time. Do it from a distance, so there's less likelihood of witnesses, and no personal contact with the targets. Kill three more offenders a few days later, to make it seem like the targets are random. Write a note to the newspapers, explaining the goal of ridding Chicago of perverts. Then disappear into legend.

Swanson even thought about the far future, forty years from now, making a deathbed confession and stunning the world. Explaining he did it all for his precious Jen. Making a grand speech about how it is every private citizen's duty to protect the people he loves. Along with the right to bear arms, there is a responsibility to use those arms for truth, justice, and the American way.

It would have been a damn good speech.

But Munchel had to fuck everything up. Now TUHC are cop killers. Instead of being admired by millions, they'll be hunted forever, chased to the ends of the earth. They'll be called psychos instead of vigilantes. In the TV movie, Swanson will be played by Harvey Keitel or Christopher Walken, instead of Ben Affleck or Bruce Willis.

It's all gone to hell. Best to get it over with as quickly as possible.

Swanson sights down the night-vision scope, looking into the dark house through the front bay window. He's moved ten feet to the right, away from the spot where the cop came close to hitting him. The stretch of grass he's on is slightly elevated. Not quite a knoll, but raised enough so he can see into the living room and look down from a slight angle.

He sees green. A world of blurry, indistinct, phosphorescent green.

Though he doesn't admit it to the guys, the starlight scope isn't the easiest thing to use. With Swanson's whole field of vision monochromatic, the only way to identify people is by shape and movement. Earlier in the night, Swanson put three rounds into a chair, thinking it was a crouching body. And he also discovered that the house has a cat in it, which kept darting back and forth, messing up his concentration and his aim.

The ever-increasing wind has also been a factor, throwing off several shots that were otherwise on the money. That fat cop should be dead three times over. Swanson knew Pessolano felt the same frustration, because the Desert Storm vet had been only fifteen yards away, and Swanson heard him swear after every miss.

Swanson also knows he's jerking the trigger. Every shot, the butt of the TPG-1 slams into his shoulder. The area has been tender for several weeks, from all of the practice, and the bruise hasn't ever healed. After the dozens of rounds fired tonight, it hurts like crazy. Swanson flinches every time he fires, and this tiny movement is throwing off his aim.

Add in the pressure of getting done quickly, and the fact that Swanson isn't a very good marksman to begin with, and it's no wonder he hasn't been able to hit anything.

But that is all about to change. The next person who appears in Swanson's scope is going to die. He can feel it.

Swanson blinks, takes a deep breath, and adjusts his grip on the TPG-1. He aims the starlight scope on the hallway, ready to shoot the first thing that moves.

Something blurs past his line of fire. Swanson adjusts, finding the figure again, watching it disappear into the garage. He holds there . . . holds . . . holds . . . holds . . .

The figure appears again.

Swanson fires.

He misses—the target is moving too fast. It's the woman cop, and she has the rifle. She ducks behind the couch.

Swanson pulls back the bolt, ejecting the empty cartridge, loading another one. He re-aims at the sofa and puts a bullet through the middle, where she was just a second ago.

I got her, he thinks. *I must have.*

Movement, in the lower right quadrant of his scope. He adjusts, sees someone squatting by the window.

The woman cop.

Swanson pulls the trigger. Nothing happens. He didn't load the next bullet yet.

Stupid bolt action rifle. Why didn't Pessolano buy semiauto—

Swanson feels a sharp tug in his chest. He hears the shot at the same time.

Did she just—?

The pain runs Swanson over like a truck. Someone has him in a giant nutcracker and is squeezing his ribs, making it impossible to draw a breath. He touches his breastbone, looks at his fingers.

Blood. A lot of blood.

This isn't happening. This can't be happening.

Swanson crawls away from his gun. His breath comes back, and the oxygen burns and stabs at his insides. A weak cry escapes his throat.

He fumbles in the darkness for his belt, finds his radio, brings it to his face.

". . . shot . . ." he manages to whisper.

No one answers.

". . . I . . . got . . . shot . . ."

No reply. Why won't they answer?

Swanson looks into the woods. Where's the truck? Where did they park it? He has to get to a hospital. Has to get there so they can take this bullet out of his chest.

"I didn't catch that, Swanson. Can you repeat?"

He stares at the radio. Presses the talk button.

". . . shot . . . been shot . . . need . . . help . . ."

The radio falls from his hand. Swanson coughs, feels something wet come up. Everything is getting all topsy-turvy. He isn't going to make it to the truck. He isn't going to make it another foot. He wants to lie down, go to sleep. Swanson falls onto his face, and the universe explodes into a Technicolor panorama of agony.

Swanson moans, manages to roll off of his tortured chest and onto his back. He stares up into the night sky. Each time he inhales he wants to die. He wants, *needs*, to talk to Jen, to tell her he didn't mean for it to work out this way. This isn't the ending he planned on.

"Swanson?"

It's not the radio. Swanson's eyes drift to the right, land on Munchel, standing next to him.

"Jee-zus, man! You got yourself shot." Munchel stares back at the house. "I knew she was good. Glad I only gave her three bullets."

"Doc . . . tor . . ." Swanson wheezes.

"Hell yeah, you need a doctor. Shit, I can see blood bubbles coming out the hole in your chest. You are seriously fucked up."

Swanson wonders why Munchel is just standing there. He should be dragging him to the truck, or shutting off the cell phone jammer and calling an ambulance.

"Hos . . . pit . . . tal . . ."

Munchel leans over. His face looks huge, and his expression is grim. "See, here's the problem with hospitals, Greg. They have to report gunshot wounds. How quick do you think they'd connect a rifle slug in the chest with what happened tonight in Chicago?"

". . . won't . . ."

"Sure they will."

Swanson forces it out. ". . . won't . . . tell . . ."

"Oh, I get it. We drop you off, and you don't mention us at all. Even when you're on trial for all of those dead cops that I killed. You don't say anything at all about me or Pessolano. Is that right?"

Swanson coughs. His mouth feels hot and wet. He can't believe Munchel wants to talk this much while he's dying. The talk can come later. Right now he needs help.

"Do you promise you won't rat out your buddies, Swanson? Can I get your word on that?"

Swanson thinks he nods. Or maybe he just imagines he nods. Either way, he feels himself being dragged. To the truck. To doctors. To safety.

He closes his eyes, hopes that Jen is there in the hospital when he wakes up.

Pain forces Swanson's eyes back open. He feels like there's an airplane parked on his chest.

It's Munchel. He's standing on Swanson's rib cage.

"Can't use a bullet," he says. "Pessolano might hear."

Swanson can't draw a breath to answer. He tries to push away Munchel's legs, but he has no strength left.

Death doesn't come quick or easy. It's takes close to five minutes. Swanson feels every second.

I'M PRETTY SURE I hit the sniper, or at least came close. I set the
rifle down, find the wall switch, and flick on the living room lights.
They'll have to change scopes again, giving me time to—

She comes at me in a blur. My mind registers the glint of a knife
blade, and I instinctively throw both hands up over my head, forming
an X with my wrists to block its downward path. Then I spin, sweep-
ing my right leg out, tripping Alex.

Alex lands hard but recovers fast, rolling to the side, getting her
feet under her. The knife is from the rack on my kitchen counter. A
cheap set, flimsy blades, but they're serrated and insanely sharp. She's
chosen a paring knife. Alex switches her grip to underhanded, blade
up. She's fought with knives before.

I cast my eyes around for a weapon, settle on a sofa cushion.
It won't do much, damage-wise, but it's thicker than the knife
blade.

Alex's eyes are cool, dispassionate. She feints once. Again. Then
lunges.

I block the knife with the cushion, feeling it puncture the fabric,
twisting hard to try and catch the blade. She pushes harder, swiping at
my face with her free hand, catching me on the cheek.

I stumble back, managing to keep hold of the cushion. She comes at me again, but this time I kick at her shin, driving my heel into the spot below her knee.

Alex roars. Then a gunshot thunders over our heads, making a divot in the ceiling.

Harry, in the hallway, pointing my Kimber at us.

"Hey! Mrs. Hyde! Hold still so I can hit you!"

Alex must not feel threatened by Harry's left-handed shooting, because she ignores him and comes at me again. Personally, I feel extremely threatened. Chances are high Harry will shoot me instead of Alex. I've witnessed firsthand how bad he is lefty. Adding codeine and vodka to the mix isn't going to improve his aim.

Alex strikes, hard enough for the knife tip to penetrate both sides of the cushion. She muscles forward. I double back, smacking into the wall behind me.

Another *BOOM*. A hanging picture of my mother shatters, Harry's shot hitting her in the head.

Alex presses her whole body against the cushion. I feel the tip of the blade poke against my stomach. I shove back, but she's bigger, stronger. I suck in my gut, trying to avoid being skewered. It isn't working. The knife jabs me again, and I feel it break the skin.

"I'm going to gut you," Alex says, spittle flecking off her lips. "And then feed you your intestines."

Rather than push against her, I move sideways, letting her keep the cushion. The knife pierces the wall. I hit Alex in the ear with the heel of my hand, putting my weight into it.

She staggers. I pivot my hips and kick her, hard. Alex's hands are still wrestling with the cushion, so she can't block my blow. The top of my foot connects with her unprotected kidney, and I feel the impact in my fillings.

Alex drops the knife and the cushion, her arms pinwheeling to keep her balance. I advance, fists clenched, sensing my chance to put her down for good. I rear back and unleash a vicious right hook.

Alex recovers faster than I expect, and she sidesteps my punch. Then she grabs my extended arm and uses my momentum to hurl me across the room.

I kiss the carpet, look up, and see Harry aiming the gun right at my face.

"Wrong target!" I scream at him.

I roll away a millisecond before he pulls the trigger.

"Sorry, Jackie!" he yells.

I get to my knees, vision squiggly, head pounding.

"Mom! Take the gun away from Harry!"

Then Alex is on me again. I endure a kick to the shoulder that makes my whole arm go numb, then I duck another that would have broken my neck. Adrenaline and reflex have been controlling my actions, both of them fueled by fear. To survive, I need to think rather than just react. Alex is bigger, faster, stronger, and a better fighter. I can't win going toe-to-toe with her. I need a weapon.

Asking Harry to throw me the gun isn't a wise idea. He'll miss. Plus, he still needs it for defense.

The kitchen has knives, pans, a rolling pin, but nothing that will give me a distinct advantage.

But the garage—I have power tools in the garage.

I crawl around Alex, use the wall to stand up, and then sprint for the doorway.

I make it to the door, see some potential weapons on the workbench, and then fly past it when Alex prods me from behind. I bump into some stacked boxes, bounce off, and turn to face her.

She's on the balls of her feet, dancing back and forth, hands up in a sparring position. Her head rolls on her neck, like Muhammad Ali loosening up before a title bout.

"Afraid?" she says. "You should be."

I am afraid. I'm more afraid than I've ever been in my life. But that doesn't mean I'm ready to quit.

I adopt a fighting stance, my feet apart, my fists in front of me.

Alex moves in. She works the jab, hitting my upraised arms, pain stacking upon pain stacking upon pain. When I try to circle toward the workbench, or the shovel sitting in the corner of the garage, Alex cuts me off. When I return blows, she easily sidesteps them. We both know I'm outclassed, but I'm going to go down swinging.

"I'm going to take you apart, Jack. Piece by piece. It all comes down to conditioning."

"You should be more concerned with moisturizing," I say.

Alex snarls, then unloads on me. I bunch my shoulders, take the hits, wait for her to tire.

She doesn't tire. And my arms are getting so sore that soon I won't be able to punch back.

I back away, feel the boxes behind me, reach around and throw one at her.

She dodges it.

I tear into the box beneath it, hoping for a weapon, coming out with a crooked branch to an artificial Christmas tree. Why couldn't I be Jewish? Menorahs are solid, heavy, perfect to bash someone's head in.

Alex slaps the branch from my hand, throws a right at my cheek. I duck it, then swing a big haymaker that catches her, full force, on the chin.

She wobbles backward, dropping her hands. I follow up with a kick, but I'm disoriented and only strike air. I try again, connecting with her side, but there's no power behind it, and Alex shrugs the blow off.

I cast my eyes on the workbench. Lunge for it.

Alex's leg shoots out like a piston, catching me in the cheek. I sprawl backward, onto my ass, not able to tell up from down.

Then she's on me.

Her first punch lays me out, and while I'm on my back she stomps on my stomach, so hard I can feel organs shift. I roll to the side, blind instinct guiding my actions, and receive a few more kicks to the body. When I reach the automatic garage door I feel like I've spent an hour in a cement mixer.

I cover my face, Alex kicks me in the body. I protect my body, she goes after my head. I curl up fetal, unable to defend myself, unable to fight back.

I'm being beaten to death. And there's nothing I can do to stop it.

Pessolano stares down at Swanson's lifeless body. For some reason he thinks of his mother, lying in her casket. He bends down and crosses Swanson's hands over his chest, and then gently closes Swanson's eyes. Pessolano wishes he had a lily, or a Bible, or a rosary, to place in Swanson's hand. He fishes around in his vest and comes out with a granola bar. He presses that into Swanson's fist.

"We'll avenge him," Munchel says. "We'll kill every last one of those assholes."

Pessolano stands. He hopes Munchel doesn't see the tears on his cheeks. He turns away and discreetly wipes them off.

"We can't leave him here," Pessolano says into the woods. "Soldiers don't leave their dead behind."

"We won't. But we're in a combat situation right now. We'll give him a hero's funeral. I promise. But after the war is over. We have to finish this first."

Pessolano nods.

"I think we should rush the house," Munchel says. "Break in, flush them out of hiding, and blow their goddamn heads off. You've got those Desert Eagles in the truck, right?"

"Yeah."

Pessolano has two Magnum Research Mark XIX Desert Eagle .50 AE handguns. They're massive weapons, weighing over four pounds each, capable of stopping a charging bull with one shot.

"Let's do it, man. For Swanson."

Munchel claps his hand on Pessolano's shoulder.

"For Swanson," he agrees. He wipes away another tear and clears his throat.

"Look," Munchel says. "I know this is a tragedy, but Swanson would want us to soldier on. Right?"

Pessolano nods. He's choking up a little bit.

"One of us should stay here, keep an eye on the house, and the other should go get the truck, bring it back."

"Shouldn't we, you know, say a few words first?" Pessolano gestures at the body.

"Yeah, sure. I suck at this kind of shit."

"Please." Pessolano sniffles. "For Swanson."

"Shit. Okay. Yeah, sure. Uh, oh Lord, our friend Greg Swanson was a good man who wanted to rid the world of perverts. He was a hero, and he'll be missed. But me and Paul are going to fuck up those fucking motherfuckers responsible, and make them choke on their own fucking blood."

"Amen," Pessolano says. "I'll go get the truck."

ALEX GRABS MY SHIRT, jerks me to my feet. I try to lift my hands, try to push her away, but I don't have the strength. Physical or mental. I'm broken, bleeding, beaten, finished. It's over. I'm done.

"That's all you've got?" Alex asks. She's not even breathing heavy.

My eyes dart around the garage, but I have no idea what I'm looking for. Nothing can help me. I'm past pain. Past exhaustion. Deep down, I know I need to keep fighting, know I'm dead if I don't. But there's nothing left in the tank. I can't even stand up, and my knees wobble and give out.

Alex picks me up again.

"You're pathetic, Jack."

I hear gunfire, coming from the house. Harry, shooting at codeine apparitions. *Dummy*. He needs to save the bullets.

"You know, I built you up in my head as this supercop. I considered you a worthy opponent. No one had ever beaten me before."

She squeezes my cheeks together, like I'm a child.

"You got lucky, Jack. That's how you beat me. Luck."

Consciousness is slipping away. A slap brings me around again.

"Say it, Jack. Say you got lucky."

I close my eyes. Alex slams me into the garage door.

"Tell me you got lucky!"

"I . . . got lucky."

Half of Alex's face breaks into a smile. I start to cry. Not for me. For Mom. For Latham. For Herb. And even—I hate to say it—for Harry. None of them deserve this. This night of horrors was supposed to end with the good guys winning.

Alex is right. Human beings are just animals, and all animals are selfish. And I selfishly want the people that I love to be okay, and I weep because I'm not going to get my way.

"Perfect," Alex whispers. Her horrible face gets close to mine, and it looks like she's going to kiss me. But she doesn't.

Instead, she sticks out her tongue and licks away a tear.

"Hey! Frankenbitch!"

We both turn.

Harry McGlade is standing in the garage. The Kimber is in his left hand, pointing at us. His right hand is still attached to the refrigerator door, which is resting at his feet, the hinges shot off.

"Let my little sister go!"

Alex snakes her forearm around my neck, putting me between her and the gun.

It's a mistake. I'm a physical wreck, and a mental disaster, but you don't need muscles or brains to execute a judo flip. All you need is leverage.

I jerk my head back, snapping it into her nose, then immediately lean forward and to the right, throw her over my hip.

Alex tumbles ass over head, releasing me, flipping onto her back. I take three steps toward Harry and fall at his feet.

"Shoot her," I mumble.

He drops the gun, grabs my arm.

"Out of bullets."

Harry drags me and the refrigerator door back into the house.

"Hold on . . ."

I stop, spin around, and pull the door leading to the garage closed, turning the dead bolt, locking Alex in.

A shot pings through the living room window, whizzing past my face. We kneel side by side, propping up the stainless steel door like a shield. It's not tall enough to cover us completely, leaving the humps of our backs exposed as we crouch behind it.

"Thanks, Harry," I manage.

"Mom made me. I think she loves you more."

Everything starts to spin. I rest my forehead on Harry's shoulder. He looks at me.

"Jesus, Jackie. You got your ass kicked."

I run a hand over my face, which is a mass of swelling and pain.

"You don't need more blood, do you?" he asks.

"I think I'll be okay."

Then everything gets really blurry and the darkness takes me in its arms.

THE CAB SPITS PHINEAS TROUTT out in front of a house that isn't Jack's. According to the taxi driver and his electronic address finder, hers is the next one down the road. Phin prefers to walk the rest of the way. On the phone, Jack sounded scattered. If something is going down, Phin prefers to sneak up on it rather than announce his presence by getting out of a car at her doorstep.

It's cool, dark, quiet. Jack lives in a woodsy area, practically a forest preserve. Phin walks alongside the winding road, not thinking about why Jack called him. There's no point in speculation. Especially since he'll know the reason soon enough.

A *pop!* pierces the calm of the night.

Gunfire. Far away.

Phin reaches behind him, retrieving the revolver he has shoved into the back of his belt. The gun is a .38, a scratch-and-dent that has probably been involved in crimes dating back to the 1960s. It was all Phin could get on such short notice. He picked it up an hour ago, off a gangbanger selling Thai stick to Wrigleyville yuppies in an alley off of Addison. Phin relieved the dealer of his gun, his stash, and eight to ten teeth.

He squints at the revolver in the moonlight, swings out the cylinder, counts six rounds. The gun is old but looks clean, cared for. Phin hopes it can fire. He breaks into a jog, holding the weapon at his side, finger off the trigger.

Another gunshot. Closer than before, but still a good distance away. Then another. Phin stops, scans the trees around him. Sees nothing. He moves to the tree line, alert, cautious.

Jack has privacy out here, that's for sure. He walks another hundred yards before he sees her house in the distance. A few interior lights are on. Four cars are parked in the driveway. As he gets closer, he sees that two of the cars have been shot up; windows broken, wheels popped.

Now Phin does lapse into speculation. Jack's a cop. Phin is not. If she has people shooting at her, why didn't she call other cops?

Phin can think of two reasons.

One, because the people shooting at her are cops.

Two, because someone Jack is with wants Phin specifically.

Phin hasn't been a criminal for very long, but he's managed to pack a lot of crime into just a few years. He's made enemies. It isn't inconceivable that one of them is using Jack to get to him. Though they don't see much of each other, Phin considers Jack a friend. It's a strange friendship, centering around occasional games of pool, but there's mutual respect. And strangely, considering their opposing vocations, there's also a sense of trust. Someone may have picked up on that. Someone bad.

Another shot. Phin sees a muzzle flash, maybe two hundred yards away, in the woods across the street from Jack's house. He heads for it.

A vehicle, coming up the road behind him. Phin hears it before the headlights come around the bend. He ducks into the trees, watches it pass. A truck, a Bronco or a Blazer. Single driver, tearing ass toward Jack's house. It stops in the street. Phin can't see what's happening—he's still too far away.

He cocks the .38 and creeps closer, moving slow and silent.

'M RIGHT ABOUT JACK being lucky. She might very well be the luckiest bitch on the planet.

I yawn. It's not from boredom. I can't remember many days in my life that have been more exciting than this one. But fatigue is setting in. I'm tired. Sore. Part of me is tempted to get the hell out of here, find a nice bed-and-breakfast someplace quiet, murder the owners and spend a few days just relaxing.

But I'm not going to leave without killing Jack and Company. Plus there's still the matter of the gun nuts surrounding the house who can't aim for shit but still have managed to complicate things. I counted three. They're using bolt action rifles with suppressors, and a variety of ammunition and scopes. Not pros. Anyone with military experience could have wiped out everyone in the house a long time ago. Hunters, maybe. Or wannabe soldiers.

Whoever they are, they seem angry at Jack, and I don't expect they'll give up any time soon. I'll have to deal with them eventually, but first things first.

I pick up the gun Harry dropped and I'm not surprised to find it empty. I toss it onto the workbench.

Then I check the door to the house. Locked. It's one of those security doors, a solid wood center sandwiched between metal plates, steel or aluminum. The jamb and frame are heavy-duty as well. I can't kick it in, because the hinges are on this side.

I spy the automatic garage door opener next to the door. I could open it, run outside, and find another way into the house. But then I'd be opening myself up for target practice.

I glance at the door to the house again. Maybe there's a key for the dead bolt in the garage somewhere. I check the workbench and see something even better than a key.

I walk over to it, feeling a warmth well up inside me, the same warmth I always feel when I have a chance to kill someone in an exciting new way.

It's not gas powered, unfortunately. It's electric. But Jack has thoughtfully provided me with a fifty-foot extension cord, easily long enough to reach the hallway bathroom where everyone is hiding.

I pick it up. It feels natural in my hands, like something I was born to hold. I smile.

Then I search around for an outlet, so I can plug in my new chain saw.

A BEE IS IN THE CAR with me. A giant bee, the size of an egg. It buzzes around my head, and I try to get out of the car but the doors are broken. I'm terrified of bees, because I'm allergic to them. So when it lands on my shoulder I can't swat it because I don't want to get stung, and it stares at me with malevolent eyes, knowing I'm helpless, knowing it can kill me whenever it wants to.

The car crashes into a tree and begins to roll down the side of a hill. I open my eyes, panicked and dizzy and hurting all over.

I'm not in a car. I'm on the floor, and Harry is shaking me.

But I can still hear the bee buzzing.

"Wake up, Jackie! We're in some shit."

I look over my shoulder, see a chain saw sticking through the door to the garage. The buzzing blade is gradually cutting away the door-knob and dead bolt.

I try to stand up, and Harry drags me back down. There's a *ping* and the refrigerator door in front of us vibrates from a bullet impact.

"We're pinned down," Harry says. "Can you move?"

I nod, and that simple movement causes everything to go black again. More shaking from Harry.

"Dammit, Jackie! Stay awake!"

"Breaker," I mumble.

"What?"

"Circuit . . . breaker."

"Mom!" Harry screams. "Cut off the electricity!"

I glance back at the door. The chain saw is really throwing off some sparks. It's almost pretty, like fireworks.

I close my eyes and think about the Fourth of July.

MARY STRENG HEARS the chain saw in the garage. She sticks her head out of the bathroom, around the refrigerator, and sees it cutting through the door.

She knows the chain saw is electric. Knows they need to trip the circuit breaker.

Mary also knows that the circuit breaker is behind a small child-proof door. When you have rheumatoid arthritis, *childproof* is synonymous with *adultproof*.

She looks at Herb, sprawled out on the bathroom floor, clutching his leg in a codeine/pain fever dream.

Then she looks at Latham, who doesn't appear much better. His eyelids are halfway closed, and he's white as milk.

Neither one of them can make it to the fuse box.

A woman screams, "Mom! Cut off the electricity!"

But the woman isn't Jacqueline. Mary looks in the hall again.

"Mom!"

It's Harry. Apparently his voice goes up a few octaves when he's terrified.

Mary tries to think of an answer, comes up blank, and hurries down the hallway, into the laundry room. She hooks a finger into the cruel metal ring on the circuit breaker door. That simple act alone brings agony. Even with the codeine, and the vodka, Mary's hands have never hurt so badly.

And it's about to get worse.

Mary sets her jaw and tugs, fast and hard.

It's like sticking her hand in a furnace.

The door doesn't budge.

She eases up, tries to change fingers. Her hand is shaking so much she can't get ahold of the handle. Mary switches to lefty.

"Mom! I'm too pretty to die!"

Harry again. That guy certainly is a complainer. Must be Ralph the sailor's genes.

She hooks her left index finger in the ring, closes her eyes, and jerks her whole arm back.

The pain takes away her breath. But the door swings open.

Mary releases the handle, reaching for the breaker, but the spring engages and slaps the door closed.

"SHE'S ALMOST THROUGH!"

Now both of Mary's hands are trembling. She tries her right hand, then her left hand, and can't grip the damnable metal ring. Despair mingles with anguish, and Mary curses herself for being a worthless old woman, of no use to anyone, not even able to—

On the dryer, atop a stack of sweaters, is a coat hanger.

She snatches it up, puts the hook through the metal ring, and pulls like hell.

The door swings open.

Mary reaches inside the panel and jabs at the main breaker switch, plunging the house into darkness and silence.

11:11 P.M.
MUNCHEL

AGAIN WITH THE GODDAMN LIGHTS. Munchel sighs, wondering why the military doesn't make a scope that works in the daylight *and* the nighttime. Then soldiers wouldn't have to switch scopes every three goddamn minutes.

He sits up, rubs his eyes, and sees Pessolano in the truck up the street.

It's about damn time.

Munchel stands, stretches, and begins to walk across the grass toward him. The wind is still strong, and has dropped a dozen degrees, hinting at the harsh winter doubtlessly drawing near. Once he spreads the word to the soldier-for-hire underground that he was part of the Chicago pervert murders, he expects his services to be in great demand, fetching premium dollars. Munchel decides that his next merc gig will be someplace warm, like Bosnia. Or Atlanta.

Munchel pauses, briefly, at the corpse of Swanson, and grins at him.

"You gonna eat that, Greg? No?"

He reaches down and plucks the granola bar from Swanson's cold, dead fingers, and tears the wrapper open with his teeth.

Cinnamon raisin. Munchel's favorite.

"You want some, buddy?"

He breaks off a corner, bounces it off Swanson's face.

Predictably, Swanson doesn't protest. Though Munchel wouldn't be surprised if the former TUHC leader did suddenly sit up and start bitching, complaining that his piece isn't big enough, or that they should just leave the cop alone and run to Mexico, or some other bullshit.

Munchel continues onward, and finds Pessolano poking around in the back of his Bronco.

"You got any fleece in there, man? It's colder than a penguin's nuts out here."

Pessolano pulls a small stack of clothing from the cargo bay.

"That don't look too warm."

"It's Dragon Skin. Tactical body armor. Stronger than Kevlar."

Pessolano takes Munchel's TPG-1, trading it for a vest. Munchel rubs the fabric between his fingers.

"It's thin."

"But it can still stop an AK-47. Maybe . . . if Swanson had one on . . ."

Pessolano stows the rifle. He looks like he's going to start bawling again, and Munchel doesn't think he can stomach another display.

"He's in a better place," Munchel says, popping the rest of the granola bar into his mouth. "Where are the Desert Eagles?"

Pessolano reaches into the truck again, comes out with an aluminum suitcase with combination locks on the buckles. Munchel waits, becoming progressively annoyed as Pessolano keeps screwing up the numbers. The dummy finally gets the case open, revealing two huge nickel-plated handguns, nestling in individual foam compartments.

Munchel whistles, reaching for a gun. The damn thing has to weigh more than five pounds. You could kill a person just by hitting him over the head with it.

"This is the Desert Eagle Mark XIX," Pessolano says. "It uses fifty-caliber Action Express rounds—the biggest handgun bullets on the market. Same length as a .44 Magnum, but wider. It has almost eight times the stopping power of a nine millimeter. What it hits, it kills."

"Can it go through the Dragon Skin?"

"I wouldn't want to try it to find out."

"How many rounds does it hold?"

"Seven. And they're really expensive, so don't waste them."

Munchel spins, aims at the house, and squeezes the trigger. The *BOOM* is so loud it feels like someone slapped him in the ears, and the recoil jerks his arm back.

Awesome.

"I said they're expensive!" Pessolano screams.

Munchel grins at him. "Shit, man. I'll write you a check."

He helps himself to the box of bullets, popping the clip and adding two more. Seven plus one in the throat. Pessolano says something, but Munchel can't hear him through the ringing in his head.

"Huh?"

"How do you want to do this?" Pessolano yells.

Munchel considers it. Everyone is holed up in the hallway, behind the refrigerator, except for that crazy bitch with the chain saw in the garage.

"We bust in the front door," he says. "I'll take the house. You take the garage."

Pessolano nods, then he spends a minute untangling his bullet-proof vest, trying to get it on. He's like a child, unable to find the arm-hole. This convinces Munchel that Pessolano is lying about his military experience. Munchel doesn't have a problem with lying. He lies to his mama, about when he's going to visit her next. He lies to his foreman at the English muffin factory, about being sick when he's actually just hungover. He even lies to hookers, telling them he works for the CIA. But Pessolano's lies are dangerous. Munchel is supposed to trust this guy with his life, have full confidence that Pessolano has his back.

How good can he watch Munchel's back when he can't even put on a simple vest?

Munchel decides he isn't going to work with Pessolano again. True, the man has some cool weapons and equipment, but someone of Munchel's professional stature shouldn't associate with amateurs.

Munchel straps on the Dragon Skin, finishing before Pessolano does. He spreads his hands, to show Pessolano how easy it really is, and then hears a gunshot come from the trees behind him. At practically the same time, he feels a slap in the back.

He drops to the ground, crawling to the other side of the truck, adrenaline raging. Pessolano scurries beside him.

"You hit?"

Munchel nods. He allows Pessolano to turn him around, examine his back.

"Vest stopped it. You hurt?"

Munchel shakes his head. It feels like he's been snapped by a rubber band.

Holy shit, he thinks. *I actually got shot.*

I got shot and I survived.

He can picture himself in a seedy bar in South Africa, playing poker and drinking rotgut with a bunch of other mercs, casually mentioning how he got shot on his first job. A crazed smile appears on his face.

"He's in the woods," Pessolano says. "If we rush at him from two sides, we can flush him out. You ready?"

Munchel nods, feeling invincible.

"Let's do it," Pessolano says. "On my count."

Munchel doesn't wait. He stands up and charges straight into the trees.

PHIN

PHIN RETREATS INTO THE FOREST, moving fast. He's lost one-sixth of his ammunition, along with the element of surprise. All he's gained is the secure knowledge that his recently acquired revolver sucks. He'd been less than fifty feet away, aiming directly at the man's head. The bullet hit the lower back instead.

At least the gun didn't explode in my hand.

From the short amount of time he'd observed the two men, Phin didn't get the impression they were cops. They aren't soldiers either, despite their camouflage outfits. And Phin doesn't recognize them, though he didn't get a good look at their faces.

But it really doesn't matter who they are. The only thing that currently matters is that they're coming after him. And they have much better guns.

Phin ducks under some low-hanging branches, jumps over a fallen tree, and finds himself in a small clearing. He jogs around the edge of it, kicking up dead leaves. Then he cuts back into the woods and heads back toward Jack's house, approaching it on an angle.

He steps onto Jack's property, on the southwest corner of her house. It's completely dark. He can hear the men fumbling through the forest behind him. Phin jogs across the open stretch of lawn, energy fading. When he reaches the window by the garage, Phin considers his options. He can go for help, but by the time help arrives the yahoos with the Desert Eagles might kill Jack.

Of course, she might already be dead.

He can continue to play hide-and-seek, try to pursue his pursuers. But Phin has no training, no military experience. He can fight, and he can shoot, but that's the extent of his commando skills.

Or he can break into the house, grab Jack and whoever else is inside, and try to herd them all to safety.

That seems best. Phin fishes out a pocket flashlight, attached to his key chain, and peers in the garage window. He sees stacked cardboard boxes. Phin strips off his T-shirt, wads it up against the glass, and smacks the cloth with his gun. There's noise as the glass shatters, but not too much. He clears away the big pieces of glass, spreads his shirt over the pane, and climbs inside, wiggling between the wall and the boxes.

Phin holds his breath, listens. Hears nothing.

The boxes are all various sizes and weights. He tucks the revolver into the back of his jeans and wastes a few minutes finding his way through the cardboard maze, picking up, climbing over, and shifting all of Jack's crap. When he finally makes it to the middle of the garage, a space opens up, and he sighs in relief.

That's when someone hits him in the head with a shovel.

Phin stumbles forward, then falls to the right, feeling the wind of another swing sail past his face. He waves his mini-flashlight, sees the shovel coming at him again, and rolls out of the way.

Phin gets on all fours, reaches around his belt for his gun.

It isn't there.

He scuttles backward until he has some room to get to his feet. His head hurts, but it's bearable. He does a quick sweep of the floor with the light, looking for his dropped gun but not finding it, then raises the beam to view his attacker.

Alexandra Kork.

Now it made sense why Jack called. Alex forced her to. Once upon a time, Alex almost killed Phin. Apparently, she wants another chance.

"Hello, Alex. You're looking well."

Alex smiles, but the scarred side of her face doesn't move. She holds up a hand to shield her eyes from the flashlight beam.

"I like the bullet holes," she says, pointing the shovel blade at the healed pockmarks on his torso. "Sexy."

Phin and Alex begin to circle each other.

"Those your friends outside, standing guard?" he asks.

She shakes her head. "No. Jack is Miss Popularity tonight. Apparently she collects enemies. She's got something about her that really pisses people off."

Alex moves in closer. Phin steps back, out of range.

"They're coming," Phin says. "Two of them."

"They've been shooting at the house for almost three hours. They can't hit shit."

"They're not using rifles anymore. They've got handguns. If they get in the house, we're all going to die."

Alex stops moving. Phin can see her working it out in her head, can see she doesn't like the odds any better than he does.

"What's the situation inside?" Phin asks.

"No ammo. No guns. Where's yours?"

"If I had one, you wouldn't be standing there right now. How many people are in the house?"

"Jack. Her mom. Her boyfriend. Her partner. And Harry."

Phin tries to sound casual, tries to keep the hope out of his voice. "Is Jack okay?"

Alex smiles again.

"Got a little crush on her, Phin? Isn't she a bit old for you?"

"Is she okay?" Phin asks, harder.

"I kicked her ass, but she's alive. Everyone in there is pretty beaten up. In fact, I shot Latham. Maybe he won't make it, and you'll have a shot at your secret crush."

Phin realizes he took too much time navigating the boxes. The men are going to bust in here any minute. He can't afford to waste time sparring with Alex.

"You've got to make a choice, Alex."

"Really? What choice is that, Phin?"

"Those guys are going to come in and kill anything that moves. They've got Desert Eagles. You ever see one?"

"I had one. Beautiful weapon. It can shoot a hole through a brick wall."

"They're coming, and they're coming now. You and I can go a few rounds while they're sneaking up on us. Or we can figure out how to defend ourselves."

Alex snorts. "Are you serious? You want me to help you?"

"Either help, or leave. I don't have time to deal with you right now."

"The enemy of my enemy. Is that what you're saying, Phin?"

"Make your choice."

Alex stares at Phin for a moment. Then she starts to laugh. It's a genuine laugh, and she shakes her head in obvious disbelief.

"Life certainly throws a few curves, doesn't it?" she says.

Then she drops the shovel.

I DON'T TRUST PHIN any more than he trusts me. And I'm sure that if he gets his hands on one of those Desert Eagles, the first thing he's going to do is blow my head off.

Which, of course, is the first thing I'm going to do. I just have to make sure I get one before he does.

I turn up my palms and say, "Okay, we're on the same side. Now what?"

Phin shrugs. "You were in the marines. I was hoping you'd tell me."

"Any good marine knows when to fight and when to retreat. We should retreat."

"You go ahead. Run east. I don't think I saw them there."

Which probably means he saw them in the east. Or maybe not.

This is going to be an interesting alliance.

"Okay," I say. "Tell me what you saw."

"Two men. They're wearing vests, and each has a Desert Eagle. They took them out of the back of a Ford Bronco parked down the street."

"Any more weapons in the Bronco?"

"I couldn't see."

"Keys?" I ask.

"I don't know."

"Did they put their rifles in the Bronco?"

"I heard rifle fire, but didn't see any guns."

Which means the rifles might be abandoned on Jack's property somewhere. Why did the shooters ditch their rifles? Out of ammo? Or do they figure they'll finish the job with the handguns, then pick them up later?

I can remember where the shots came from. If I did a perimeter check, I might be able to find a rifle. And unlike those knucklehead snipers, I hit what I aim at.

I stare at Phin. Of course, he may be lying. Maybe he knows where the rifles are, and plans on getting one for himself.

Detente is a bitch.

"How about a third shooter?" I ask.

"I only saw two."

Phin lowers his eyes to the floor. He's looking for something.

I bet it's a gun. He must have had one, and dropped it during our scuffle.

"We need a plan," I say, moving a bit closer to him. If he finds the gun and makes a move for it, I'll punch him in the throat, break his windpipe.

"I'm all ears."

"They have two choices for entry. Front door, and the patio door. Patio door is thick glass, might be tough to break through. Front door is smarter. Two shots at the lock and a swift kick, and they're in."

"Maybe they'll split up," Phin says. "Each take an entrance."

"The house is dark. They might shoot each other. Did they have night-vision scopes or goggles?"

Phin shakes his head. "Not when they were chasing me."

"Then they'll probably stick together. We need to get inside, set up an ambush."

Phin points his light to the left, moving the beam across the workbench. He rushes to it, grabbing Jack's .45 that I threw there, pointing it at my head.

"It's empty," I say.

He pulls the trigger. Nothing happens.

"Sorry," he says. "Had to make sure. No offense."

"None taken. Check around for a crowbar, or something to pry the door open."

He searches the workbench. I come up beside him and also search. We keep an eye on each other, in case one of us finds a potential weapon. I see Phin's eyes linger on a hammer.

"The door is steel," I say. "Hammer won't help. If you pick it up I'll grab the shovel again, which is longer and heavier and can do more damage."

"I'll attest to that," he says, rubbing the bump on his head.

We both leave the hammer alone. In the dust under the workbench is a rusty old car jack. The handle is a removable lug wrench, steel, two feet long. It's not a crowbar, but one end tapers, like a screwdriver. I put a hand on it the same time that Phin does. Together, we bring it over to the front door.

"It isn't big enough for both of us," Phin says, indicating the bar.

"You're the big, strong man," I say, releasing my grip. "Be my guest."

I hold the flashlight, and Phin sticks the flat end into the doorjamb, under the still-protruding chain saw. He gets a solid, two-handed grip on the bar, and leans back.

The muscles in his arms and back bulge, twitch. Phin's a good-looking guy, and it's been a long time since I've seen a man without a shirt. On impulse, I trace my finger across his lats.

He flinches, spins around.

"Easy, tough guy. Just admiring the view."

His eyes are hard. "Don't touch me again."

"I'm too ugly for you, huh, Phin? Can't handle a few scars?"

"You were ugly long before you had the scars, Alex."

Asshole. When I get my hands on a gun, my first shot is going to remove his sanctimonious balls.

Phin goes back to it. The door frame creaks . . . bends . . . then the door pops inward, and I'm highly amused to see Jack Daniels burst through the doorway and descend on Phin with a knife clutched in her hand.

JACK

I SEE AN ARM RAISE UP, moving to block my knife, and I adjust the arc, getting in under it, aiming for the neck—

It's Phin.

I try to put on the brakes, but momentum drives my strike onward. Phin's eyes get wide and he jerks his body sideways. The knife tip nicks his chin, and then I bump into him and he catches me before I fall onto my face.

We both stumble backward, and then I tense up and lift up the knife again when I see Alex standing directly behind him. She's smiling her half smile.

My energy is nearly gone, but I struggle with what little I have left, fighting Phin to get at the murderer over his shoulder.

"Easy, Jack!" Phin says, holding me back. "We called a truce."

A truce? Is he out of his mind?

Alex steps closer, pinches my wrist and twists, making me release the knife.

"We can kill each other later, Jack," Alex says. "Those idiots outside, they're getting ready to come in. They're armed. We aren't. We need to come up with a plan, and quick."

I can't believe this. And maybe if I wasn't so damn tired and banged up, I'd stage a protest. But it makes a warped kind of sense. If the snipers break in, we have no way to defend ourselves. Alex is actually the lesser threat. For the moment, at least.

"Don't trust her," I say to Phin, keeping my eyes on Alex.

"I won't."

My chest feels damp. I glance down and notice Phin is bleeding on my shirt. I touch his cheek.

"Sorry," I say. "Does it hurt?"

He smiles. "I'm tough."

"I know. Thanks for coming."

"We're friends. You call, I come."

I'm strangely moved by that, but being a hard-edged homicide cop I respond with a strong, curt nod. Phin, however, holds me closer, actually hugging me. I give him a perfunctory pat on the back, wondering what the hell he's doing, but not minding it terribly much. His skin is cool to the touch, and he's got the barest hint of aftershave, something that smells like pine. No, it actually is pine. I brush a pine needle out of his hair.

His breath is on my ear, soft and warm. He whispers, "I dropped a .38 somewhere in the garage."

I nod, slightly so Alex doesn't notice. Then we mutually disengage.

"Hey, sis! You kill the bitch yet?"

Harry, from the living room.

"There's been some, uh, complications, Harry," I say over my shoulder.

"What complications?"

Harry's not going to be pleased. I'm not either. Phin and I lead the way back into the house.

"Hey, Phin," Harry says. "Welcome to the rave. You bring the Chex Mix?"

"Hi, Harry. What's with the refrigerator door?"

"I'm neurotic. My shrink says I have a hard time letting go." Then Harry notices Alex, and his eyes narrow. "What the fuck? You make a deal with Satan?"

"The snipers are coming," I say, and the words taste lousy on my tongue. "We need her help."

"What we need," Harry says, "is to pound a stake through her heart, cut off her head, and bury the body on hallowed ground."

"We can finish up our business later, sweetheart," Alex says to Harry. "Where's the circuit breaker?"

I stare at her, suspicious. "Why?"

"They'll probably come in through the front door. We soak the carpeting with water, strip the covering off the end of an extension cord, wrap it around something metal, and put it in the puddle. They walk in, we hit the breaker, fry both of them."

"They teach you that in psycho school?" Harry says.

Alex coolly regards him. "I should have cut your tongue off instead of your hand."

"Why don't you come over here and say that, so I can bounce this refrigerator door off your goddamn—"

"Enough," I interrupt, giving Harry the palm. I actually like Alex's idea. "What if they're wearing rubber-soled shoes?" I ask.

"One of us stands by the door with a hose, soaks them when they come through the door."

"Won't it trip the breaker?"

"Circuit breakers are tripped when there's resistence or surges. All we're doing is running current. It will work."

"We need to hurry." Phin is staring out the front window. "They're coming."

"Get the hose and the extension cord in the garage," I tell Phin and Alex. Then I hurry to the kitchen, turn on the sink, and fill a six-quart cast-iron pot with water. It's really heavy, almost too heavy to lift. But I muscle it out of the sink and carry it at waist level, waddling to the front door. I spill the water all over the floor and set the pot down.

"Got the hose," Alex says. "Phin is stripping the extension cord. I don't think he trusts me with a knife."

"I wonder why."

I take one end of the hose, and hand the other to Harry. "You're on squirting duty. Make sure you stay out of the wet spot."

"I always do."

I bring the hose down the hall, peek in on my mother.

"You okay?"

Mom nods, but she looks terrible. She hands me the flashlight. I check out Latham and Herb. Both are semi-conscious, and they also look terrible. Then I make the mistake of peeking at the vanity mirror, and I look worse than everyone. Sort of like DeNiro at the end of *Raging Bull*.

"Oh, Jacqueline," Mom says. She reaches up to touch my face, and I flinch away.

"It's not as bad as it looks."

It's the truth. All of the pain has sort of combined into a dull ache. Unpleasant, but bearable. Maybe I simply don't have any energy left to devote to hurting.

I give Mom a quick peck on the cheek, and then it's on to the laundry room. I set the flashlight on the dryer and turn off the water valve that leads to the washing machine. I unscrew the hose coming out of it, attach the garden hose, then put the water back on.

"Dammit, Harry! Quit it!"

Harry is apparently soaking Alex. If I had a sense of humor left, I might have smiled at that.

"Tell me when to hit the power," I call down the hallway. "How are you doing, Phin?"

"Power cord is stripped. I'm plugging it in."

"Wrap the stripped end around the cast-iron pot, then step away."

I fight the circuit breaker door, manage to get it open, and poise my finger above the main button. A wave of vertigo hits. I ride through it without losing my balance.

In the silence that follows, I have a chance to think about a lot of things. One of those things is retirement.

Ever since I was a kid, I wanted to be a cop. It didn't take a psychoanalyst to figure out that my desire came from my parents. My mom was a cop, and she was my hero. My dad wasn't in the picture, and his absence left a void in my life. I wanted to emulate my mother, and I became a control freak as a defense mechanism. The more control I had in my life, the less chance of being surprised, of getting hurt. My desire to protect myself, and my mother, evolved into a desire to protect others.

After a few years on the Job, I realized I couldn't really protect anyone. It wasn't any particular incident that stood out, any key moment that led me to this conclusion. It was just the day-to-day grind of seeing people getting hurt, all the time, without being able to save them.

I accepted it. If I couldn't protect them, then at least I could catch the ones who were hurting them.

I've caught a lot of bad people in my twenty-plus years as a cop. I know I've done a lot of good.

But now, here I am. I became a cop to protect others, and now I can't even protect the handful of people who are more important to me than the rest of the world put together.

Alex was right. It's my fault we're all in danger. If anything happens to Mom, or Latham, or Herb, or Phin, or even Harry, I won't be able to live with myself.

I make a decision. A big decision. If we get out of this—no . . . *when* we get out of this, I'm going to hang up my gun. Retire. Draw a pension and get married and gain weight and spend life enjoying it instead of trying to fix it.

"Jackie!" Harry yells. "Alex just ran out the back door!"

No real surprise there.

"Phin went after her!"

"Did he finish the wires?" I call.

"No!"

Dammit. "Mom! I need you!"

Mom shuffles into the laundry room.

"Press the breaker when we tell you to."

I trade places with her, holding open the panel door until she can get her finger on the button.

"I don't like this plan," she says.

There isn't time to argue. I hurry back into the living room, spy the extension cord in a tangled pile on the floor.

A noise at the front door—someone trying the knob.

"Hurry," Harry says. He's got the hose in his hand, bent in a kink.

Something slams into the door. It shakes, but holds.

I find the end of the cord, stripped to bare wires. I reach for the cast-iron pot.

Three gunshots, incredibly loud. The door rattles.

I wind the wire around the pot handle, then scurry off the damp section of carpeting just as the door kicks in.

Two men in camouflage dress storm into my living room. They each have a huge handgun. One is wearing yellow aviator sunglasses. The other is the sniper I saw at Ravenswood, which seems like so long ago.

"Now!" I scream.

Harry hits them with the hose. The lights go on. There's a spark, a crackling *ZAP*, and the smell of smoke and ozone.

The snipers flinch.

Neither of them fall.

It didn't work. Sweet Lord, it didn't work.

They look at each other, then turn their guns on me.

PHIN

WHEN ALEX RAN OUT the back door, Phin knew where she was heading.

To find a gun.

Phin takes two seconds to decide that Alex with a sniper rifle poses a bigger threat than the two guys with their Desert Eagles, and he rushes out after her.

He tears through the kitchen, out the patio door, into the backyard. Phin looks right, then left, sees Alex dart around the corner of the house. He vaults a lawn chair and pursues.

She only has a twenty-yard head start, but she can run like a rabbit. Phin, though lean and muscular, is not in good shape. He's been in remission for a while, but it's more a stay of execution than a full pardon. The pancreatic cancer is still there. It's shrinking, bit by bit, thanks to chemotherapy. But the pain hasn't gone away, and the chemo comes with a slew of symptoms that rival those caused by the disease.

Phin supplements his prescription drugs with many that you can't find at your local Walgreens, and these have also taken their toll on his body. He can pace Alex, but he can't catch her.

She reaches the street, then cuts left, heading toward the Bronco. All of the running Phin did earlier tonight has pretty much tapped his reserves, and he falls farther behind, his breath ragged, his muscles crying out. The night air is cold, tingly, on his bare chest. He chances a quick check over his shoulder, sees the two men at Jack's front door, trying to kick it in, and hopes Alex's electricity booby trap is legit, not bullshit.

Alex gets to the Bronco, tries the driver's-side door. Locked. She runs around to the back, and Phin closes the distance, hands out in front of him, leaning on the truck's hood when he gets there, taking big gulps of air so he doesn't throw up.

The rear door must be locked as well, because Alex sprints away without getting inside, running across the lawn and blending into the night. Phin is too wiped out to follow.

Gunshots. From Jack's house. Phin sees the two men bust in the front entrance. He watches them walk inside, sees the lights go on.

Sees nothing happen.

Alex's trap is bullshit after all.

Phin puts his face up to the tinted glass of the front window, tries to get a look inside the truck. There's a rifle in the front seat, a big one with a scope. He does a quick 180, scanning the ground for a brick or rock or something to break the windshield. There's nothing but grass.

Phin puts his back against the driver's door, clenches his hands, and fires his left elbow backward against the glass, like a piston. He does it once, twice, three times, hard as he can.

The window remains intact.

He wants to try it again, but he can't—he's pretty sure he just broke his elbow.

THE FRESH AIR FEELS GOOD. Liberating. The rhythmic slap of my feet hitting the ground, the stretch of my muscles, the wind on my cheeks. I bet I could run five miles without breaking a sweat.

Phin is behind me, but he gives up when he reaches the truck. Wimp. I should have beaten him to death while we were in the garage.

No biggie. There's still time.

I'm running so fast I almost miss the rifle. It's on a grassy hill, only a few yards off the road. I sprint to it, slide alongside like I'm stealing second base, and snatch it up in my hands.

It's a beauty. Bolt action, suppressor, bipod, night-vision scope, cheek pad, palm support, padded butt plate. A better weapon than the M40A1 rifle I trained with in the corps. I get behind it, assume the position, load a round, and point it back at the Bronco. Phin is crouching next to the side door. An easy target. I consider putting a round through his leg, but notice he's cradling his elbow, already hurt.

I'll get to him in a minute.

I swing the barrel around, aiming at Jack's house. I can see Harry through the front bay window, sitting on the floor and clutching his hose. Those two sniper idiots, standing there, pointing their guns. The trap must have tripped the circuit breaker. I figured it might do that. They should have held the breaker button in and kept it there; then the current would have kept flowing. But I saw no reason to share that little tip.

I nudge the rifle. There's Jack. She actually has her hands up over her head. Like she's surrendering.

As if that's going to help her.

"You are dust," I say, quoting Scripture. "And to dust you shall return."

My Bible-thumping father would have been proud I remembered that. I grin, caress the trigger, and fire.

PESSOLANO

"HOLD ON. We're on the same side."

The woman cop is standing a few feet away, her hands raised. Pessolano can't make out her face in the dark, but her voice is strong and sure.

Pessolano doesn't feel strong *or* sure. After chasing that blond guy through the woods, he's exhausted. He's also cold and wet, having just been squirted with a hose. Part of him knows that he needs to kill everyone in the house, then get out of there. But another part, a bigger part, is having some difficulty. Shooting someone from a few hundred yards away feels detached, kind of like playing a video game. The distance is emotional as well as physical. Shooting someone at point-blank range, someone with her hands up, someone *surrendering*—that's more like murder than war.

"You're called The Urban Hunting Club, right?" she says. "You kill perverts. I'm a cop. I kill perverts too. We're both fighting for the same cause."

Munchel isn't shooting her either. Pessolano wonders if he shares the same doubts. If he thinks this might be wrong too.

"You got nice legs," Munchel says to the cop. He sounds breathy, excited.

Pessolano stares at Munchel. His friend has a wild look in his eyes. A scary look.

"Thank you," the cop says. "You're the one from Ravenswood."

"Yeah," Munchel answers. "Did you like that? You almost got me a few times. You ever in the military?"

"No. Just the police."

Munchel takes a step closer to the cop. "You nailed Swanson right in the heart. He died in a whole mess of pain."

"You gave me the rifle."

"I wanted it to be a fair fight."

"Would killing me now be a fair fight? I don't have a gun."

Munchel licks his lips. "Maybe I'm not thinking of killing you right now. Maybe I'm thinking of something else."

Pessolano stares at the cop. She does have nice legs. And to the victor, the spoils.

Right?

The man on the floor, the one holding the hose, clears his throat. Munchel points his gun at him.

"You got something to say, tough guy?" Munchel demands.

"If you do anything to my sister," he says, "would you mind if I took a few pictures?"

Munchel begins to laugh. Pessolano starts to laugh too, but instead he starts to choke.

What the hell?

Pessolano cups his hands to his throat, vaguely aware that he just heard a gunshot.

I just got shot. Who shot me?

When Pessolano pulls his hands away, they're filled with blood. And something else. Something stringy that looks like a peach pit.

It's my Adam's apple.

Pessolano drops to his knees. He glances at Munchel, who is looking back at him, mouth hanging open, eyes wide.

Behind Munchel, Pessolano sees the man on the floor lifting up a big board. No—it's a refrigerator door. The man rams the door into Munchel, driving him across the room and up against a wall.

Pessolano turns, sees the female cop running away, toward the garage.

Pessolano looks down, watches the fountain of blood raining in front of him, aware that it's coming from his neck.

Pessolano tries to take a breath, but his throat is blocked.

There's no pain. Only that same sense of detachment, as if this is happening to someone else.

Then, another shot.

Pessolano feels it burn right through his right thigh, snapping the bone in half.

He falls forward.

Now there's pain.

Soul-searing, unbearable pain.

Pessolano tries to scream. *Has* to scream. But his clogged throat won't let him.

Another bullet.

The other leg.

Pessolano writhes on the floor, his brain overloading on unbearable agony. Agony that can't possibly get worse.

The next bullet blows off a good chunk of his arm.

The agony gets worse.

Pessolano is beyond reason now. Detachment has led to the keenest sense of self-awareness he's ever experienced. He exists now only as raw, exposed nerve endings, millions of them firing at once.

When his other arm gets shattered by a bullet, his body finally diverts its remaining resources to Pessolano's brain, giving him a brief moment of lucidity. A flood of thoughts assault him:

Please let me die.

Shoot me in the head.

Make the pain stop.

And then he thinks of something odd. Incongruous.

If they made a plastic green army man toy that looked like I do now, maybe I would have followed a different path.

That's the thought bouncing around in his skull as his life blessedly fades away.

IT DOESN'T WORK, as Mary expected. As soon as she presses the circuit breaker, it pops right back out. Mary presses it several times, with the same results.

No *ZAP*. No cries of men being electrocuted.

Which means Harry and Jacqueline are completely vulnerable.

Voices, coming from the living room. Jacqueline's voice. Then a man she doesn't recognize.

Mary has no weapon, and even if she had one she wouldn't be able to hold it. The OxyContin has made her light-headed, and it's dampened some of the pain, but she still can't open her hands.

Mary heads down the hall anyway.

As horrible as the last few hours have been, Mary has learned something about herself. *Old* and *useless* are not synonyms. Age does not equal feeble. And even though Mary is beaten, bowed, and has been around for a long time, she's far from helpless. Her daughter needs help. And *dammit*, she's going to get some.

Mary slips past the refrigerator, moves quietly to the edge of the living room, pausing next to the wall. She sees two men in army fatigues, holding very large handguns.

They're pointing these guns at Jacqueline.

Mary gets ready to call to them, to draw their attention, and then the taller man gets shot in the throat.

Jacqueline doesn't waste the opportunity. She runs into the garage.

Get away, Mary thinks. *Bring help.*

But knowing her daughter, Jacqueline won't leave until everyone is safe.

I should have raised her to be less considerate.

Then Harry rushes the other man, and there's a scuffle. Though Harry McGlade is—what's a good word? *flawed*—Mary has grown fond of the guy. She hurries into the living room to lend a gnarled hand. Mary abandoned him once, and won't follow that particular path again.

More sniper fire. The man who was hit in the throat gets shot several more times, not in any vital spots. It's so appalling that Mary knows Alex must be behind it. While Alex is preoccupied with that, Mary gets close to Harry, to push against him and keep the man pinned to the wall. But then the sniper gets a hand free, and he fires at both of them.

Mary gets knocked backward, Harry smacking into her.

She has no idea if she's been shot, or if Harry's been shot, or perhaps even both of them.

PHIN

ALEX HAS FOUND A RIFLE.

She's fifty, maybe seventy-five yards from Phin. He can't see her body in the dark, but he can pinpoint her muzzle flash. Phin watches her fire at the house. Watches one of the gunmen fall. Watches Alex take the guy apart, limb by limb. Deliberately. Cruelly.

It's a sneak preview of what's going to happen to him, to Jack, to everyone in the house.

Phin shuffles along the asphalt to the front of the truck, out of Alex's direct line of sight. He can't bend his arm at all. His elbow is busted, or something in it is torn.

The pain is bad.

He seriously considers digging into his pocket, taking out the pot he stole from that Wrigleyville banger, and eating as much as he can. Marijuana is a marvelously effective analgesic. Phin is an expert when it comes to analgesics. The past few years of his life have been dedicated to a singular purpose: the numbing of pain. Physical, mental, and emotional.

After his terminal diagnosis, Phin dropped out of society. He left his job, because it was meaningless to work when you've been given a death sentence. He left his fiancée, because he wanted to spare her the torture of watching him die.

Since he had no hope for the future, he began to live day by day. Sort of like a dog.

That's not a negative comparison. Dogs live in the moment. They don't think. They don't dwell on the future. They exist to meet their base needs. Eating. Sleeping. Breeding. Surviving. No worries. No regrets. Minimize effort, maximize pleasure.

Phin tried to do the same. He lost himself in drugs, liquor, and whores. When the money ran out, he robbed dealers, gangbangers, pimps, and criminals. That led to hiring himself out as a rent-a-thug, solving problems for people who didn't want to go to the police.

It worked. He was able to blot out his pain.

Then he met Jack. She arrested him after a fight with a group of Latin Kings. Later, he and Jack ran into each other at a neighborhood bar, and began to play pool on a semi-regular basis.

Which would have been fine if it didn't go any further. But, unfortunately, they became friends.

Phin didn't expect it to happen. He didn't *want* it to happen. Friendship involved responsibility. Phin's only responsibility was to himself, to his indulgences. To avoiding pain.

Yet Jack calls, and he comes running.

Just like a dog.

Phin shivers. His bare chest is gooseflesh, cold to the touch. The smart thing to do is to eat the weed, run into the woods, and try to find a hospital, a bottle of tequila, a few grams of coke, and a clean hooker. Forget Jack. He owes her nothing. He isn't going to be around long enough to regret the decision.

Run away, he tells himself.

But he doesn't run. Instead, Phin stands, crawls onto the hood of the Bronco, and gets up to the windshield. He's wearing gym shoes. The rubber soles aren't hard enough.

But he knows something that is hard enough. Something that routinely cracks car windows.

Friendship sucks, he thinks.

Then he shuts his eyes, rears back, and slams his forehead into the glass.

It brings out more stars than the ones currently occupying the clear night sky, but he manages to crack the windshield—a spiderweb pattern the size of a dinner plate. He didn't break through, but it's a start.

He waits for the dizziness to pass, realizes it isn't going to, then spins around on his butt and drives his heel against the crack. Again. And again. And again. And again.

The spiderweb gets larger. The window bends, indents. Then his foot busts through.

Phin continues to kick, widening the hole until he can slip inside, avoiding cutting himself on the glass while climbing into the front seat.

His head hurts. So does his arm. And the tumor on his pancreas feels like a piranha trying to eat its way out of his insides.

But when Phin touches the sniper rifle, he can't help but smile.

"The truce is over, Alex," he says.

JACK

I GET TO THE GARAGE as fast as I can, which isn't very fast. The house feels more like a ship, rocking to and fro in the waves, making it challenging to stand. I stop in the doorway, feel for the light switch, and stumble over to the workbench.

I'm looking for the gun Phin said he dropped.

The light is just a single bare bulb, maybe a sixty-watt, and my loopy vision is further impeded by a black eye that's puffed halfway closed. There are boxes strewn about the garage floor. Some Christmas decorations. A few books. I don't want to let go of the bench because I'm afraid I'll fall over, but I don't see the gun from where I am. I'll have to go searching.

I take two steps toward the mess, moving a box aside, peering beneath it. Nothing. The floor is cold, causing me to shiver. From inside the house, more gunshots.

Sniper fire.

I wondered if it was Phin who saved my life, grabbing one of the sniper's rifles when he ran outside. It might have been Alex, who didn't want anyone else to kill me because she was saving that particular pleasure for herself. Either way, I caught a break. Now I needed to capitalize upon it.

I kick away a piece of cardboard, almost lose my balance. No revolver underneath. A faint breeze tousles my hair, and I follow it and see the broken window, hidden behind the stacks of unopened boxes. If Phin dropped the gun in that maze I'll never find it.

More gunfire. But this is from inside the house. It's loud, even louder than firecrackers.

The Desert Eagle.

I don't want to think about what that implies, but I do anyway. Even if the refrigerator door is thick enough to block the bullets, at close range the shooter can aim around it.

My last image of Harry McGlade—of, God help me, my *brother*—was of him charging the Ravenswood sniper, trying to save me.

I hope Harry's okay.

MUNCHEL

WAR IS HELL.

First Swanson bites it. Then Pessolano gets shot in the neck. The cherry on top is getting whacked full-body with a refrigerator door.

The blow knocks the wind out of Munchel, ramming him into the wall, sandwiching him against it. Like a true soldier he manages to hold on to the Desert Eagle. Unfortunately, Munchel's arm is at his side, immobile, the door pinning his wrist. He can't raise the gun, and has no leverage to push away from the wall.

A second shot whizzes through the window. Munchel jerks at the sound, but he isn't the one who gets hit. Munchel stares at Pessolano writhing on the ground—the man's leg looks like it has sprouted another knee in the middle of the thigh.

Another shot does the same thing to the opposite leg. Pessolano clutches at his throat, making a face like he's screaming, but no sound is coming out. Munchel is horrified. It's too much to watch, too much to bear. He squeezes his eyes closed and wiggles, trying to twist away from the refrigerator door. With a grunt and some hip action, Munchel frees up enough room to get his gun arm loose. He brings the gun around, shoots behind the refrigerator door where he guesses his attacker to be, the Desert Eagle sounding like cannon fire.

The one-armed man pinning him to the wall backpedals. Munchel fires at him twice more, his bullets pinging into the door as the man falls. Munchel has no idea if he hit the guy or not, but he takes a quick last look at Pessolano, sees his friend's remaining good limb get turned into cube steak by more sniper fire, and decides he doesn't want to be in this room any longer.

He sprints away from the big bay window, out of the living room, following the path of the chick cop through the kitchen and to a doorway. Munchel finds her in the garage, her back to him, rummaging through a large stack of boxes.

James Michael Munchel raises the big Desert Eagle. It's time to end this.

JACK

NOISE, FROM BEHIND ME. The Ravenswood sniper charges into the garage, and when he raises his pistol I throw myself forward.

Two shots in quick succession, both missing. The sound is painfully loud in the enclosed garage, echoing off the concrete floor. I tumble over a container of books, roll, and land on my butt, my body forcing a trench between two stacks of boxes. The single bare bulb hanging from the ceiling isn't strong enough to penetrate the crevice I'm in, so I can't see a thing.

I cover my head and wait for the sniper to start firing again.

He doesn't. Instead, he starts kicking boxes, knocking them over, swearing and yelling. A crack opens up between crates, and I see he's brandishing a knife now. One of those survival models, long and unwieldy, with a serrated blade. His face is a picture of anger and frustration.

"Come out of there, you split-tail bitch!"

I get on all fours, back away. There's a breeze coming from my left—the broken window. Maybe I can make it outside. I crawl toward it, keeping low.

He pushes through ahead of me, cutting off my escape. He's only a few feet away. He grins, baring yellow teeth.

"There's my girl. Stay down. I like that position."

If I got scared by creeps talking trash, I would have quit the Job after a week. Threats don't bother me much. Knives, however, do.

"Where's your friend?" I ask. I hold out a hand, touch the wall, keeping an eye on the blade.

"Casualty of war."

I keep my voice even, keep the fear out of it. He seems like a guy who would be turned on by fear. "You don't seem too upset about him dying."

The man smiles. "He knew the risks."

I stretch up onto my knees.

"Is that was this is?" I ask. "A war?"

"Life is a war. We have to fight for every little bit we get."

"War is for soldiers," I say. I shift my weight back onto my toes. "You're not a soldier."

He points the tip of the knife at me. "I AM a soldier!"

I lean back into a squatting position. "Soldiers don't kill innocent people. They don't threaten girls with knives. What's your real job? Construction worker? Assembly line at a factory?"

I see that hits a nerve. The sniper snarls and rushes forward, slashing. I leap at him rather than away, getting inside the swing of the blade, throwing a hard right into his stomach and then driving him backward with my shoulder. We get tangled up, push through some boxes and up against the workbench.

I latch both hands on to his wrist, keeping the knife away. The Ravenswood sniper fights against my grip, then suddenly seems to realize he has more than one hand, and uses his free one to punch me in the face.

I hold on tight, tucking my chin into my chest. He hits me on the side of the head—in the ear—and my legs give out. Then he connects with my cheek and I release his knife hand, falling backward, my consciousness slipping away.

"I don't work in no goddamn factory, bitch!" he screams. "I'm the best goddamn soldier you ever met!"

He switches his hold on the knife so it angles down, raising it up over my head.

I'm in no condition to stop him.

I'VE GOT HARRY in my sights. He engaged in a brief tussle with the remaining sniper, the sniper shot at him, and Harry fell onto his back, right on top of Mom. I can't tell if either of them got hit or not. He's still moving, but doesn't seem to be in any particular hurry, which might indicate an injury.

Let's make it worse.

I consider where the first bullet should go. Foot? Knee? Balls.

No. His other hand.

I'm such a little stinker.

I aim, adjusting for the wind, visualizing the shot like I learned in basic training.

Then a patch of grass explodes just a few feet to my left, accompanied by a *BANG!*

Phin found himself a rifle.

He obviously can't shoot for shit. I'm less than a hundred yards away. Hell, with these guns a blind preschooler could shoot the shine off a penny from three quarters of a mile. I switch position, sight his blond head in the rear window of the Bronco, and squeeze the trigger a fraction of a second after I see him ducking down.

Crap. Miss.

No problem. He got lucky. And luck doesn't last forever. Jack has learned that particular lesson well tonight. Phin will learn it too.

I eject the round, seek out the backpack full of clips that the snipers have so graciously left me. Without taking my eyes off of Phin I select one, my fingers feeling to make sure it's loaded. It's empty. I try another. Also empty.

The whole bag is filled with empty clips.

Phin fires again, and it kicks up a clod of dirt only a few inches from my hip.

Rather than dwell on the misfortune of unfolding events, I decide to get proactive. I detach the night scope and stick it in my pocket. Staying on my elbows and toes, I inch backward down the slope of the small hill I'm perched on, stopping periodically to tuck down and roll left or right. Phin keeps shooting at me, keeps missing, and then I'm out of his line of fire, on my feet, and sprinting toward the woods adjacent to the road.

Shooting isn't the only thing the marines taught me. I can also sneak like a cat.

I cut right, make my way through a hundred yards of trees, then circle back and head for the Bronco, slow and low, silent as death.

MARY

MARY OPENS HER EYES.

She's lying on the floor, and there's tremendous pressure on her leg, accompanied by a dull ache.

A bullet wound?

"I need a fucking vacation."

"Harry?"

That's the pressure. Harry's fallen on top of her.

"Mom? You got those codeine pills on you? Gimme about ten."

"Were you shot?" Mary asks.

"I don't think so. Only holes I got in me are the ones that are supposed to be there."

"You're on my leg, dear."

"Oh. Sorry."

Harry moves, and the pressure is replaced by the pins and needles sensation of blood returning. Mary sits up and rubs her leg with both palms.

Gunshots. From the garage.

Jacqueline.

Mary looks around, spies the large handgun on the floor next to the dead man. She crawls over to it, clasps it between her hands. She tries to curl her fingers around it, but they won't cooperate.

"Give it here, Mom." Harry takes it in his left hand and points it at the refrigerator door. "Stand back."

Mary obeys. Harry fires at the door handle, and it shears away, releasing his prosthetic claw.

"Should have done that to begin with," he says. "Where's Jack?"

"Garage, with the other sniper."

Harry puts a protective arm around Mary, hustles her into the kitchen.

"Stay down, Mom. I'll be back in a second, right after I give that son of a bitch a lead enema."

Harry gives her a quick kiss on the cheek, then runs off.

That's my boy.

THE SPLIT-TAIL is at his mercy, and Munchel likes the feeling.
He likes the look of defeat on her battered face. Of submission. She's resigned herself to death at his hands.

But he's not ready to kill her yet.

He backhands her, and she doesn't even try to block it. Such a far cry from the cocky cop who almost shot him.

Munchel grins. It's always been a secret shame of his that he hasn't ever had sex without paying for it. But he's going to now. Her face is all bruised and puffy, but she's got good legs, a nice ass. He's going to ride this bitch like—

"Hey! Rambozo!"

Munchel whips his head around. Sees the man with the bionic hand standing in the doorway. In his real hand is Pessolano's Desert Eagle.

"I wanted you to see it coming," the man says.

Munchel backs away, his hands up in protest.

The man fires six times in rapid succession.

Miraculously, the first five shots completely miss.

Unfortunately, the last one doesn't.

It drills Munchel in the stomach, and feels like getting hit with a miner's pick. Munchel doubles over, dropping the knife, falling to his knees, and then to his side. He curls into a fetal position, clutching the fire in his belly. This isn't like the other time he got shot, that wussy slap in the back. This is awful.

He lifts a hand to his face, sees the blood.

But I'm wearing body armor, he thinks. *This isn't fair.*

"You okay, sis?" The man bends down next to the cop, helps her up.

"I'll live. Where's Mom?"

"I'm here."

Munchel looks left, watches an old broad come into the garage. They all share a group hug. It's a big happy goddamn Walton family reunion, and he's lying here in agony, bleeding to death.

"Help me," Munchel whispers.

The bionic guy walks up to him, squints. "You're lucky I suck lefty. I was aiming for your head."

"It hurts."

"I can fix that," the man says. "Don't worry. I won't miss this time."

Munchel feels the barrel press against his forehead. His bladder lets go, soaking his fatigues.

"You . . . you have to help me," Munchel states. "You're a cop."

"She's a cop," the guy says. "I used to be a cop, but they kicked me off the force for not following the rules." The man grins. "I'm not big on rules."

Munchel's entire being is focused on the cold steel between his eyes. This isn't how things are supposed to end.

"I'm begging you. Don't kill me. Please please please don't kill me."

"Do me a favor. When you get to hell, give Hitler a kick in the balls and tell him it's from Harry McGlade."

He cocks the Desert Eagle.

"No!"

"Harry, don't."

The split-tail. She won't let him do it. Thank God.

"You want the honors, Jackie?"

"Don't waste the bullets. Alex is still out there."

"Gotcha. How about I use the chain saw? See what this guy had for breakfast?"

Munchel starts to cry.

"Go find the cuffs, Harry. Check the kitchen."

"Your house, your rules." He hands the gun, butt-first, to Jackie the cop, then trots out of the garage.

"Call an ambulance," Munchel whines. "Jesus, it hurts."

"That might be a problem," Jackie says. "Some assholes cut the landlines and are using a cell phone jammer."

"Roof," Munchel says. "Pessolano threw it on the roof."

"Where on the roof?"

"Somewhere over the garage. Switch it off. Call for help."

"Was it just the three of you?" she asks.

"Yeah. Me, Pessolano, and Swanson."

"If there's another one of you idiots out there, I might get killed, and then I'll let Harry go Black and Decker on your ass."

"I'm the last one. I swear. Find the jammer." Munchel moans. It feels like he swallowed a hot coal. "Jesus, the pain is getting worse."

Jackie pats him down, taking the Desert Eagle from his holster, and his wallet from his back pocket.

"James Michael Munchel," she says, reading his driver's license. "You have the right to remain silent."

Munchel tunes out her spiel. He doesn't give a hoot about his rights. He's focusing on something else. Something only a few feet away.

Harry returns with a pair of handcuffs. Jackie snicks a bracelet onto his wrist, and then they drag Munchel across the floor over to the workbench.

Perfect, Munchel thinks.

Harry tries to pull Munchel's fist away from his burning gut. Munchel fights it as hard as he can.

"Please! I'll bleed to death!"

"Don't worry about it. We'll get the stains up with some bleach."

Harry wrestles his hand away, but again the cop stops him.

"Just cuff the other end to the leg of the bench. It weighs a ton. He's not going anywhere."

Harry obeys, locking the cuff around one of the metal pipe legs, above a crossbeam so Munchel can't lift the leg to escape.

But Munchel has another way to escape. The real reason he wants his hand free is because he spotted something under the bench, next to a cat litter box, only a few feet away.

A revolver.

Munchel should be able to reach it if he stretches. Then he can shoot away the cuffs, kill everyone in the house, and use Pessolano's truck to get to a hospital.

But he can't do it while he's being watched. Everyone has to leave the garage first, give him a little privacy.

James Michael Munchel groans again, biding time until he gets his chance.

MIDNIGHT

JACK

UNCHEL'S DESERT EAGLE is predictably empty, but Harry's has two bullets left. After I make several threats, he reluctantly gives me one.

"This sharing thing is new to me, sis."

I eye him. "You accepted this whole sister thing pretty quickly, don't you think?"

He shrugs. "Give a starving man a cracker, it's a banquet."

That's more insight than I thought Harry capable of, but I figure we can hold off on this discussion until we get our blood tests. And I have a couple of drinks in me.

"You okay?" I ask Mom.

She nods. "I'm going to check on Latham and Herb. Which one of you is going on the roof?"

"Jackie is." Harry chews his lower lip. "Heights scare me, Mom."

I put my hands on my hips. "Give me a break. Do you remember riding in a helicopter not too long ago?"

He nods. "I remember. It scared me."

"I'm not leaving my mother alone, McGlade."

"I'll watch her."

"I'll watch her. You'll get your ass up on the roof."

"We can play rock, scissors, paper, to decide," Harry says.

"That's ridiculous."

"It's fair. You ready? On three."

I can't believe I'm doing this. "Fine, Harry. One . . . two . . . three."

I hold out my fist. Rock.

Harry holds up his metal claw.

"Paper covers rock, Jackie. I win."

"That's not paper!"

"You want to discriminate because I'm differently abled?"

I consider popping him in the nose with my rock, but that isn't going to get him on the roof. I turn to my mother for support, but she shakes her head.

"You kids work it out amongst yourselves," she says.

I consider calling Harry a name, like sissy or coward, but I hold off. The sissy coward just saved my life, so the insult probably won't stick.

"Fine," I say. "I'll go."

"Don't be sore, Jackie." Harry raises his prosthesis. "Want to try two out of three?"

I stick my finger in his face. "Just protect Mom, McGlade."

"No problemo."

I give Harry my back, leaning down over Munchel. Ignoring the perp's protests of agony, I turn him over and unbuckle his holster. Then I slide it off of him and cinch it around my waist. There's a surreal quality to my actions, the combination of unremitting pain and fatigue. This has been an intense night, and it isn't over yet.

The Desert Eagle goes in the holster, and I take a deep, steadying breath.

"I'll need help getting up on the roof," I say to McGlade. "Or do I have to ask Mom to give me a boost?"

Harry smiles. "I'm here for you, sis. Let's do this."

"What about him?" Mom asks, indicating Munchel.

I look at the holes in the garage door, and the broken window on the side wall. Too many ways to see inside here, too many angles Alex can attack from.

"He stays here. But I want you in the bathroom, Mom. It's safer."

The three of us walk back into the kitchen, keeping our distance from the living room window. But the lights are on, and I catch a glimpse of the dead sniper lying by the front door in an incredibly large pool of blood.

"I forgot to mention," Harry says, "it looks like our buddy Alex found a rifle."

I escort Mom quickly down the hall, peek in on the boys, find them still alive, and press on to the laundry room, where I left the flashlight. I stick it in my holster belt, then stop by the bathroom again on my way back.

"I'll just be a few minutes," I say to Mom. "This is almost over."

"I hope so, Jacqueline. This might not be the right time, but I'm thinking about moving back into the city. Would that be okay?"

I smile. "We'll call a Realtor in the morning, Mom. Stay put. Harry will be by soon."

We hug again, and I hurry back to the kitchen. Harry is at the kitchen table, holding his cell phone.

"Just erasing the picture of your head," he says. "And another one I took up your skirt when you weren't looking."

I open the patio door and step outside, Harry in tow. The night has continued to cool off, and the wind blows through my hair and makes me shiver. It feels good, clean, almost energizing. Hopefully it will be energizing enough to get me on the roof.

"I'm going to climb up onto the veranda," I tell Harry.

We push a lawn chair to the corner of the patio, and I stand on it. Harry braces himself against the post and bends down. I step onto his back and get my chin up over the top of the veranda. On any other night, I could have easily pulled myself up. But this small effort by itself has turned the world into a carousel, spinning me around and around. I take a few seconds to control my wobbling.

"Anytime now," Harry grunts.

"You have to lift higher."

He straightens his back, and I rise another few inches. It still isn't enough.

"Push me up with your hand," I say. Then I add, "Your real one."

The aforementioned hand lands solidly on my ass, and he squeezes. I freeze up.

"McGlade, there's so much wrong with what you're doing right now."

"I'm not enjoying it either, Jackie. You're not exactly heroin chic."

Fighting words. "Are you saying I'm fat?"

"No. Of course not. You're . . . what's the opposite of anorexic?"

I remind myself I only have one bullet and need to save it.

"Never discuss a woman's weight with her, Harry."

"Tell that to the loop of intestines bulging out of my side. It's so big I can twist it into balloon animals."

He grips lower, onto my thigh, and lifts. This is enough for me to get my upper body onto the veranda. But I'm having a little trouble swinging my leg up.

"Okay, Harry. Push on my—"

"Oh shit!"

Suddenly McGlade is gone and I'm alone, legs dangling. I slap my palms against the wooden slats of veranda top, trying to find something to grab hold of. All I find are splinters. If Alex is down there with Harry, I'm an easy target with my ass hanging over the ledge. I reach for the holster, ready to drop down and—

"Sorry, Jackie." Harry is beneath me again, his hand pushing against my feet. "Your damn cat just ran past me, into the house. Scared the hell out of me."

He shoves me, and I manage to finally get my whole body up onto the veranda. I lie on my back for a moment, staring at the stars in the night sky. My heart is beating wildly, and I try to summon up enough saliva so I can swallow.

"You okay?" Harry asks.

I'm about as far from okay as a girl can be, but I say, "Yeah. Get back in the house and keep an eye on Mom."

"The cat's in the house."

"McGlade . . ."

"Fine. I'm on it."

I wait, but don't hear the patio door close. I twist my head and peek down through the slats. Harry is still standing there.

"Move it, Harry."

"Yeah. It's just . . ."

"It's just what?"

He shrugs. "Maybe I should be the one on the roof."

Unbelievable. "Little late for that now."

"Just . . . just be careful, Jackie. I was an only child my whole life. I'm not anxious to be one again."

I'm grateful I'm up here, because his tone implies he wants to hug me again.

"Don't you have anything you want to say to me, Jackie?" he asks.

"Yes, I do, Harry."

"Go ahead."

"Are you listening?"

"I'm listening. I'm here for you. Say what you need to say."

"Here it is: Get in the house and watch Mom."

Harry nods. "I understand. You've got all of these new feelings, and it isn't easy to—"

"GET IN THE DAMN HOUSE!"

"Got it. I'm going."

Harry goes back into the kitchen, closing the door behind him. I sit up, then carefully get to my feet. The veranda is flat on top, and I'm able to keep my balance. Walking from the veranda to the roof is a bit more problematic, since the roof is on an angle. Not a steep angle, but too steep for a woman with multiple injuries who was shot in the head a few hours ago.

Standing isn't going to happen. Crawling on the rough shingles hurts my knees. So I settle for a sort of sliding scoot, navigating the roof on my butt. I tug the flashlight from my belt and flick it on, giving this side of the roof a quick scan. I have no idea what a cell phone jammer looks like, or even how big it is. I'm guessing it doesn't look like dead leaves; that's all I see.

I make my way toward the garage, my bare feet brushing the gutters, methodically checking every other scoot for anything that looks electronic. I make it to the end of the house, maneuver over the corner of the roof to the side of the garage, and still find nothing.

Unless Munchel is lying, the only place the jammer can still be is on the front side of the house—which is where Alex is waiting with her sniper rifle.

I pause, switching off my light. There hasn't been any shooting for a while. That might mean she fled the area. Or it might mean that she's just waiting for me to come into view.

I rack my brain for other options, and can't come up with any. I have to find the jammer, the sooner the better.

Either I get shot, or I don't, I think. Not much in the way of rationalization, but it's all I have to work with.

I scoot over the corner, facing my driveway, and notice an SUV parked down the road. There's a big hole in the windshield, and its headlights are on.

I can't make out who's inside, but lying on the ground, near the passenger door, is Alex. My first hope is that she's dead, but that's dashed when I see her slink closer to the front of the truck.

244 · J.A. Konrath

If she's sneaking up to it, there must be someone inside. Everyone in the house is accounted for. That leaves Phin.

I have to warn him.

I draw the Desert Eagle, figuring I'll fire one in his direction to get his attention. But that will leave me unarmed.

Alex sneaks closer.

I switch on my flashlight, wave it over my head, and yell, "Phin!"

I don't know if he hears it. But Alex does. She turns her head, waves at me, then begins to climb the hood. She's going to go in through the hole in the front windshield.

Phin came here because of me. I have to do something.

Without considering the wisdom of my action, I kick my legs out over the edge of the roof and brace myself for impact with the ground.

12:07 A.M.
PHIN

H E KNOWS ALEX is in the dark somewhere, stalking him. Phin can't find her. And until he does, he's stuck in the Bronco. This truck is a mobile arsenal, with enough ammunition to overthrow a small country. He can't carry it all back to the house in one trip. And if he abandons it, there's a chance Alex will appropriate the ammo for herself.

Hot-wiring a vehicle is beyond Phin's criminal ability. All that remains is sitting here, trying to spot Alex, and keeping an eye on the front of the house.

He's tired, and in pain, and worst of all, sober. This gives him an unfettered chance to dwell on a future he isn't going to have, which hurts more than his cancer and his elbow combined.

Living without hope is a shitty way to live.

He considers the grass in his pocket again. That would help take the edge off reality. But he needs to stay sharp. For Jack.

On the other hand, Jack is his friend, and she wants him to be happy. He's not happy sitting in a truck in the middle of the night, shirtless and shivering, with a broken elbow and a cancerous pancreas, throwing a major pity party for himself.

He sticks his hand into his jeans, touches the bag.

Leaves it there.

Phin isn't sure why Jack inspires this loyalty in him. Is it a crush? Or maybe something more?

Phin kills the thought. He has no future. He has no hope. There's no room for love in his life.

For his own protection, he needs to prove that he doesn't care. The easiest way to prove it is to get high right now.

But he still doesn't pull out the bag.

Rather than dwelling on what that means, Phin turns the headlights on so Alex can't approach from the front. His rifle is loaded, and so is a shotgun he found in back. He uses the night scope to check the rear again, and the woods to the side. Then he shifts in his seat to watch Jack's house.

There's a light, on the roof. It's waving around, and then he hears Jack cry out, "Phin!"

A warning cry.

Phin jerks around to the front, spotting Alex on the hood. He fires the shotgun through the hole in the windshield, hitting nothing but sky, and she rolls to the side.

The gun bucks in his hands, and he can't rack it again with a broken elbow. He wedges the butt between his legs, the barrel touching the ceiling of the truck, and moves to pump it with his right hand. Before he has a chance to, Alex pours into the cab.

She doesn't go for the gun. She goes for Phin's injured arm, grabbing and twisting until all he can see is a big red ball of blinding pain. He yells, hits her in the head with the stock, but there's no force to the blow.

Phin pulls away, raises up his foot, but there's no room in the front seat to kick her. Alex lets go of his arm, but then she's wrestling with the shotgun, her two hands versus his one.

She's winning, and he can't hold on much longer. Rather than release his grip, Phin pushes forward, forcing her through the front window, climbing on top and pinning her back to the hood.

Phin lets her have the shotgun—she can't use it on him while they're grappling. His knee digs into her solar plexus, and his good hand locks onto her throat. He squeezes to kill.

Alex rakes her fingernails across Phin's eyes, but he shuts them tight, concentrating on crushing her windpipe.

Then she finds his elbow again, and yanks on it so hard that something else snaps.

Phin cries out, rolling off of Alex, landing face-first on the cool grass. The shotgun skids across the hood and falls in front of the truck, between the headlights.

Alex is closer. She scrambles for it, reaching down.

BAM!

The shot doesn't come from Alex. It comes from behind them.

Jack.

The cop is only twenty yards away, jogging over with a huge handgun pointing in their direction.

Alex does a diving roll, then tears off into the woods, leaving the shotgun behind.

Phin crawls to the shotgun, pumps it with the butt on the ground, and fires it into the darkness after Alex. Jack staggers up behind him. She's panting.

"She's unarmed," he tells her. "You can go after her."

"No ammo," Jack says.

"Take the shotgun."

Jack reaches for it, goes wiggly, and collapses right onto Phin's lap.

"YOU LITTLE YELLOW-EYED BASTARD. The first bullet is going in your skull."

Munchel slowly extends his hand, reaching for the revolver for the ninth time.

The damned cat hisses and lashes out its claw, tunneling three more deep scratches along Munchel's wrist.

He jerks his hand back again and swears. Munchel's arm is bleeding in so many places it looks like he stuck it in a blender. The pain almost rivals the pain in his gut. Over twenty scratch marks and three bites; one he's sure went all the way down to the bone.

The revolver is only a few feet away, just within reach. But it's right next to the litter box, which the cat is standing in. Every time Munchel reaches for it, the cat draws more blood.

Worst of all, the horrible feline seems to actually be enjoying itself. As if this is some sick game. Munchel tried waiting for it to use the litter box and leave, but it just sits there, yellow eyes sparkling, daring him to make another move.

Gunshots, outside. Munchel isn't concerned with that. His entire world has become his arm, the gun, and the cat.

Munchel tried yelling. Tried slapping his hand on the floor. Tried talking sweet. Tried begging. He even tried nudging the litter box, but that's the move that provoked the biting, and he isn't going to attempt it again.

Munchel's lower lip trembles, and the tears come. His stomach is getting even worse. It's not even about escaping anymore. Even if he shot off the handcuffs, he wouldn't have the strength to get to the truck.

Munchel wants the gun for another reason. His final request. He wants to shoot that split-tail and that one-armed guy who did this to him. And the cat. He really wants to shoot the cat.

Then he'll use the gun on himself and end this terrible pain.

Just do it, he thinks. *It's just a cat. If it scratches you, no big deal. You're going to die anyway. Be a soldier and do it!*

Munchel extends his hand toward the revolver for the tenth time. He shows no fear, and doesn't hesitate. The cat watches him, unblinking, as he gets within ten inches of the gun.

Eight inches.

Six inches.

Four inches.

Two inches.

Munchel grabs it! He lifts the gun up, his index finger seeking the trigger, and then there's a blur of yellow fur and the cat has all four claws *and* its teeth locked onto Munchel's hand. Munchel can't help it—the cat hits a tendon or something that makes his hand pop open, causing him to release the gun. He screams, reining his arm in, lifting it up to beat the cat against the underside of the workbench. But before he can, the cat releases him, hopping back into the litter box.

The pain doesn't abate. It feels like the cat is still clawing, still biting. Munchel looks for the gun, and sees it's even farther away now.

And the cat, the damned cat, is licking Munchel's blood from its paw.

There's some noise, from the opposite side of the garage. Munchel swivels his neck around, and through a gap in the boxes he spies someone climbing in through the window.

It's the woman. The bad-ass woman who was trying to kill the split-tail cop. She navigates the boxes and walks over to Munchel, staring down at him.

The woman has a killer body, but her face is Phantom of the Opera. Still, she's trying to kill Jackie. She could be a possible ally.

"We both want the cop dead," Munchel says.

The woman lifts her foot up, lightly touches her toe to Munchel's stomach. He howls, all thoughts of a possible alliance being wiped from his mind. Everything gets bright, then dark.

"It's your stomach acid," she says. "It's leaking through the bullet hole, and dissolving all of your other organs. Bad way to die. Takes hours."

She moves her foot up higher, nudges his shoulder. Munchel wonders if maybe he blacked out for a few seconds.

"What happened to your hand?" she asks.

Her eyes track from Munchel's arm to the litter box, then to the revolver. The woman's face twitches.

"Kitty won't let you have the gun? That's pretty damn funny."

The woman bends down, looks at the cat, and says, "Scram."

The cat hisses, then bounds out of the garage, back into the house. The woman picks up the revolver.

"Is this what you wanted? So close, but so far. That must have been awful for you."

Munchel knows what he has to say, but can't bring himself to say it.

"Let me take a wild guess." The woman crouches next to him, wipes away one of Munchel's tears with her thumb. "You want me to shoot you. Right?"

Munchel nods, and manages to add, "Please."

"Normally, I'm a merciful chick. But you and your boys—well, you really fucked up my plans for the evening. So I think the best thing for both of us is for you to die in horrible agony."

She's not going to help him. But maybe he can force her to.

"I'll . . . I'll scream," he says. "I'll scream that you're here."

The woman straightens up and places her foot on Munchel's stomach again, taking his breath away.

"No you won't. Because I can make it worse."

She reaches over his head, onto the workbench, and grabs two items: a funnel, and a bottle of liquid drain cleaner. She drops them next to Munchel.

"You make a sound," she tells him, "even the tiniest sound, and I'll fill you up with something that hurts a lot worse than stomach acid. Got it?"

Munchel nods, pissing his pants once more.

"Who has the keys to that truck outside?"

"Pess . . . Pessolano."

"He the guy in the living room?"

Munchel nods again, wishing he would die.

"Inside. Are they armed?"

". . . the guy, Harry . . . he's got a Desert Eagle . . . only one bullet."

"Anything else?"

". . . no . . . please . . ."

She finally takes her foot off his stomach. Then she swings out the cylinder on the revolver, slaps it back in, and cocks it, heading for the doorway to the house. Before she goes through she looks at Munchel.

"Remember," she says, putting a finger to her lips. "Shhh."

Munchel closes his eyes and focuses all of his energy on being very, very quiet.

I WAKE UP WITH MY HEAD in Phin's lap. He appears concerned, an emotion I've never seen from him before. It softens his features, making him look like a different person.

"What happened?" I ask. The lawn is cool beneath my legs, and my various aches and pains are a little less acute.

"You passed out. After you jumped off the roof to save me."

"I landed on an azalea bush. And I landed funny."

"Are you hurt?"

"Not that kind of funny. I think the plant got to third base."

"Frisky, those azaleas. Did it buy you dinner first?"

"No. Not even a glass of wine. Where's Alex?"

"She ran into the woods."

I try to sit up. Phin helps. I'm groggy, but I can function.

"She might head back to the house," I say. "We have to get there."

"She's unarmed."

"That doesn't mean she isn't dangerous."

Phin nods. "Good point. I think we can handle her, though. Let me show you."

He hands me the shotgun, then sticks his head in the passenger door of the truck and presses something on the dashboard. Then he walks around to the rear door and opens it up. Inside are two sniper rifles, half a dozen handguns, and box after box of ammo.

"I couldn't bring it back to the house all by myself, but if we both load up, we can manage. Unless Alex is driving a tank, she won't be able to get to us."

"Let's hurry."

There's a metal suitcase lined with foam, with cut-out impressions for the two Desert Eagles. I tear out the foam and fill the suitcase with bullets. Phin finds a duffel bag, and we pile in the guns and more bullets. We barely cram everything in.

I reload the Desert Eagle, Phin adds a few shells to the shotgun, and then I help him strap on the duffel bag, which weighs a ton. The suitcase and both rifles are mine to carry.

Satisfied we haven't left a scrap of ammo behind, we head back toward the house.

My load is cumbersome, unwieldy, and after a few steps I have to rest. Phin urges me on. You never realize how big your lawn is until you're hauling a hundred pounds of ordnance across it. I really hope Mom doesn't change her mind about moving back to the city.

"I still have to find the cell phone jammer," I tell Phin between labored breaths. "If you cover the front, and Harry covers the back—"

My words are cut off by the sound of gunfire, coming from the house.

KORK

THE REVOLVER IS A .38. There are five bullets in the cylinder. That's more than enough.

I creep into the house, silent and powerful. After a little hiccup in the plan, I'm back in control. Harry and his single-shot Desert Eagle don't concern me. Even if he manages to get a shot off, he'll most certainly miss.

I slip into the living room and grin when I see the cast-iron pot with the wire attached. Idiots. Then I kneel down next to Pessolano. His pants are a bloody, sticky mess, but I manage to fish out the keys to the Bronco. I shove them in my pocket, then concentrate on the hallway.

I hear whispering. Coming from the bathroom, behind the refrigerator.

I pause. Shall I shoot to kill? Or is there time for a little fun first?

I decide to play it by ear.

I bend down low, measuring each footstep, careful I don't make a sound. I feel most alive during moments like this. I'm in control, a hunter stalking her prey. It's what I was born to do.

"She's in the house! She has a gun!"

Dammit. That sniper idiot. I thought I paralyzed him with fear, but he must have been made of stronger stuff than I assumed. I meld into the shadows, pressing my back up against the wall.

"Is that you, Alex?" Harry asks.

I wonder whether or not to answer, decide there's no harm now.

"It's me," I say.

"Found yourself a gun, huh?"

"Yep. And I have more than one bullet, Harry. Where should I shoot you first? I'll let you decide."

"Come a little closer and I'll tell you."

I laugh, then take a step forward.

"You think you can hit me left-handed, Harry?"

"I don't have to. Mom has that particular honor."

Another step. "That old lady with the crippled hands? She can't even hold a gun."

"She's not holding it. I am. She's aiming for me."

I stop in my tracks.

"Mom's an expert markswoman. She taught Jack how to shoot. Isn't that right, Mom?"

"Stick your head out, Alex," Jack's mother says. Her voice is strong and sure. "I'll teach you how to make some mincemeat pie."

I back up. Maybe they won't hit me, but maybe they will, and a .50 bullet in capable hands is not something to take lightly. I'll sneak back outside, come in a different way.

I head for the front door, and see Jack and Phin heading toward the house, their arms filled with weapons.

Shit. I buzz through a few quick scenarios in my head. I shoot at them, kill one, and the other rushes the house with superior firepower. Or I get lucky, kill them both, and Harry pops up behind me and puts one into the back of my head.

Maybe I could win with a better gun and more ammo, but a smart girl knows when to fight and when to run. It's running time.

Still, I can spare *one* bullet.

I get down on a knee, support my wrist with my free hand, and draw a bead on Jack's head. Then I wait for her to get within range. If she's too far away, I'll miss. If she's too close, that will give Phin a chance to catch me.

Fifty feet seems to be a good distance.

I'm a little disappointed that it will end this way, but I can come back for Harry and the others later. Let them mourn Jack for a few weeks. Settle back into everyday life. Then I can surprise them with a return visit, after I've finished with the other thing I've got planned.

Jack reaches the fifty-foot mark. I line up the sights.

"Bye-bye, Lieutenant."

I squeeze the trigger.

Jack remains standing.

I missed.

It's the gun. The gun's aim is off.

Damn, that is one lucky lady.

Phin stops, pointing the shotgun at the house. It's time for me to go. I hurry back into the garage, hearing the shotgun thunder behind me. The sniper is on the floor where I left him. His eyes get comically wide when he sees me.

"I thought we agreed to be quiet."

"I'm . . . I'm a soldier . . ." he stammers. "Soldiers don't make deals with the enemy."

"Soldiers also die badly," I say.

I don't have time to savor it, but I make good on my promise and manage to jam the funnel in, along with half the bottle of drain cleaner.

His screams follow me through the maze of boxes, over to the side window. And that's when I see Jack rush into the garage.

Maybe her luck has finally run out.

JACK

A SHOT BURIES ITSELF into the lawn a yard ahead of me.

"She found my gun," Phin says. "Go, I'll cover you."

I don't argue with him. All around us is open land. The only cover is near the house. Phin aims the shotgun and fires, and I move as fast as I can, beelining for my front door. I feel like I'm running in slow motion, my feet in quicksand, each step harder than the last. But the thought of Alex in the house with the people I love makes me discover reserves I didn't know I had left.

I make it to my porch without being shot, wheezing and dripping sweat. I drop the gear, pull the Desert Eagle, and go in low, keeping a two-handed grip on the weapon.

The living room is clear. I hear screaming, can't pinpoint it.

"Harry!"

"We're fine!" he yells from the bathroom. "Alex took off through the garage!"

I rush over to the garage door, get a quick peek at Munchel on the floor, his stomach wound leaking bloody foam. He's the one screaming.

I look past him, see Alex heading for the side window. I fire twice, missing as she dives through.

I can't let her get away.

I hobble between the boxes, crouching low if she decides to fire at me, sticking the barrel of my gun out the window and jerking left and right to see if she's hiding on either side.

Alex comes up from below.

She grabs my wrist and squeezes like a vise. I keep my grip on the pistol but can't aim it toward her. I sense, rather than see, her gun hand coming up, and I reach blindly and latch on to it, stiff-arming the barrel away from my head.

Alex tugs, dragging me out of the window, broken glass scraping against my stomach, hips, and legs. I fall on top of her, each of us trying to gain control of our weapons without letting the other do the same, my face inches from hers as we both grunt and strain.

She rolls, swarming on top of me, straddling my chest. Slowly, inexorably, her gun begins to swing toward my face. There's nothing I can do to stop it. I'm injured, close to passing out again, and Alex is so big and so strong and so damn evil. She's not a human being. She's a force of nature.

Her gun bears down on my forehead.

"After I kill you," she says, "I'm coming back for your friends and family."

I'm not scared.

I'm enraged.

I hear a yell—a bone-chilling, animalistic yell. It's coming from me. And then I open up my palm, letting the Desert Eagle drop, flexing my biceps and grabbing hold of Alex's hair and yanking her head so hard I give the bitch whiplash.

Alex falls to the side, off of me, and I shove her gun hand away and get my knees under me. Then I make a fist with my left hand and hit her square in the nose.

I can feel the cartilage crack under my knuckles. Her gun goes off, shooting into the night sky well over my head. She rolls with the punch, and I scramble to my feet, ready to lunge in under the gun and rip out her heart with my bare hands.

But she doesn't attack. She runs.

The monster runs away.

I scan the ground, find the Desert Eagle, and snatch it up, but she's already sprinting around the corner.

"Jack!"

Phin, at the garage window, shotgun in his hand. He looks sort of fuzzy around the edges, and I feel my legs start to wobble.

"Make sure she doesn't get back in the house," I tell him.

Then I go after her.

12:17 A.M.

KORK

I'M STILL SEEING STARS from where Jack popped me in the nose, but I don't let it slow me down. I run around the back of the house, adrenaline pumping, rounding the other side, sprinting straight for the Bronco. I quickly look back, see that Jack is fifty yards behind me.

She's persistent. I'll give her that.

She also has a bigger gun, and by now so does everyone in the house. I've got to get the hell out of here.

I slide on my belly across the hood of the truck and through the broken windshield. I wiggle myself into the driver's seat, push the key in the ignition, and have a bad moment when the truck doesn't turn over.

It's the battery.

I check to my right. Jack has stopped less than thirty yards away. She's in a shooter stance, aiming the big Desert Eagle at my head.

I kill the headlights, press the gas pedal, and crank it again.

The truck roars to life. I make a U-turn, burning rubber on the street and kicking up dirt and grass when the wheels go off the road.

I duck down right before Jack puts three shots into the driver's-side window, peppering me with bits of glass. I keep the pedal pressed down, feel the tires grip the asphalt again, and continue to stay low until I'm at least two hundred yards away.

I tap the brakes when the road reaches an end, jerk the wheel right, and speed down the street and through a green light. Then I force myself to slow down.

I raise a hand to my nose, wipe away some blood, and it causes a spike of pain. I check the glove compartment, find a box of tissues, and wedge a wad up each nostril even though it makes my eyes water.

It hurts. But my ego hurts more. I had her. *Had her.* But when it came time to punch her clock, I got greedy and tried to draw out the moment, talking when I should have been pulling the trigger.

It's not entirely my fault. There were unforeseeable circumstances. If it weren't for those idiot snipers, I'd still be back at the house, controlling the situation, having some fun.

But what's done is done. No point dwelling on the past.

Besides, this isn't over yet.

Not by a long shot.

I WATCH ALEX TEAR DOWN the road, and the Desert Eagle all of a sudden weighs a hundred pounds. I let the gun drop to my side, and a strangled sound that's a cross between a laugh and a sob comes out of my mouth.

She's gone. Alex is gone. And everyone I care about is still alive.

I walk back toward the house, but I don't feel weak. I don't feel hurt at all. For the first time all night, I feel pretty damn good.

I meet up with Phin on my front lawn.

"We'll get her," he says.

I meet his eyes. "I know."

We enter through the front door. Harry is standing guard with a Desert Eagle. He blows out a big breath when he sees me. "That was some pretty intense shit. Who needs a beer?"

"I could use something stronger," Phin says.

Harry nods. "Mom has some codeine, and I think there's vodka left."

"We're not out of this yet," I say. "We still need to find the jammer and get some help."

"Phin and I will take care of it," Harry says. "Don't bogart the vodka."

They head outside. I head to the bathroom, and Mom embraces me.

"Is she gone?" she asks.

"Yes. I still need to go outside, guard Phin and Harry."

I look at Herb, who is sitting up. His color has returned. He's trying to open a pickle jar.

"Don't eat those," I say, taking the jar away.

Herb frowns. "Harry said they were good."

I ask Mom to find something else for Herb to munch on, then go to Latham. I touch his forehead, and he opens his eyes. His fever has gotten worse.

"Did the good guys win?" he asks.

I nod.

"I wasn't worried," he says. "Not with you here to save us."

"Ambulance is coming soon," I tell him. "We're all going to be okay."

"I love you, Jack."

"Love you, Latham."

"Love you more."

"No, I love you more."

Herb's mouth is occupied with what appears to be a wedge of cheddar cheese, but he says, "For crissakes, I'm trying to eat here. Kiss him already."

I smile, kiss Latham, and then hurry back into the kitchen. The screams from the garage have stopped. I take a peek. Munchel is dead. Then I go outside and witness the spectacle of Harry on Phin's shoulders, reaching for the veranda.

"Dammit, Phin, push!"

"You want me to climb up there on my own, then pull you up?"

"Could you do that? Please?"

I lend two hands to the cause, and we manage to get McGlade onto the roof. And he had the audacity to comment on my weight. Everywhere I touch him, it feels like pizza dough.

"What's it look like?" Harry calls from above.

"No idea," I answer. "But it's probably around front."

I turn to Phin. "Any wants or warrants out on you lately?"

"I don't think so. Worried about fraternizing with a known criminal?"

"Hell no. I was going to talk to a judge friend, get everything dropped."

Phin smiles. "Can that apply to any future indiscretions I may commit? There's a liquor store near my house just begging to be robbed."

"Thanks, Phin."

I give him a hug, since this is the Night of a Thousand Hugs anyway. His skin is freezing.

"Aren't you cold?" I ask.

He holds me tighter. "Not anymore."

"Hey!" Harry yells. "I found a tennis ball! You play tennis, Jackie?"

I pull away from Phin, feeling a little awkward.

"I think Latham has some shirts inside. I'll get you one, when Harry comes back."

"Thanks."

Harry farts around on the roof for a few more minutes, then yells, "Got it!"

He tosses the jammer down. It's a black box, about the size of a walkie-talkie. I hit the off switch, and pull out the battery just to be safe. Then I turn on my cell phone and see those beautiful signal bars.

I call 911, give the operator my badge number, and request as many cops as possible. I also ask for six ambulances, and for an APB to be put out on a red Ford Bronco with a hole in the windshield.

Then I go to find a shirt for Phin, and a change of clothes for me.

The first cop arrives in four minutes. A minute after that, six more cops arrive. Then the ambulances come. All the swirling lights on my front lawn make it look like a Fourth of July fireworks display.

I give some very brief statements, and then oversee the loading of my friends and family into the ambulances. Mom. Latham. Herb— who fights with the paramedics to hold on to the cheese. Phin. And Harry.

"Mom invited me over for dinner next week," Harry tells me as they're strapping him to the gurney. "It will be nice to hang out with you when someone isn't trying to kill us."

"Looking forward to it," I say.

"Does she like flowers?" he asks. "I've got forty-nine Mother's Days to make up for."

"She loves flowers, Harry."

Only after Harry is carted off and everyone is safe do I allow my guard to ease up and finally let them put me into an ambulance of my own.

"I have a cat," I tell one of the paramedics. "He isn't good with people."

"We'll catch him, make sure he's okay."

"Might be wise to call animal control, let them help you."

He passes along the info, then takes my vitals.

"Helluva night, huh?"

I laugh. It feels good. Real good.

"You have no idea," I say.

M Y NOSE STOPS BLEEDING. I pull out the tissues, wipe away some of the extra blood, and make myself presentable. Then I ditch the Bronco in an alley behind a convenience store, jog six blocks to the ER loading dock, and sit down on a bench and wait.

This is the nearest hospital to Jack's house, so it makes sense they'll take the injured here.

The first ambulance arrives, and two paramedics hop out and open up the rear, pulling out someone I recognize all too well.

The .38 is lousy, but I don't miss at point-blank range. Both emergency technicians drop, either dead or dying. I walk up to the gurney, taking my time, enjoying the moment.

"Thought you got away, huh?" I ask. "Life's like that sometimes. Just when you think you're in the clear, something blindsides you."

I cock the gun and half of my face smiles.

"Any last words?" I ask.

All I get back is a defiant stare.

"Nothing? I was hoping for something witty."

"She'll find you."

"I certainly hope she will. And just to make sure she goes looking . . ."

I aim for the head, and hit what I aim at.

Some people run out of the ER, wondering what's happening. Time to go.

I run off into the parking lot, find an old guy looking for his car. We make a quick swap. I get his car keys, and his wallet, which contains eighty bucks and a few credit cards. In return, he gets a chop in the throat that breaks his windpipe, and a final resting place in his own trunk. A much better deal for me than for him, but life isn't all that fair.

I pull out of the parking lot, considering my next move. It's too risky to stay in the area. Plus, I have other things to do. While incarcerated, I did a lot of planning. *Big* planning. Some of it involved Jack. Some of it didn't.

I need to get started on the stuff that didn't involve her. But that doesn't mean I still can't keep Jack in the loop.

I pass several police cars on the way out of town, but they leave me alone. After driving for a bit I check into a suburban hotel using the dead man's American Express.

I yawn. It's been one hell of a day, and I'm exhausted. I strip off my clothes, take a hot shower, and climb into my first real bed in a long time.

The sheets are warm. The pillow is soft.

I fall asleep dreaming of the many deaths to come.

JACK

OPEN MY EYES when I realize the ambulance has stopped. I look over my shoulder. The paramedics are gone.

I get a feeling—a bad feeling—and reach up to unbuckle my straps. I open the rear of the ambulance and see the parking lot is a tangle of emergency vehicles, most of them cops.

A paramedic comes up alongside me.

"You don't want to see this."

I push him off, hurrying toward the nexus of activity near the rear of the hospital.

A cop is setting up some crime scene tape.

Oh . . . no . . .

I grab a nearby uniform and yell, "Who is it? Who's dead?"

He doesn't answer. Two more cops see me and begin to walk over, but I duck under the tape and see the dead EMTs, and there, on the gurney . . .

"NO!"

I become another person. Someone without any control left. Someone overcome by emotion. I rush over to the bloody body, punching anyone who tries to stop me, screaming and screaming because I just can't stop.

Someone jabs me with a needle, and my consciousness floats away, and all I can think is that I failed, I failed, I couldn't protect everybody, dear God I'm so so sorry . . .

JACK

I'M MEDICATED. Something strong that makes it hard to stay awake.

People come and go all day. Doctors and nurses. Cops. People I care about.

I have nothing to offer them. Nothing to give.

My hospital room fills up with meaningless flowers. Friends. Police officers from around the country. Strangers who watched the news.

Captain Bains even shows up, offers his condolences. Tells me to take as long as I need to recuperate.

He even offers to help with the funeral arrangements.

I decline.

"We'll get her," he tells me. "We've got the Staties involved. The Feds. Every cop shop in Illinois and the surrounding states."

His words don't reassure me. I know they won't get her. I know, because Alex has already gotten away.

She's told me as much.

Before Bains arrived, one of my floral arrangements began to ring. Inside the planter was a cell phone.

I picked it up, and read the text message on the screen.

SO SORRY FOR YOUR LOSS, JACK.
I'M IN MILWAUKEE.
COME GET ME.

Along with the text was a picture. A shot of Alex, a half smile on her scarred face, standing in front of a restaurant.

I don't share this information with the captain. Maybe I will later. I'm not sure. It depends on whether or not I'm going to stay a cop.

I look at it now. The phone. My direct link to the person who hurt me worse than anyone has ever hurt me before.

COME GET ME.

"You can bet on it, Alex. You can bet on it."

Acknowledgments

Big thanks to the following people. You've helped me immeasurably, and I won't soon forget. (Apologies to those folks I forgot.)

William E. Adams, Augie Aleksy, Tasha Alexander, Feo Amante, Brenda Anderson, Patrick Balester, Sarah Bewley, Dave Biemann, Irene Black, Michele Bradford, Wendy Brault, Tisha Britton, Lynn Burton, William Conner, Gail Cooke, Jim Coursey, Tammy Cravit, Blake Crouch, Josephine Damian, Terri Dukes, Chris Dupee, Audrey N. Durel, Jane Dystel, Barry Eisler, W. D. Gagliani, Miriam Goderich, Norman Goldman, Terri Grimes, Jude Hardin, Joe Hartlaub, Linda Holman, Kay Hooper, Adam Hurtubise, Eileen Hutton, Bob Hutton, Steve Jensen, Cynthia Johnson, Jon Jordan, Ruth Jordan, Richard Katz, Nick Kelly, Maria Konrath, Talon Konrath, Chris & Mariesa Konrath, Laura Konrath, Mike Konrath, John Konrath, Amy M. Krueger, Michele Lee, Meredith Link, Brenda C. Long, Maggie Mason, Joseph P. Menta Jr., Brenda Messex, Jim Munchel, David Omo, Henry "Hank" Perez, Paul Pessolano, Barbara Peters, Jeanine Peterson, Sharon L. Pritchard, Pat Reid, Heather M. Riley, Terry Robertson, J. Greg Robison, James Rollins, Marcus Sakey, Judith Saul, Terri Schlichenmeyer, Rob Siders, Wendy K. Smith, Shaun A. Sohacki, Greg Swanson, Linda Tonnesen, Leslie Wells, Matt Wilhite, Lloyd Woodall.

And special thanks to the many booksellers, librarians, interviewers, bloggers, reviewers, and booksellers (they deserve to be thanked twice) who have embraced my series. I owe every one of you a drink.